To Bill

MW01181197

NETTLERASH, CUSH
AND UNIONSUITS

NETTLERASH, CUSH AND UNIONSUITS

Fay Whisenant Trayler

A Hearthstone Book

Carlton Press Corp.   New York, N.Y.

Preface

Anyone who writes a family story settles more and more into an acceptance of himself as each member in the story so long as he is writing. Then when he comes face to face with them outside his sphere of activity, his studio, his office, or any other name he gives it, he has just a little trouble separating himself from their personalities as he sees them, which may be far wide of the innermost pictures they have of themselves. This office is a little-used bedroom. A pecan wood desk is heavy with notes, files, and lesser used books. The double bed holds the more frequently used thesaurus, the manual to an overused word processor, and a dictionary caged by bookends, plus a disk file, stacks of reference material sent in by various family members, and uncounted versions of assorted chapters, et cetera. Lurking in corners and niches are the personalities of others, ready to step into the very being of the narrator without regard to whether she would or not. When she patently is attending her own thoughts, those waiting egos recede into the shadows. When she portrays, by means of words, their heights of joy, or depths of despair, they juggle with her intent to prove fair, not to inflict an emotion foreign to them where it doesn't belong.

Thank you immensely, brother and sisters, and children of any kinship, for your input. Humbly we ask for grace and propitiation for any instance in which toes were trod on.

Our parents instilled in us codes of behavior that have caused the writing of our story justly and truly to be much easier, and there would have been no story without them. So bearing those facts in mind, shall we dedicate this to Daddy and Mother?

Honoring JESSE LAFAYETTE and LUCEILLE FAWCETT WHISENANT, we submit this true narration, the Whisenant saga. ❧

NETTLERASH, CUSH AND UNIONSUITS

Chapter I

As far as I personally am concerned, this began on July 23, 1919. Rumor says Marshall, Texas, is one of the hottest locations one can imagine at that time of year, but the heat didn't bother me. No one believed I'd live: Mother, Daddy, Daddy's mother, nor the doctor, when he joined them. A home birth wasn't unusual in those days, but here was a premature baby. I was well wrapped in a wool blanket, all four or so pounds of me; a heater was lighted; and they sat in front of it, holding me, all night long. Mother was fond of saying, "Fay got warm the night she was born, and hasn't been cold since." I'll tell you one thing: I never felt unwanted by my family.

But this is not an autobiography; it's an unfinished story of a family of ten. Mother and Daddy would be well over a hundred by now. They are no longer with us. And Jessie, the oldest of the eight of us, preceded them after years of invalidism. The remaining seven of us range in age from 61 to 73. Although Julius Lemar, my one brother, will be 74 before the written story is finished.

Mother quite deliberately duplicated Daddy's initials, J.L., when she named Lemar. She chose Julius because she liked the name, but Lemar was of Mother's own making. The L stands for Lena—one of Mother's four living sisters; the E stands for Edith, Daddy's only sister; M stands for Mary; A for Anna; and R for Ruth—Mother's remaining living sisters.

And so Julius is the oldest surviving member of the J. L. Whisenant family. We, the surviving crew of our generation, do indeed have a gabfest when we manager to get two or more of us together. It's been nearly a year since the last all inclusive gathering at a fiftieth wedding anniversary, and I nearly have to put on earmuffs just to think about that meeting of children, grandchildren, and great-grandchildren.

I will begin with Mother, since there was a tendency to protect her because she was the shy, weaker one. Most of us were grown before we realized how strong she actually was. If she wanted to say something, she spoke. However, she believed that man was the head of the family and ranked number one. She willingly yielded it to him; but I honestly believe that Mother was the more poised, the more sure of the two of them. If for any reason they should have met royalty, she would have known whether to curtsy, to shake hands, or leave the choice to the king and queen; and she would have played her part as regally as they did theirs. Oh, Daddy would have done all right. Afterward he would have been the one to tell the story over and over while Mother would have alluded to it only to those acquaintances who warranted that knowledge of her private life.

Mother was born to Daniel and Jessie (Sims) Fawcett, in Ashdown, Arkansas, on October 13, 1886. When she was tired, in later years, she insisted that, while she didn't know it, she was convinced that she was born on Friday the thirteenth. Grandma and Grandpa lost one daughter, at the age of fourteen, and a son in infancy. Luceille Marie, my mother, was the oldest child to attain adulthood. That spelling of Luceille indicated a few drops of French blood in their veins although she was mostly English, Irish, and Scotch. She had the blooming complexion of those people; blue eyes with a touch of gray in them; and very dark hair which did not begin to gray until she was in her sixties.

Daddy, Jesse Lafayette Whisenant, was born on April 7,

1886 to John Wellington and Julia Isabella (Payne) Whisenant. He had spoken very little about his mother to us since her death when I was about six months old—she actually died on Dan's second birthday. He felt it so keenly that Mother could never give Dan a birthday party. Feeling that that was unfair, she never gave parties for any of us. Daddy was born in San Angelo, in south Texas. His older brother died of rabies incurred when he went to scare a dog off the porch and it scratched him on the leg. That left Daddy the oldest. He also had a sister and three brothers. Daddy was one eighth or so German. Produce—fresh vegetables, of any kind—were his life's work. He planted radishes every third week from early spring until winter. He raised every feasible crop he could and shipped in what he could not.

Nettle rash is two words, but it will always be one to me, nettlerash. When we were growing up, it referred to any rash caused by a reaction to something eaten or brushed against or deliberately applied. We didn't know what a histamine or an antihistamine was; we just dodged all contact with the offending agent, if we could figure out its identity. Due to allergies, our sister John often lived on vinegar poured from a bowl of onion and cucumber slices over hot fresh-made biscuits. Biscuits were quick and easy to make. Why should we waste money on enough bread to feed a family of ten plus an assortment of friends? Besides, Daddy liked the biscuits better. After a few days of a greatly restricted diet, Johnny usually could again eat whatever the rest of us were eating. Poison ivy caused a different rash. So did fresh mustard and okra when they inflicted their tiny spines on us. There still were a multitude of rashes known simply as nettlerash.

Before I was old enough to remember anything, Daddy and Mother had upped stakes and moved to Eastland, Texas, nearly one hundred miles west of Fort Worth. Oil had been discovered in nearby Ranger late in 1917, and the town was now booming, making the area ripe for Daddy's business. When I was three or four, I now recall, Daddy was constantly driving new cars home. Shiny black Fords. I must have been grown before it occurred to me that when the old car was clean and polished, it was new to me; and I can still see myself racing from the sand pile to the back door of the house to call in to Mother that Daddy had bought a new car.

Jessie was born in Marshall, Texas, on July 16, 1912. She was given Daddy's name, but of course it had the feminine spelling. It seems that Grandma Whisenant was jealous. She firmly believed that Jessie was named for our maternal grandmother. Mother said she wasn't to Daddy's kinfolk; and while I thought it more prudent not to ask, I wondered if she related that same story to her own family. Jessie was lithe, and both physically and mentally quick. She was the only one of us to have such lovely dark brown, naturally curly hair. Since both our parents had blue eyes, we all had them of one shade of blue or another.

During all this time Daddy's business was growing, and frequently customers would call the house to inquire or, possibly at Mother's instigation, place an order. She was a poised home secretary. Naturally Daddy took office calls as well. As far back as I can remember, we had a typewriter in the house, but I never saw Mother typing anything. I assume that she was able to type, for they met when they still were students at Tyler Commercial College. Also Mother's fingers fairly flew over the piano keys. Perhaps by the time I came on the scene there were no longer enough hours in a day for her to type a business letter.

Daddy used to receive mail on stationery adorned with a picture of a perfectly shaped and colored apple, complete to its upstanding bright brown stem and one perky green leaf. It was on the upper left (I think) corner of the paper, and we children all loved it. If we were around when one of the letters was discarded, we eagerly salvaged the apple for our "collection." At one time in our lives, likely all eight of us fought for those pictures, but not more than three of us at a time. I wonder today if some fruit company is still using that emblem.

Lemar had the distinction of being the only one of our generation to be born in Arkansas. A friend of today, Joyce Stroud, whose husband was born in Scotland, Arkansas, stands firm that it is proper to refer to the natives of that state as Arkansans; but we had long ago acclaimed Mother and Lemar to be Arkansawyers. Right or wrong, they'll always be that to us. Lemar was born in the small town of Morris Ferry, on July 19, 1916. A few years later the county court house and all the records burned. Then came a time when he had to show his birth certificate. There was very little difficulty due to the circumstances, however. He had the sandyish hair common to our family and was "obviously a Whisenant." How many times we have heard that said about one or another of us!

Chapter II

Daddy's business was part retail, part wholesale. Often he went to the large produce houses in Fort Worth or Dallas and bought produce for resale. Frequently one or two of us children would go with him. Various trips left a variety of memories. Meals might be cantaloupe, bananas; apples, grapes; nuts, crisp and tasty raw vegetables, topped off with a Coke, or a candy bar, maybe even both. Once when Dan and I were quite young, we accompanied Daddy. As we were small girls we always spent some time in the offices among the secretaries. After a period of chat followed by a period of boredom, there was little left to do but nibble at our finger-nails.

One compassionate secretary put a stop to that pursuit for all time. She suggested that it wasn't a good idea, and then she told us about a little girl who became ill. The doctors couldn't heal her, and decided to operate to see what could be wrong. They found, and removed, (here you must cup your hands together) "this many fingernails which the child had chewed off and swallowed!" So the secretary would be quite careful not to bite her nails any more if she were us. And so were we after that.

Many times we weren't home until after dark. Highway 80 had not had any of her kinks straightened out yet. It began to climb and circled partway around Ranger Hill. Today as I went from Borger—in the Texas Panhandle—to Stinnett, which is the county seat, I saw the old road climbing up the side of the hill while I drove on the wide, smooth, level new one very near by; inevitably I recalled Daddy's navigating Ranger Hill on those nights. When we reached it, Daddy was usually tired and inclined to doze off; therefore we were instructed to chatter, sing lustily, prod him if need be. Nothing else so effectively cuts off the flow of words as does being told to talk, of course. When we failed him, Daddy would get out the hardest peanut brittle planks he could find to buy. We were taught to eat quietly. Believe me, it is impossible to eat rock-hard candy silently. It echoed all over the cab of the truck. Daddy did have an alternate ploy on hand though, and if we had not already lost our ability to be vocal, that exploit made sure we did: he would open the door, stand on the running board (if you don't know what that is, ask your grandparents) and drive. The wind blowing in his face would keep him awake. I've no idea how long that hill was, but it couldn't possibly be as long as it seemed in those days.

We always got home safe, and Daddy even had one or two certificates awarded to him as the safe driver of the year. I'll wager no one on the awarding committee ever met him on that hill.

Daddy's territory included Eastland, Olden, Ranger, and Morton Valley. Because Olden was dependent on the petroleum industry, plus the feeding and clothing of those who worked for the oil company, we called it a greasy spot in the road. Morton Valley was basically a crossroads with a store and a few houses. In our vernacular, Daddy "worked" a town. He went to all the stores and to some large restaurants to sell to the managers. If Mother asked him if he were through for the day, the answer might be, "I haven't worked Olden yet." We were so used to his running in and out more than once most days, almost always eating every meal at home, that we were nonplussed by our school mates whose fathers (a mother only rarely in those days) were at home only mornings and nights.

Daddy occasionally began to gain weight, but he refused to allow himself to get really heavy. Some days he had his coffee at home and only one or two cups in town. Other days he drank uncounted cups. Then as if he didn't get enough in the restaurants he visited, the produce managers frequently seized the opportunity to go have a cup while they discussed business with him. The first time I heard about his keeping an eye on his weight, he told Mother, in my hearing, that he would have to cut the cream in his coffee as he had reached 186 pounds that day. You'd think losing weight by that ploy would have been hard, but it apparently worked for him.

The first house I remember us living in was—how odd, I could drive to it this day if it's still there, but I don't remember ever hearing the street address—it was behind the Church of Christ in Eastland, and faced south. The church building faced east, and it looked across the street to the courthouse block. The house sat north and south, and had a long continuous porch along three sides, the west, the south, and the east. We spent many happy hours on that porch, dry ones usually. One large bedroom had two double beds in it, and maneuvering space besides.

Speaking of the old place reminds me of one sin Dan and I committed. On a Sunday morning, or so I'm told (I was too young to remember) we spotted the communion trays through an open door of the church and wandered over. Dan is some year and a half older than I and can faintly recall it. We held our own private tea party and trailed off home again. I do not know why we were not at church, but maybe John was ill and Mother was pregnant, enough to keep at least part of the family at home. As Daddy taught classes, he was probably at his church—he was strictly Baptist then.

I don't remember much about my battle with the chicken pox, but I do know that I was thoroughly drilled that I must not scratch. I was three or four years old. I lay for what seemed like hours lifting first one leg and then the other quickly straight up into the air. As they sideswiped one another, I was given at least slight relief from the burning itching that I thought I would never be free from.

At times Mother and Daddy, singly or together, appeared in my twilight zone of memory, vague, misty figures, standing by the bed. That twilight zone was caused more by my tender age, I'm sure, than by my condition or the time of day, although the room may have been darkened. If Lemar or any of our sisters were about, I've forgotten them.

When I was five we had the measles. Those side by side beds stood us in good stead then; either Mother or Daddy or Jessie would let us walk along the smooth curved metal at the foot of the beds. With them to keep us upright we walked all the way from the north end of one to the south end of the other. What relief to stretch our bodies and rid them of the imprint of rumpled bedclothes. Dan, John, and I all were speckled at once. Lemar and Jessie had already had them. We were not particularly affluent, and our beds were not brass, but by far the most of us have never yearned for that old style of bed, brass or otherwise.

Often during our early years a car would drive up, and its horn would sound. Someone would say, "We just wanted to see the twins." There were no twins in the family, but Dan and I were close enough in size to fool people if they were careless observers. I just grew into the knowledge that they meant us. After a time, we didn't bother to point out that there were no twins; and by the time we were seven or so, no one ever suggested it anymore. Our fame was gone.

Mother's sewing was quite probably at least part of the reason for the assumption that we were twins. I do not know at what age it started, but Mother made many of our clothes alike. When I was a first grader, we each had dresses with gathered skirts and short puffed sleeves, gingham, black and white checks, with collars, sleeves, and pockets of red and white checks. People frequently pay more attention to the clothes than the wearer of them. About the time we sported those eye-catching dresses, Mother made "Sunday" dresses for Luceille and Mable. Luceille's was of sky blue rayon and it had a bertha which Mother had professionally knife-pleated before attaching it to the dress. For Mable she chose pale pink, and it too had knife pleats. Somehow Mother had made the short sleeves from the pleated material.

Although the order of some events is vague in my memory, I remember when we moved. We must have spent a normal day with friends that day, only to go to a new house at the end of it. I was young enough to accept a strange house with a shrug as long as my bed was there.

Some very happy memories from the time we spent in that house by the church are because of Daddy's occupation. For a few years he owned and operated an ice cream plant and we had only to go past the church yard to the corner, cross the street and walk one full block, cross the second street, and go left a short distance to be at the plant. It was hot, humid, rather noisy, and utterly fascinating to us.

During those days, Mother didn't buy sugar, but merely sent some of us, armed with a big can, to the plant. Daddy would fill it with sugar. We had biscuit or cornbread with 99 percent of our meals, and we used lots of baking powder. Calumet sold it in gallon size cans, ten pounds or more—Vickey, who manages a large school cafeteria, says it would be nearer fifteen or twenty pounds. Its metal lid fitted neatly over the can to a depth of an inch or more and was quite sharp at the edge. It made a good storing and carrying can. I realize today that Daddy would not have filled it completely for the smaller delivery crew. Often Dan and I had the coveted chore, for Jessie and Lemar were in school and John and Luceille were too little. We would pause mid-point in that first long block, joyfully remove the lid, and eat pinched up bites of sugar from what remained in the can. Once after we had done that, we didn't shake the can well but put our small hands on it and gave it some whirls meant to erase the telltale signs of our feast. Too gently we whirled the can back and forth in the same way one rolls a pencil between his palms. It moved to the right and to the left satisfactorily, we thought.

The first thing Daddy said after he lifted the lid and saw our still intact fingerprints was, "I see someone likes sugar." Dan and I exchanged one quick guilty look, but when Daddy raised his head to look at us, there was a warm smile on his face.

Today one can buy half gallon cartons of neapolitan ice cream or mellorine in any grocery store. Daddy produced and sold individually wrapped bars of a strip of vanilla, one of chocolate, and one of strawberry that actually tasted like strawberries. There were times when he brought a block each for five to seven children at the end of the day.

Daddy was an active member of Rotary International, and the secretary of the local Rotary Club. They met on Monday nights. Almost invariably he brought home a pocketful of balloons, enough for one or two apiece. Occasionally he failed to lay them out before retiring—we were always abed before he came in. Then our crestfallen faces would remind him the next morning, and one of us would be sent flying to the front closet to retrieve them from the inside pocket of his suit coat.

The Clarks lived across the street from us. Ann was close to my age, and Gilbert was nearer Dan's. I cannot say if it was because their parents were younger than ours, or if it was because they with only two children could live a different lifestyle, but our parents didn't visit. Still all the neighborhood children played outdoor games together. There was a brassy child from a few doors away who was often around. Edna (I'm unsure of that name) talked ninety miles an hour to anyone and everyone. Dry saltine crackers were a favorite outdoor snack, and what I see the most easily in my mental pictures, is her holding her cracker under the faucet in our back yard, and turning the water on. I still shudder at even the thought of eating those soggy crackers. Though she denied that they were soggy, I could never believe her.

Sometimes when we played games of tag or hide-and-seek, I would blunder into a tree or turn a corner too short, and wind up in the house in tears. So it happens to every child. But once in the house I might choose the wrong door of two side by side. As I was the only one to see the second door, I wound up wearing glasses before I started school. I still have them, round lenses with narrow black frames and gold ear pieces.

I stopped running into things, but I had a tendency to go to school without my glasses. Many times Miss Maybe sent me home for them. At some time I just ceased to wear them; it was possibly during the Christmas vacation, or at the end of the school year. When, grown and married, I decided it was again time to correct my vision, the ophthalmologist informed me that I was using only one eye, and that it might be too late to save the other. He adjusted my sight easily though; apparently I had fallen into the habit of using each eye alternately for whatever chore faced me, and neither one was unused.

Lemar was always tough. He was making a slingshot. Slingshots were different weapons to us. They had one end of a rubber or leather strap tightly fastened to a stick while the other end was fastened to a holder for the missile; the second band was also fastened to the holder but not to the handle. Rather, it was held with the handle, and the entire outfit was circled around to gather momentum. The untied end was then released to project the rock toward its intended target— which frequently was not what it hit.

A piece of it slipped from his grip when he was testing it

for strength and length. Suddenly blood gushed out of the wound he had inflicted on himself. Fortunately the eye was not injured. It was I who was dispatched to the house to get a cloth for the mopping up so he could finish the job.

He felt it was rotten luck that I couldn't find one and Mother and Daddy asked what I was looking for. After a few words between them, it was decided Daddy had better check to see if it was severe enough to need a more sterile approach than a seven or eight-year-old boy could handle for himself out of doors. It only took a couple of stitches to close the gash up, but Lemar hasn't forgiven me yet for the necessary delay before his return home to complete his weapon.

Chapter III

Three weeks before I turned five, for reasons unknown to us, and with Jessie, nearly twelve, in charge, we children (Dan, Jessie, Lemar, John, and I) went one morning to visit the Alfords, some family friends. I recall Chester was there, but I don't know whether he was the son or the father, nor can I associate any other name with them. We were outdoors when Mr. Alford came and told us that we had a baby sister. We jeered in disbelief.

"Yes, you do. She's about this long," he persisted and measured by sawing a large forefinger across a huge forearm somewhere above the wrist.

We broke out in a babble of conversation—well, really of overpowering statements to one another; and that's all my almost five-year-old memory retained. But it was true. I remember later, at home, some discussion of what to name our new arrival. It was Jessie who suggested naming her for Mother. There was some earnest discussion, and the idea won in spite of Mother's protest. So the baby was named Luceille. Through the years we called her—as well as Luceille—Ceal, Silver, Lucy, Luce, and Cilla.

After the first somewhat darker hair was gone, Luceille was a cotton-top like most of the rest of us, and had a very fair complexion. I remember her having a huge abscess in a gland below the jaw, on the left side of her neck. It meant several trips to the doctor to have it drained. We were often too noisy—we made them tough in those days—and the babies learned to sleep through everything; but we sympathized sincerely with her during that ordeal.

Dan was the nearest to me in age of all my siblings, and she and I were best friends as well as sisters. She was named for Grandfather Fawcett, but Mother dropped the iel in favor of a shorter name. It was handier, easy to spell and easy to write, and always an ice breaker with the newly met. Dan has been widowed twice. Her second husband's name was Felix Sawicki. She sold real estate for some years through a Bastrop, Texas realtor, and since the customers were not truly comfortable with her surname, her business cards bore Mrs. Dan on them, and that they did like.

Jessie came along in Marshall, Texas; Lemar arrived in Arkansas; and Dan was born in Marshall. It turned out that the Arkansas fling didn't work out as well as they had hoped. I suspect Daddy and Grandpa Fawcett were both too domineering to work close together. Knowing that Grandma called Grandpa "Mr. Dan" may have fostered that suspicion. It may have been that the area just was not ripe for the business.

Dan was born on January 27, 1918. She had a slightly more rounded face than most of us did, and was both a very pretty baby and quite healthy. Again Mother and Daddy produced the baby before the doctor arrived to superintend the birth; and again all was well. Never did I hear Mother make any remark about Dan being a problem as a baby or growing child. Nor did Mother have a tendency to whitewash our sins.

I was the next born, and this time Daddy had his mother to help before the doctor arrived. Mother had made plans to honor Grandfather Whisenant by naming the baby for him. She found herself unable to do so. Looking at the tiny pale and supposedly dying infant, she felt compelled to choose a name suitable for what she thought looked like a little fairy and remembered that a fay is a fairy. Thus I became Fay. I was taunted with "living to spite our parents" by my siblings in those serious discussions which invariably take place among two or more children without any necessary reason. I should have been an August child, and surely gave them great trouble for some months. I think Dan took me under her wing as soon as she was allowed near me; I can almost hear Mother tell her to go "peep in and see if the baby's all right." It was automatic for me to follow her lead for years.

We left Marshall while I was still a baby, and John was born in Eastland. Mother used to speak of a house that they shared with one of Daddy's brothers and his wife: Mother and Daddy had certain rooms for themselves and their young brood; and our uncle and aunt had the rest. The back porch was without partition, and was entered from two kitchens. Our aunt was undoubtedly a stickler for reality. This was the clincher, and, believe me, it scandalized our mother; my aunt would sweep precisely half of that porch when she reached the back of the house with her broom. Not so Mother; she swept all of it, possibly sanctimoniously. Since I was always writing something, I stored lots of such juicy tidbits and sneaking suspicions in my memory genes.

John had the darker hair that most babies were born with— but she didn't shed hers. As it grew, she became a cotton top with dark ends on her hair; and strangers used to query how it had got burned. At some time between the ages of one year and eighteen months, she was taken to town by Daddy for her first haircut. Tears came to Mother's eyes for years whenever she told us about that haircut. She told us that she hardly recognized her own child when Daddy lead her into the house.

John was named for Daddy's father, and for sixty odd years

she has answered to John, or Johnny, which is more frequently bestowed on girls. Of course she too has had odd experiences due to her name.

One day when I was three or four, Mother sent Lemar and Dan to a neighborhood store across the street from us with a warning to be extremely careful crossing the street. She missed seeing the tag-along: me. I followed them. A local doctor's wife saw the two small children, slowed carefully, and kept an eye on them. But she didn't see me. I was knocked down by a fender. Mrs. Burns was shocked and almost ill at what she'd done. She saw that I was cared for and apologized copiously even though it wasn't her fault. She bought and presented to me a "mama" doll, the first one we had ever seen. What a marvel, a talking doll!

I still remember the morning the three of us, Lemar, Dan, and I, were in the yard with it when Mother called us to come in for a minute. There was no one in sight except a lady and a small child nearly a block down the street. We put my doll under an orange crate we were using for a table and went in. We were soon back in the yard, but there had been time enough: the doll was gone, and there was no one at all in sight. We never saw the doll again, but the scar on my lip was a constant reminder.

Jessie, Lemar, Luceille, and I all have July birthdays. That was good as at that time Texas children had to be seven on or before September first the year they began school. School filled our lives for eleven years. So we were young for our grade levels. If a child was seven by the end of the first semester, and if there was space for him in the first grade room, the parents were allowed to pay tuition and start him early. Dan's birthday fell after the end of first term, and Mother was furious. She wouldn't have minded the money, and she hated that, "Dan will be eight years old when she starts to first grade!" Of course Dan wasn't the only one, but we didn't mention that.

Dan enjoyed school, and after she could read a bit she decided to teach me to read. We had some old primers around in spite of the fact that the state furnished our books, and she taught me one word at a time at first. She would circle it, for instance, and I was to circle it every time I saw it on the page. Each time I got it right I was rewarded with a grain of Puffed Rice. Although I preferred Grape Nuts, I was delighted, and I reveled in our lessons and my reward.

Another set of Mother's and Daddy's good friends (very likely the best) were Jack and Mable Meredith. When one of the families visited, they arrived after breakfast but stayed until it was time to begin cooking supper. The noon meal was dinner and we enjoyed it en masse. One of the joys of that day was usually whole wheat bread—bakery bread—to give the adults more visiting time. Since the Merediths too had a flock of children, you can imagine the loaded tables.

We younger ones sometimes sat on upended orange crates or apple boxes. Other times we waited for the second tables for our turn. If you've never eaten while perched on such a seat, you've missed out on one of the most poignant hazards of childhood: "Schooching" to a more comfortable position and having a tiny bit of the back of one's leg or buttocks get caught in the crack of the make-do chair as it gave slightly in the process. Everyone but the two mothers and the unwary victim laughed before he could stop himself. It never kept any of us from eating, however.

Down one side of the yard on Seaman Street were what we called firebushes. They were round and symmetrical and had almost pointed tops. They were actually pale green annuals, three or four close together allowed one to push his way in between them to a hiding place, or a "house" for a small child. They were like separate conference rooms when there was company to match the homefolk. They were put to good use as hiding places in games and bases for leaping out to frighten the unaware.

One morning when Luceille was a year and a half old, we woke up to a still house and the sound of a kitten crying—which couldn't be, for we hadn't any dogs or cats. Daddy's brother Addie, remember, had died of rabies; and two of our cousins, his brother Maynard's children, had barely survived the agonies of diphtheria which presumably cats had carried to them. After some cogitation we got out of bed and went toward the kitchen to ask Mother about it but Mother was not there! We wandered around, in and out of everywhere except my parents' room. When the door to that room was closed, one just didn't burst in.

I'm sure each minute was an hour long that morning, but at last Daddy came out to inform us that we had a brand new baby sister. I was still young enough to have to have each I dotted and each T crossed, and wanted to learn more about the cat before I accepted the fact he had presented us with.

"That wasn't a cat. It was your new sister crying," he assured me. Talk about something being too much to believe! I could easily have been floored with the proverbial feather and I only really believed him when I saw the evidence.

This time the baby's hair was a little darker than John's, and did indeed prove to be definitely brown later on. Mother chose her friend's name, Mable, for our new family member. It was an established fact that Mable Meredith was loved; and her namesake was loved. The fact that the name unfortunately rhymed with a number of words, one of them extremely common, didn't occur to us until a rather awkward child of the same name but some years older than our Mable suffered in school because she was exposed to some couplets of very poor taste. We were piously abstemious about such cruelty; unless we were quite angry with her and our parents weren't in evidence.

One winter, after we got old enough to play out of doors

without someone breathing down our necks to be sure that we didn't wander into the street, old enough to walk to school unaccompanied, we met and soon came to despise a most necessary (in Mother's and Daddy's eyes that is) evil: One piece underwear, unsightly, complete with long sleeves, long legs, and dropseat. As they were worn over other underwear, we wore them more than one day. Long sleeves over them kept the sleeves comparatively clean; and long cotton stockings, bulging with the ribbed ankle cuffs, which had been smoothed and folded tight before being encased, strove masterfully to keep the exasperating lower extremities clean. On the first day they weren't too bad, but from then on they became quite unrepentantly more difficult for wee fingers to control and hide. Nevertheless, each year the day came when we had to don them, our odious unionsuits, until we were brave enough and mature enough to declare war against that tyranny that decreed we should wear them.

Chapter IV

When there are seven children in the family, childhood diseases can't be a total surprise. I'm sure John's scarlet fever was first doctored just as a flu: sniffles, headache, and fever. But when the doctor declared her highly contagious and seriously ill with a disease which was prone to leave after-effects, Mother and Daddy and the health authorities girded up their loins. Mind you, the doctor called on John at the house where he made that diagnosis, and no one else's child caught it while she hurt, whined, and coughed in their faces. Today provisions are made in the doctor's office for the contagious child if the parent warns them on or before arrival. I can recall when they didn't.

We were quarantined. Official notices were prominently displayed. A bed was added to Mother's and Daddy's bedroom, which was off limits to the rest of us, for John. Not only that, but no one was allowed to leave the yard except Daddy. Mothers and fathers rarely have scarlet fever anyway. Only family and very few exceptions were allowed on the premises. The doctor came. The iceman entered through the back door, and we stayed out of the kitchen until he left.

The rash, protruding and infectious, left only John's face uncovered; and then the peeling process lasted a long time. Toward the end of three weeks, we sometimes were allowed to step into the room, stand at least twelve feet from her, and carry on a witty thirty-second conversation. How that could have so added to our intelligence, I don't know, but we felt quite smart when we returned to what by then was the normal way of life and the rest of the family. Before three weeks had passed, a neighbor stopped on the walk along the edge of the yard and handed an Easter basket to either Dan or Lemar; we stayed on the grass, and care was taken that there was no contact. Even at that age I felt that the care was due more to respect for the law than from fear. The gift was rather small, but it contained enough candy eggs that we each were given several. We had taken it to our parents to distribute as we were directed.

Before any of us were allowed off the property, the house had to be fumigated with a germicide that was calculated to kill everything except our souls. It must have; none of the family, no neighbor, no business caller caught the disease. Nor did we ever know where John met up with it. Today it is not the problem it was then. Penicillin and other antibiotics protect us from the dread of infected ears or sinuses.

At last I was old enough to start school. We still lived in the house on South Seaman, on the southeast corner of an intersection. Across the street from us lived the Tillies. They had two daughters, Margie, my age, and an older one. Most of the block, however, was taken up by the school and its grounds. Jessie, Lemar, and Dan were poised older students, but Margie and I were as excited as children ever got over such a major step in their lives.

Our teacher, Miss Maybe, made a few comments about the new lives we were starting; then, when another teacher came to talk to her, she told us to write our ones times tables. We looked at one another in consternation until the gabfest was over. We felt fortunate that she didn't ask to see what we had produced. Today I wonder whether Miss Maybe was new to her profession that she didn't realize that we'd not understand what she meant, or if she was being sly and perhaps laughing silently at us while they chatted.

Miss Maybe's company left, and she asked how many of us could read. A scattering of hands went up, mine among them. She called us up one at a time, and had us read a page to her. There were five of us, and we all read our assignments quite to her satisfaction. She pointed to a row of chairs, one behind the other on one side of the room.

"Go sit on that row. You're in the high-first." Wow! Just imagine the conversation at noon while we were gathered around the dining room table.

When I was about six or seven months old, I was put in the baby bed sound asleep, and Mother and Daddy went outside to round up some baby chickens and get them safely above any water level from the rainstorm that was taking place. When they returned to the house, I had obviously woken up, cried, and then pulled myself up by the bars of the bed and managed to fall overboard. A good bit of blood was smeared around, and they thought I was dead at first.

Closer examination showed that I was not, but those two teeth I had sported were now on the floor beside me. Signs indicated that I had pulled up, surely begging for attention all the time, and cried myself back to sleep at the refusal. Dan and Lemar were taking naps; Jessie was at school. Mother couldn't relate the story without crying all over again, and she saved my teeth. When I cut my permanent ones, she told me the story and handed over the first ones. I showed them off and bragged happily about my new ones. For a few weeks I was Exhibit Number One; but then I lost the baby teeth, and my day was over.

Older students never did like to be told to walk on the streets and sidewalks rather than through yards. The Tillies bore the brunt of their cutting through. Likely there were fences that blocked that tendency beyond their yard; but for whatever reason, traffic continued to pass right through it. They complained to the school. Much of the daytime traffic was obedient; but evening traffic, much of it the same boys, continued to track through at night on their way to wherever fourteen and fifteen year-old boys go after dark.

Equally determined, Mr. Tillie strung a rope from a tree to the house, just far enough above the ground for the big boys, failing to see it, to fall over. I don't know how many boys it caught; but on the first evening, before Margie went to bed, she dashed madly around the house. Poor thing, the rope was neck high to her. She had a painful brown rope burn from ear to ear; it began on the underside of her chin, and was as wide as her neck was long. Besides that, she was flung ignominiously to the ground when all the slack in the rope had been taken up by her rush. The rope was removed.

During the later part of that year, Mother would place Mable on a quilt spread on the front lawn. Mable loved it, but of course she had to be overseen. That was Dan's and my job. Each day one was on duty as baby sitter while the one off duty could play with the neighborhood children. Neither Lemar nor Jessie had that hour or so of duty. As our Mother and Daddy were always fair, this meant that they had a duty that I didn't see. Of course Jessie may have had to rest or perhaps couldn't lift a plump baby at that time.

During my first year at school I was introduced to a radical new concept: doctors could cut you open and take part of your insides out, and it didn't kill you. Jessie had to have an emergency appendectomy, and, although only few of us knew the word then, it was traumatic. Making bad matters worse, somehow every stitch in her incision became infected. I don't really know how long she was in the hospital, surely not so long as it seemed. But surely longer than patients averaged even then. Then when she was dismissed, she could not go to school for a time. The doctor came daily to dress her side. Soon he turned that job over to Mother before Jessie was at last pronounced well and allowed to return to school. If Jessie had not been a quick learner, she may have had trouble.

Miss Maybe really disappointed me one day. A girl from another first grade room dropped her cookie, a recess snack, on the playground. We didn't have to have milk or juice all together in the room; we were allowed personal taste and to be hungry or not as our own tummies dictated. We did have to wait for recess time. I must have laughed at the other child and angered her, for she told my teacher and hers—who were having another gabfest—that I had hit her, and said that I was "the boss of the world!" When I denied this, Miss Maybe merely told me to go on and play, to behave myself and not to say such things again. But I noticed they didn't challenge my accuser. That was the only trouble I had with Miss Maybe, however; nor did I get a bad mark in deportment on my report card.

In fact, the only time I ever received a poor grade there was when I was a sophomore in high school, and received a startling B- in what I think may have become attitude by that time. The teacher was Miss Bryson, and by then I had years of theme and short story writing behind me, not always assigned work. Mislaid commas, misplaced colons, errant semicolons, even split infinitives hindered me from reading smoothly and must therefore hinder others; so I learned to put them where they belonged. I was rather shy, but I was generous with my understanding of such things. When Miss Bryson was grading papers, she sometimes sent another student to me for help.

The day after we received our report cards, Miss Bryson asked if anyone had any questions before lessons started. I raised my hand, and given the green light asked why she had given me a B- for my behavior. I felt that she welcomed the opportunity to tell me in front of the class that I thought I was smart; I was always telling other students what to do.

I didn't argue back; that wasn't my style; but neither could I hide how I felt. I was dumbfounded and flabbergasted. Throughout the day most of the students sympathized with me, and Mother and Daddy dismissed it from their minds. They knew me too well.

It was only two or three days later that a student went to Miss Bryson for help while she was grading a pile of our themes. Engrossed in what she was doing, she said, clearly and quite loud enough for the entire room to hear her, "Why don't you go to Fay? She can help you with that." Perhaps hearing her own voice did it—I do not know—but she looked up with a surprised look on her face, and found every eye in the room focused on her. Hurriedly she dropped her eyes to her desk. Neither of us ever mentioned it again, but the other students cackled gleefully about it later. It was the last unfair grade I ever got from her.

Airplanes were biplanes in those days, definitely the forerunners of today's monsters, with each one sporting four wings. It was a few years later that monoplanes began to be seen and were always distinguished in conversation by their proper cognomen: monoplane. Alas! Now "airplane" conjures up visions of all kinds—and in their foreground, a has-been which, these days, is called a biplane!

One day when I was seven, an airplane landed about two blocks from our house, in an intersection and out of gas. I was not allowed to go across streets without permission yet; so I couldn't just go and see it. Lemar and Jessie went. I don't know if Dan did. No one else was old enough. A girl my age came back by the house on her way home. She had been to see it or perhaps had just passed by, but cheerfully she told Mother that it was dangerous, that she ought not let us go near it. Mother muttered and fumed every time she thought about it for years. It was extremely disrespectful and very ill-mannered of a child her age. Today I still can feel the thrill of mixed awe and fear I felt when we went to see that marvelous machine. I never believed man was meant to reach the moon in spite of that; I didn't even allow that some day he might do so. But years later it happened! The fact that I do not understand aeronautics is the basis of my doubts.

"Black bottoms" was the name given to swampy areas with rich black soil that was sticky when wet. Well and good, but while I was in the first grade, someone invented, for young girls, black sateen bloomers. They were certainly modest; but they likely also were a laundry problem as well; for the fad did not last long. Still this old world never again saw so many black bottoms, proportionately speaking of course, as it did for the life of that fad.

Sometime during those days Daddy decided Mother should be prepared to drive in case of emergency—or desire, as he would have liked for her to go shopping and visiting as many young wives did. He borrowed a dealer's Willis-Knight, and he taught her to drive. We used to watch them drive around and around the block, and into the yard and reverse out over and over until Mother drove quite smoothly. Then he bought a dark green Willis-Knight. If Mother ever drove again when the lessons were over, I didn't know it. However, she said even when she was past seventy, that she was sure she could drive if it was necessary.

Some of our entertainment was furnished by the area in which we lived. Doodle bugs, for instance, are fascinating insects which make lovely miniature volcanic-type craters; craters that seemingly haven't a grain of sand out of place on their sloping inner surfaces. With tiny twigs we touched the disappearing center of the bottom of the pits, using the butterfly-light circular motion experience had taught us and invoked invitingly, "Come out. Come out, doodlebug, wherever you are." At times, to our delight, the knobby head broke through, signaling the approach of the creature which looked just like her name. Irrationally, when we viewed her we felt both ten feet tall and rather motherly. If we hadn't unduly disturbed her dwelling place and she didn't flee from us, we might leave it alone. If we had marred it severely, which was likely, then it was hard to walk away, and usually we would scoop deep enough to lift her up along with some of the sand. She would try to burrow back down, tantalizingly tickling our palms; we would murmur solicitously, and place her on the ground that she might reestablish a home. Never would we deliberately harm her; she is of the fairy kingdom and never herself harms a soul. (For goodness' sake, don't let Noah Webster or his underlings tell you she is a larval creation bent on trapping her lunch. That takes absolutely all the fun out of that portion of your life, unless you are one of the lucky few who knows what bits of petty entomology you can safely discard.)

Also, don't be confused after years of absence from the fairy kingdom and warn her her house is on fire. That's the ladybug, the little orange-red creature with black spots on her back and the unwavering desire to guard believing human beings from various harmful aphids. You can pick her up if you wish, but she will visit you uninvited when she sees you frequently and loses her fear. If that should happen, hold your hand up to eye level so you're sure to make contact and warn her, "Ladybug, ladybug, fly away home; your house is on fire and your children will burn." If she acts confused, it is because she doesn't speak your language, and you may blow her gently off your hand. Usually she just makes a beeline for home, and you find yourself helpless to follow her.

We lived about 130 miles west of Dallas, where Mother's sister lived. A very few times Mother boarded the train before there were too many children to handle well and rode to the city to see her sister and perhaps other members of her family. I don't remember the visits, but I remember getting motion-sick on the train. Mother would whisk me off to the ladies' room, clean me up, and put fresh clothing on me. One time she had to put Dan's clothes on me because I had gone through all of mine. I wonder if that's why she had to quit making those train trips.

Of course we all wanted our share of Mother's attention. She used to laugh sometimes after we had got a fussy, sleepy little one safely off to bed, and tell us about Lemar when he was very young. He would wear himself out, and want cuddling at just the wrong time, when the evening meal would burn if she left it. When she spoke soothingly and carried on with her work, he would sing, over and over, "Momma don't like me cause, I don't like Momma." His voice reached its highest note on me and returned to its beginning level again on Momma. Mother felt for him, loved him, and took him as soon as she could; but she never failed to be diverted by his so inadvertently placing the blame on himself.

Fall of the year means a fair with produce, homemade canned goods, cooking, and sewing displays. Daddy was a confirmed visitor to any and all fairs. In all fairness—no pun intended—he extended to everyone an invitation to go along. The fair also had rides—the merry-go-round with its bobbing horses, and the exciting Ferris Wheel, plus the half-man, half-woman, the snake handler, and the wild man.

Lemar wanted to see the wild man and I didn't. Lemar probably took me under his wing because I was the younger; I would stay close by, leaving Dan to Jessie to control. But I wouldn't go in the tent of the wild man, and Lemar, at eight or ten years old, wasn't about to miss it. Stationed nearby and bade firmly to stay put until he returned, I willingly agreed to do so. How time dragged. I can still hear myself calling, "Lemar! Lemar!! Lemar!" I thought I got extremely loud, but in the crowd and rush and laughing and yelling, it's now no wonder that he couldn't hear me. I was probably six or seven, because I found my way home at night by myself. Of course it was only a few blocks and I ran pell-mell down the middle of the pavement.

When I burst into the house and no one followed, Mother questioned me. I think she relaxed. Soon the telephone rang. She answered, and assured Daddy that I was there and safe and sound. They must have understood; it was never mentioned to me again; or if it was, I forgot it.

Daddy had rooms built onto the back of the garage and hired a lady to cook for us, Jim, bless her heart, who was a friendly, warm-faced black woman. Her husband was Leon, and we all liked them. Such odd things stick in our memories as we mature. Jim, for instance, shuddering when I licked some mustard—always French's; even today no one else prepares it so well, so perfectly spiced—off my finger. I went across later to her rooms with the end of my finger swollen to the size of a marble by a blob of mustard. I proved to her how tough I was by licking it all off. With smiling good nature she admired me, and then she shooed me back home.

Mother ate only chocolate cream pie, but she liked cobbler, ice cream, cookies, cakes. On the other hand, Jim loved to bake pies topped with beautiful meringue; and since lemon was a favorite with Daddy, she made them frequently as well. Out of the oven and beautifully browned, each meringue peak a thing of perfection, they had to be showed off.

Mother duly and honestly admired them, and answered in the affirmative Jim's, "Ain't they pretty, Miz Whiznant?"

Chapter V

In order to understand some things about our lives, we must have the proper background. Mother has told all eight of us this story more times than we can count. When she was a schoolgirl, all the other schoolgirls used to stay home on washday and help hang out clothes. Mother naturally wanted to do likewise (poor little underprivileged thing!) but was never allowed to. Neither did her parents ever explain the discrimination. Years later Jesse Whisenant asked Daniel and Jessie Fawcett if he could marry their daughter. I don't know whether Grandma let Grandpa answer, and then tacked her say-so on as a postscript or a codicil; or if she answered before Grandpa could, but her will was done.

She said, "If you won't ever let her wash."

Daddy promised. I can remember Mother washing a piece or two a few times, and I remember her doing a week's laundry with us to help once when we'd just moved. Then when we had to change laundries because an owner decided to shut up shop and retire, Mother washed, in the days when clothes went the cycle with the wash water being used more than once. Mother washed a couple of tubs full and rinsed each in fresh water. After the clothes were hung to dry, some on fences as we did not have enough line for that many, she poured the wash water through a clean cloth. Our water was spoken of as "hard" or "lime" water, and she had a ball of gypsum scum as big as an old heavy teacup. Of course she did a little delicate hand wash occasionally, but I'm sure she never did more than half a dozen tubs of laundry altogether in her life.

Daddy's shirts were "finished" at the laundry, starched and ironed beautifully, and each one folded around a "shirt cardboard." When the laundry came back to the house, those shirts were a separate bundle, very light weight compared to the flat pieces; the towels, sheets, and cup towels, were all pressed in a mangle to speed the drying and make them easier to handle. The other clothing was ironed at home.

Mother sprinkled the clothes with water and rolled them up. Then she wrapped them together in order that they would be nicely damp for the iron. Granny Hickerson, who had emigrated from her native Denmark, would come in, busily shake some of the pieces out, and throw them across the chairs: Mother always had them too wet to suit her. Next she set up the board and began to iron. Once a week until we moved to the farm this scenario took place.

I'm not sure if we knew the Hamiltons in Eastland or in Olden. They were a married couple with a grown daughter. They too were a biscuit and cornbread family. But what we recall most frequently is that they all wanted their biscuit at a different stage of "doneness." Dave Hamilton wanted his taken from the oven when they were just done, not browned at all; so Mother Hamilton opened the oven door and took his bread out of the pan. The rest continued to cook. Louise took hers pale, pale brown. They were removed second. Mrs. Hamilton's cooked until they were "good brown."

Mother and Daddy had been considering moving to a farm, although we children didn't know it for some time. Then the spring before I was eight, they began to think and talk "farm" in our hearing. Daddy looked, listened, and questioned, and once we went to a farm about a mile out of the town of Olden and walked around. There was an old, unpainted house and some plum trees nearby. Beyond them, a barn graced its lot, and just off it were some pens for animals smaller than cattle. We passed through a small wooded area which brought us to where we could see the water of a stock tank gleaming at us from behind its earthen dam.

Mother must have stayed at home with the younger ones, but Lemar and Dan and I ran and played about, fascinated. We were on a farm! After he had walked around poking here and prodding there for a while, Daddy left us there while he went off to check on something. We examined a few short rows of dead cotton and eventually picked what we could, gouging our fingers on the hard, dry bolls in the process; and stuffing it in what we assumed was a sack for that purpose. Once the cotton was picked, we poured the trashy product in a natural sandbed nearby and played in it.

Some time later, just before we moved out to the farm, Daddy sent out a lot of less than half-grown chickens in the bed of a pickup. No one told him to divide them into small lots, and they crowded too close together, resulting in the death of a good number of them. They smothered in those few miles. Of course they were still warm when the trip ended, and the men cleaned them immediately. Mother both bemoaned the financial loss and mourned the chickens. She refused to eat one bite of them.

We actually moved to Olden on Lemar's eleventh birthday—four days before I turned eight. We lived in an unpainted "four rooms and a path," but the house we would live in was begun before then. Even though we moved into the new house quite soon, we still had a path. That was because we had to bounce back some from the big financial blow before we could afford the fixtures for the bathroom. We could take a bath, in a tub sitting in the middle of the bathroom floor, and we did have four bedrooms, which was still none too many for a family as large as ours.

Olden's school was small and contained the eleven grade levels required for graduation, but had split level sections for third graders, with half of them in with the second graders and half in with the fourth graders. Sixth graders also were divided, one half with the fifth grade, the others with the seventh grade. The four high school classes had of necessity to be mostly separated. But juniors and seniors were lumped together in English classes, taking English III one year and English IV the next.

That first year Daddy figured it would be better for us to continue our schooling in Eastland. It did mean changing from East Ward to West Ward, and Jessie was in high school, by then. Lemar drove us to school in the pickup—legally—at the age of eleven. My first day in the second grade was different to say the least. My teacher explained that on the first day of school she always kept the smallest child in the room at her desk, in her lap if she was seated, and in her chair when she wasn't. So I had a ringside seat that day. There must have been some husky students in the room, for I'm neither short nor skinny—although my family insists I was skinny then.

We brought our lunches that year most of the time, but if we had an emergency, we could get a sandwich for a nickel at a nearby grocery store. It was not an unusual practice for a butcher to put lettuce and tomato and mayonnaise on bread and add a slice of lunchmeat for customers. I assume Jessie ate in a school cafeteria at the high school, for she never showed up at the grocery store. For the first few years we were proud of those sandwiches made on commercial bread, but Dan and I in later years fought for the biscuit and sausage that was so palatable at noon. Other students would eagerly have traded their lunchmeat for it too.

Even second grade has its scandals. Our scandal was part of a school-wide misbehavior. Down the street from the school was a choice house that had roses blooming riotously both in the yard and on the fence. We saw them from the pickup, but many students saw them from the sidewalk, and they began to help themselves. The resident family properly talked to the principal, and the entire student body was cautioned not to pick them, that it was against the law, and that any student who did so was courting reprisal. It slowed, but it did not stop the onslaught. There was a second warning; then came the command for every student in every room who had picked even one rose since the cautions were made to come to the office. Three or four boys and one small girl filed out of our room. Each person involved received a swat from the principal. We were duly horrified. Even a girl had been spanked!

Living in the old house was nothing like living in town had been. Mother did all the cooking now, but she began to involve Dan and me, first at breakfast. How to fry bacon, a real cooking chore, got us interested. Peeling vegetables, clearing the table, washing dishes, and becoming acquainted with the kitchen and its implements followed. The house was not piped for water, and we all were soon familiar with the galvanized water bucket. As there was no grass, both Mable and Luceille had to be carefully watched; all of us accepted our share of that responsibility. John was borderline, both watching and being watched. There were tumbles, but nothing serious; and they escaped from the yard a few times, but not once for a prolonged length of freedom. Mother saw that we had time to play as well as to help.

It was from the apple orchard which Daddy set out that fall that I learned, two or three years later, just how many green apples I could eat before I was stricken with an honest to goodness, old-fashioned stomach ache: seven did not hurt me, but eight tore me up every time. I learned which aches were bearable if one did not mention them to his parents. Useful information, that.

There were many scrub oak trees around, ample to screen some of our activities from the house. Playing on or in the pond, which we never called a stock tank, was taboo, but it was fun. Lemar was eleven, quite old and large enough to keep us restrained to the edges of the water if we wanted to accompany him. He also loved to build rafts when he could. Dumpings from unguarded movements were neither dangerous nor rare; and our parents soon learned that Dan and I could gain our feet all over the pond.

Another favorite activity was tree climbing, and Mother and Daddy preferred that to our water play. An abundance of limbs on the stubby, copiously-leafed trees made falling to the ground all but impossible. Dan and I frequently lolled among the branches of our favorite tree where she portrayed the mother of "Epandimondas," and I miraculously became the title character. It never mattered that they were a little black boy and his mother, and we were white girls; we loved him.

We usually climbed through wire fences, over them if we must, on our rambles, for we were not big enough to open the gates. Also we never dared leave a gate open. As the pigs grew larger, we began to shun their pens. Then as they became hogs and won blue ribbons, Daddy fastened them into smaller pens that we knew never to enter. Except that they lacked real freedom, they were utterly spoiled.

The fruit trees were lovely in the spring, but much of their area would soon be used for something else. The apple orchard was a loss almost from the word go, and, gradually, the trees died or were uprooted. There weren't enough plum trees to turn them into a commercially profitable crop, but the fruit was good to eat and made good jam.

The old barn and barn lot were small, and the barn was in

need of repair. Daddy replaced them with new and larger ones closer to the site of the house we were to live in; and for several years we used the old barn and lot for the pigs and horses, and the new one for the over night housing when needed for the cows and for milking. It adjoined a huge bed of gravel, and Daddy sold gravel by truck loads. We reveled in delving in the stirred up pebbles when a lull in business took place. Often we found stones with the beauty of rubies and opals and some gems for which we didn't know the names.

At one time Daddy used the area just west of the larger barn for another venture. We had hundreds of white leghorns as well as a huge nest house with many roosts. Eggs were gathered in bushel baskets, and they sold well; but the egg business took too much time from the production and selling of fresh garden produce. We ate vast amounts of chicken and loved it; which meant that plan wasn't a complete disaster. I'm sure some of the fowl were sold live, however.

Some years later, after he no longer sold gravel, Daddy also had the barn enlarged and improved, and tried dairying. But he was determined to be on schedule: milk at twelve noon and again at midnight. Alas, no one got any rest. Daddy at first set an alarm and went to supervise and help, but that waked up part of our household. The men had to show up, and that upset their households. So a sleep allowance had to be made for them. Soon it was evident that crops which needed early picking or watering were not doing very well under the present regime. Back we went to total gardening again.

It was exciting. I'd gone to school for a year at East Ward and that long at West Ward, both in Eastland; and now I was entering the third grade at Olden. What would it be like? Just like school: playgrounds, water fountains, and bathrooms cannot stay successfully hidden long. Daddy paid tuition for John, and she was enrolled for first grade.

She blended in immediately, had no problems, and was a good student. Mrs. Timmons taught first grade for years. After the first graders went home at two fifteen, she then taught history to the seventh grade.

I repeated the first half of the third grade in order that Dan and I wouldn't be in the same grade, but to me that did not matter; I loved school and there was always something to learn. I adored Dan, too, but I did not desire to be under her aegis twenty-four hours a day.

Here it took only a few minutes to walk to great picnic grounds; we had a Halloween carnival and a Christmas program as well as Christmas trees in our rooms. What joy it was to squander that quarter on the friend whose name we had drawn.

Another well-remembered teacher taught second and half of the third grade, though not my half. She was very quiet and proper, a real lady, Nan Allman. Rumor had it that her unmarried state was the result of her fiancé's death in the First World War. One Sunday when she found that she had not brought any money to church, she borrowed back the penny she had given to her great-nephew for the plate and made it her own contribution. What a conscience! Johnny watched, with great amazement at such behavior in a teacher.

Laura Simor was one of my favorite teachers. On day I overhead her tell a friend that the school board, which paid others with equal qualifications the princely salary of one hundred twenty-five dollars monthly, cut hers to ninety-five because, "after all, you'll be living at home."

On May 7, 1929, we children calmly slept right through the arrival of the next member of our family. Granny Elkins came to the house to rule supreme in Mother and Daddy's room for ten days. She showed us the baby, Vickey, when she was clean and happy, perhaps asleep, and with her blondish coif carefully curled from contact with an adult finger when wet. Her hair curled when properly encouraged, but she wore it as straight as a ruler and almost white for years. Later, with a little brushing and fussing, it was easily fixed without permanents as most of us had to have.

When Granny Elkins found out that Mother was not sure what she wanted to name the baby, she told Mother that she had a standing offer to a baby named for herself: a new dress and a dollar. Amused, Mother asked what her name was.

"Well, my name is Minnie Victoria; but the baby could be called 'Vickey' or 'Vickey Van.'"

If any of the old timers around Olden ever peruse this, they may drop dead with surprise; for while Vickey got that full title, she's always gone by Vickey. Except before bed when we rocked her. Then we sang, "Oh, Vickey; Oh, Vickey; Oh Vi-uh-kee-uh-Van!" Repeated as long as necessary to get her to quit bawling and go to sleep.

Vickey was the last of the blue-eyed, cotton-topped Whisenant children. We petted her shamefully, and Daddy was as guilty as any of us. Which was not unusual, as he had been as proud as punch of each of us in turn. Only Vickey got an undue share of petting. I'm not positive, but I think Dan made up the lullaby.

To keep the record straight for posterity: Mother would not allow Mrs. Elkins to give Vickey any gift at all.

By then baby-tending was old hat to us, and so was done with good-natured resignation most of the time, and rebelled at fiercely if it interfered with important plans, which did not always produce results. She followed us around and grew into a little tomboy like the rest of us. Then one day when she was four, in the spring, they came in after she had gone with Daddy on one of his rounds, and she was dressed to the hilt: fluffy pink dress, slip, rayon panties, slippers! We hardly recognized the child, and genuinely envied the "silk pants," as we wore cotton. From then on Vickey seemed older, no more a baby.

After Vickey was born, Dan and I took on the production of breakfast. Mother needed her rest, Daddy decreed, and as Jessie had been ill, it fell to our lot. We set our alarm for what we considered an unearthly hour. Daddy left earlier to deliver the produce ordered the day before. Dan and I would have breakfast, biscuit, bacon or sausage, eggs, and coffee, prepared day after day when he returned. We learned to pick up the sound of his truck as it rounded Eastland Hill, about two miles from the house; and that was when the biscuit slid into the oven and the eggs were poured into the frying pan. Daddy's eggs were turned over, the yolks soft. Lemar asked for (demanded) and got his beaten thoroughly and fried soft, not browned, but more like a sheet of pale tissue paper. If he did not go with Daddy, we weren't always as careful with his. I was at liberty to vary the menu, but not too often. I might add hominy, cooked in a skillet with its juice and a tablespoonful of butter and one of bacon grease until all of the liquid disappeared. Or I made thickened gravy with the bacon menu, brindled with the sausage. You know, pour most of the grease off, pour a bit of water in the pan, and boil up the tasty brown bits in the skillet. I might fix cheese and crackers; cheese, cut rather thin and slightly smaller than the salty crackers, topped them, and the whole was thrust in the broiler for browning. Broilers then were the flames for the ovens which reared up next to the stove top. We did not have to stoop to peer in at the baking goods. Now table tops are the thing, and never again can we store items under the oven safely out of the way.

Lemar used to beg for a dog, and at last was allowed to accept a puppy from a friend. He spent many hours with it, and was very upset when it became ill. The local vet feared rabies. Naturally our parents were vitally concerned; Daddy took the little thing to Fort Worth. It died, and Daddy told us when he got word of the death, but he forgot Lemar's age, and lack of adult understanding. For some days Lemar waited to be stricken with rabies, and even went so far as to tell Mother to tie him when he got ill so that he could not bite the girls. Quickly she told him that the puppy had been ill with the flu. Then Daddy apologized and re-explained. Both Mother and Jessie, who with her four year edge over Lemar had stayed around for the full story, were horrified. Neither could ever hold back her tears when they spoke of the incident.

Beginning in 1930, Texas set the age for entering school as six on or before September 1 of the current year; so Luceille began her education. The following incident happened either to her or to Mable two years later as they had very similar experiences. Going to school, we first walked two blocks to the highway, then a fair distance along the highway, followed by a stretch on cement sidewalks.

The Simors' house was along the sidewalk. Confined to the yard was a bulldog, which luxuriated in accompanying all passersby the length of his territory, barking ecstatically the while from his side of the fence. After a few months little sisters could be left behind if they tarried along the way. This day, this one was quite alone when the gate burst open. The dog dashed out, grabbed her lunch sack, and helped himself. Automatically, without waiting to see if she was hurt, the child screamed lustily. Mrs. Simor came charging to the rescue, made sure the victim wasn't harmed, and took her inside to replace the lunch: two sandwiches, fruit, carrot. Mrs. Simor asked if that was all and the child took a last look at the luscious uncut cake on the cabinet. She gave in to Satan's prod.

"A piece of cake," she said.

Of course we were scandalized when Mother got the full story out of the imp. We were most concerned about the lie and what amounted to the theft of the cake then. Today as I recall how shrewd Mrs. Simor was, I wonder if she recognized the longing and untruthfulness and still gave the cake quite gladly. She loved to make cakes, and grew famous for them. I can see her today as she made delicate swirls through the icing, and then licked the knife.

As we grew older, we often answered a knock on the back door, where most of our visitors showed up, or the call of a car horn to find a local customer wanting to buy vegetables fresh from the garden. We liked that, for Daddy would allow us to keep half of the take. If it were only a small order, we tried to be the only one to gather it in order to have a bit more spending money.

We never had regular allowances as some neighbors did, mostly those who were a part of a small family headed by a man with a good job. We were taken to town before Christmas and each given enough money to spend a small amount on each other. A great deal of thought and searching were required to make us succeed; but, resolute, we did it, often by not buying the one gift we wanted most to give to one of the family. At times there were odd little results.

One year Dan took John under her wing when it was time to wrap and label the gifts. One of her gifts had vanished. As it was Dan's gift that vanished, a third party was called in to assist in locating the lost item, a canoe occupied by an Indian boy. Though it was a man—made material, it was not called plastic. It took some time, and secret conferences with both Dan and John; but we did it. We solved a mystery made more difficult by the fact that none of us would have dreamed of taking another's gift. We might have snitched bites of his hoard of candy if we had the opportunity, but Christmas was too serious to us. The gift reflected John's level of maturity, and she hadn't aged enough to realize that Dan was too old for it. Dan had also bought one for John, and, after an inadvertent glimpse while John dived into various small bags for items to be wrapped, had assumed that she herself had been careless. She took it and hid it under the fold of her skirt. John and Ceal could play Indians together that year after Christmas.

That may have been the same year that Lemar had set his heart on a lariat which he didn't receive; he hid and cried. No one could console him, and finally Daddy drove off alone—where, none of us knew. After a long time he returned with the coveted rope. Some kind merchant had opened up to sell it to him; and earned another star for his crown. Lemar got far more good out of that lariat than its dollar value. He became very proficient for his age.

Where the road we lived on met the highway, there lived a family. Mrs. Mason was a very accomplished piano player and teacher. Mr. Mason may at one time have been an accomplished person previous to living on those acres, but he now eked out an existence on maize—all grain similar to this crop is maize to me. They raised four children. The oldest was a girl, a mother's helper type due to enforced practice, I'm sure. The second was a boy about Ceal's age. He could read the newspaper aloud easily before she could stumble through some items with help. The second girl was a beautiful child, with lovely gold curls, who could recite her ABCs at two. She loved to dry dishes, but as she had had polio she found it hard to do. She could open her left hand only by pushing it back and swinging her arm in a circle to pull it over her shoulder and turn it so that the back was toward the floor. The fingers opened wide, allowing her to insert a small item such as a fork or a toy shovel, for instance before the hand clamped tightly shut automatically. The same procedure was followed for its removal. The last child was a boy. At one time the children helped themselves to Mr. Mason's razor and totally ruined it. Mr. Mason quit shaving and grew a super-abundant, bright red beard. He became known as "Red Beard" behind his back after that.

Mrs. Mason and Mother planned together that we children should take piano lessons for helping Mrs. Mason. When she needed help, she hung a dishcloth over her back screen door. When we saw it, whoever was taking lessons was sent to help. I played only by transferring A on the written notes to A on the keyboard. Nothing ever became automatic with me like it is with typewriter keys. Oh, I worked, and I practiced, but I was a failure, and at last I quit. Jessie learned to play but from another teacher; and Mable learned while I was away at college. I don't know from whom. The rest of us failed to learn even though my sisters were more apt than I.

One day when I went to help, the crippled child endured some painful muscle spasms, began to run a fever, and lapsed into a coma. I had never seen a convulsion, and desperately I threw a towel over the screen; it went unnoticed at first, but Mother spotted it far sooner than it felt like. Earlier she had seen Mrs. Mason trudge down into the fields to speak to her husband before leaving for town, where I thought she had already gone. One of my sisters was sent to contact the parents, and they came to the house. The little girl had a high fever for some time and, at last, the doctor diagnosed her illness as some technical-sounding words, but he allowed they meant "shrinkage of the brain." She recovered bodily, but was never mentally normal again, and in a few years was sent to a state home. In the meantime, her mother had coped and had trained her lovely hair not to curl since she cried when it became badly tangled and had to be cared for.

The parents used to go to see her occasionally, one at a time; and I felt more kindly toward the mother because she never told the father that the child did not truly remember him. Mrs. Mason knew that any man who came toward the girl was greeted with loud, happy cries, "Daddy, Daddy, Daddy!" To this day, over fifty years later, I see a bright, lovely little girl with the golden curls, and, suddenly standing at her side, the older child with straight pale brown hair and the year-old mind when I think of her. And I wonder why the waste of humanity. A reason exists, but I don't know it. I lost all track of the family after I went off to school, but Mrs.

Mason contacted some of the family when we lost Jessie, and again when Daddy died.

Yes, we worked, but we played too. On a fine Saturday Lemar, Dan, and I decided to cook out. I really cannot say that Johnny was or was not included. Anyway, we wound up in the woods near the old barn where we built a fire and put on a pot of red beans to cook. It wasn't our fault that Mother Nature decided to change her mind. The wind whipped up dust and sand, and we should have had enough sense to pack it all up and go home. We didn't.

It was hard to keep the fire lighted, and the wind made a good stab at blowing all the heat "clear to Kingdom Come." I can't recall what else we had on the menu, but I do recall what poor eating those half-done beans made when we had had all we could take, were starving, and most of all were tired of fighting nature.

Mother, it turned out, could look and see how well we were progressing, how many times we climbed a tree, watch us lift the lid to taste the beans, and knew when we checked to see that the bull which Daddy sometimes let graze in that pasture wasn't coming out of hiding. We had a healthy fear of him. Mother was more intelligent than we; she would have gone home. She queried our not doing so when the wind began to get up. We weren't about to admit that it was pride.

But they really were the good old days.

Chapter VI

Jessie and Lemar were the first of us to take on the chore of milking. Daddy taught them. Then the art of milking was handed down to the next of age. It came to be Dan's job and I took on feeding the hogs at the same time. There was poison ivy on the farm, but some of us never had any trouble with it. Although we were taught to dodge it, and Dan did, she seemed to break out if she got within ten feet of it and circled away. When I was seventy, an old milk hand told me that cows brushed against it and passed it on to the humans who came in contact with them. I wish we'd known that back then. It could have saved Dan untold misery.

Jessie spent many pain-filled days with an undiagnosed problem with one of her legs. The doctor tried treating it with the cure for first one thing and then another before it was decided that she had inflammatory rheumatism. Watching the leg getting harder and harder to move, Mother had begun exercising it for her as she lay in bed. Often Jessie would cry with pain; stymied, the doctors condemned her to life on crutches when she was still sixteen. Daddy supported Mother and Jessie, however; and they refused to give up. It took a very long time. Success crept toward them, and receded; the joint loosened almost imperceptibly. Jessie walked with the aid of crutches for an extended period of time; but at last graduated to two canes. Then to a single cane. Still she persevered, and the great day came when she walked unaided.

The knee was stubborn; it would never totally straighten the leg in the future; but she conquered it by simply denying it the privilege of remaining a hindrance. She could dance and she could skate, both gracefully. She swam, and she walked miles at a time.

Oddly, one of the things I remember most vividly, other than Jessie's pain and struggle, was the illness at the same time of one of the Meredith boys. I never had the faintest idea of what his trouble was, but he died. Soon after their own troubles, I recall Mrs. Meredith coming to visit Mother. She was very apologetic because she had not come sooner both to visit and to help Mother and Jessie in their anxiety and their struggle against the pain. Mother was equally adamant that her friend couldn't have been expected to. They cried like babies then for themselves and their children. I still can feel my eyes burning in sympathy some sixty years later.

A classmate of mine, Helen, lived off the highway, near the depot, where her father was the agent. Because she had no one even near her age in the neighborhood, she begged us to stay and play with her. One time Dan and I gave in, using the excuse that I had to copy a poem to memorize, and that I had left my book at school. We had not reckoned with Johnny. When she walked home, she rubber-necked and caught glimpses of us between houses. Johnny was a tattletale that day. Although we produced our alibi at the proper time, our astute mother demanded to see the poem. After all, we were seen playing. Howard, Helen's brother, and Dan's classmate, had written it for me. That wasn't good enough either when used as a desperate bid for clemency. Mother paddled us for telling her a story. I don't suppose that she ever used the word lie in that context in her life.

Speaking of Mother's language, one time when she was in her mid-eighties, I was visiting and had been doing some of the housework for her. Finished, I told her that I intended to go to town shortly and would buy anything she had need of if she would make a list. I was allotting her ample time to check her supplies while I bathed, but I had not put it into words, and that worried her.

She hemmed and hawed a bit and finally hesitantly said, "Honey, perhaps you had better freshen up first. You are a little rank."

I promise you she thought her children were using that word as a polite way of saying dirty and smelly!

If anything can be work, we as children tend to make it so. Today I rather like to pick peas, but then it was work. Early one morning Mother wanted some for lunch. We two set out for the field, a place of lush, dark green beauty below the old house. We had picked the bucket full before Mother suddenly squawked and jumped. Those freshly picked black-eyed peas lay spilling out of their bucket.

"Fay, come over here; let's go; there's a rattlesnake," she warned me agitatedly.

I was too stupid to obey. Instead I knelt, one eye on that coiled, rattling strip of evil, and salvaged every pod of those peas. I was certainly not going to throw away the product of our labor. I'd not do that today!

In some ways we were slow learners. Daddy's old adding machine was gathering dust in a back bedroom, and John showed off by striking matches and letting some of the dust balls go up in a poof of flame. As younger ones will, Luceille decided to show off. She managed to catch the machine keys on fire. Either she or a younger watcher ran in and told Mother. Even today, Mother's bravery is extolled when John or Ceal speaks of her carrying the blazing machine outside.

In the summer time when the sun was hot and the squash were prolific, the harlequin bugs were also prolific. They struck the squash in great numbers. Each of us was given a can with waste motor oil in it and instructed to remove the bugs from the plants and drop them in the oil. How we hated it! Nor did we feel sorry for the bugs. But we felt sorry for us. It was quicker than dealing death to the individual bugs, however, and more efficient than sprays.

Of course we didn't work all the time. It's just that we remembered the freezing cold and boiling hot days and the very tiring ones the most. We had fun also, even learned to dog paddle in the stock tank, always with a swimmer who was also responsible for our behavior. Store-bought suits were too expensive for that watery playground and sure to be permanently discolored after a few sessions. So we made our own for the tank, and hoarded the store-bought ones for more public bathing—if we had a public swimming pool at that time. One of our best sources for homemade suits was Daddy's worn shirts. Romper styled suits were made with less work than more professional copy could be turned out.

Daddy sometimes went swimming with us, and Mother would watch occasionally, but I never saw her in the water, unless she felt the need to help a very young child to stand erect, or herd an animal along. When we could swim across the deep end of the tank and hold to the limbs of the old willow tree dangling provocatively far out over the water, it was a red letter day for us.

Then there were the evenings when it was warm enough to stay out. Hide-and-seek, blind man's bluff, tag, and quite fascinating, the lightning bugs—did you know that just one or two, especially the larger ones, could make the dark room appear quite light when one waked up at two or three o'clock in the morning? One gets such an impression of friendliness from the glow. We would drop them into a bottle, or jar, with a blade or two of grass, and be sure to put an air hole in the lid. The next morning, we would release them. We could always catch more through the summer.

There was room for a large number of cars between the house and garage, and behind the garage were fields. Once a storm blew the garage away. It lay in great scattered sections in the fields. With the garage missing, we could quite clearly see the Sharps' home on their farm.

All of the Sharps had been country-raised where we had been sort of transplanted. We borrowed back and forth, even visited sometimes, but mostly where our ages zigged, theirs zagged. To go between the houses across the fields was the shorter way, but it was rough walking; and often there were grassburrs and/or sticktights which we could not completely eradicate. Of course we could go out the front and walk the block to Sharp's lane, but it was a long boring journey that way. That morning we went out to survey the damage and one of their daughters shrieked at us, wanting to know if we had suffered any damage. One of my younger sisters answered that the garage was all. We didn't know then whether damage to crops had occurred. Vivian Sharp realized only then that for the first time she could see into our yard very plainly.

Mildred Sharp, the youngest child, used to come to see us frequently when she was old enough. One drawing card was the ever-present banana. We always offered her one, and she always accepted it. She ate it, peel and all. Dan gagged at the thought, and at last told our little sister to tell her she could have two if she would peel them. That did the job. Mildred ate two peeled bananas on every visit from then on.

No one seems to know why one day Vickey was the victim of Mable, Luceille, and Anna May Sharp, but they admit that she was. Those three, all older than she, tied Vickey up nice and tight and left her in the cornfield to struggle unaided and fight her way through the earlier mentioned weeds and cuckleburs to our home. Of course there was a strip next the yard that wasn't quite so bad to walk through as the cornfield. Mother made a believer out of the guilty ones that day. If you have ever walked across those dry and penetrating cuckle-burs, you will understand Mother's outrage at the perpetrators.

Mother loved buttermilk, and drank it often. During a doctor's visit one day, she told him while they drank coffee together after the business was over that she seemed to get more of a lift from buttermilk than anything else she drank. He informed her that after forty-eight hours buttermilk developed a minute percentage of alcohol, which explained the lift when she was tired. He also assured her that she couldn't become intoxicated on it.

Mother liked cane syrup too, especially when we had hot biscuits. Well and good, we all did; but when Mother imbibed buttermilk and ate syrup at the same meal, a severe headache invariable followed. She studied the changing circumstances and nailed the problem. She made a choice from then on, and ignored it if she hungered for both.

John fiercely defended her friends if we made unkind or suspicious remarks about them. We could kindly mind our own business and let her and her friends alone! While she still is quite loyal, she judges us more carefully now, and is not so quick tempered either. Luceille, on the other hand, was mild-natured and merely smiled. Somehow she always had a boyfriend, even in the first grade. One of them, Link, was from a family we knew about but didn't know.

Poor Link! He had to have a tooth pulled, and somehow his mouth became infected. In only a few days he was dead. His funeral was held in the Methodist church.

In Olden, as in most small towns, funerals for children of school age were attended by the entire student body. The three churches in Olden were Baptist, Methodist, and Church of Christ; and they were all very close to the school. The rare student who didn't attend was free to go home unless it was in the morning.

A few days later, Lemar teased Ceal about not having a boyfriend. She came back with, "I'll get me another one!" Her sweet smile flashed, and her dimples appeared, pointing out why she could be so totally sure of herself.

We had lots of fresh homegrown vegetables to eat during those years, but so did lots of other people. Still we knew that money had grown scarce, and every one of us must do our share of the work, especially if we wanted a few luxuries to accompany the necessities. Each day after school we hurried home unless we had prior permission to do otherwise. First we ate, anything we could find that we were sure was not for supper. Then we asked for "the list"—that list of produce to be gathered for the morning delivery. Typically it might be thirty dozen turnips, seven dozen mustard, nineteen dozen radishes, eight dozen onions, six bushels of blackeyes, and three bushels of spinach. The bushel is easy to understand, but dozen may mislead the bystander who sees vegetables only in plastic bags at their favorite grocery. The strings looped to our belts gave us the answer to how many we had done or to do. We carried the bunches to the vegetable house, washed them, and stacked the order neatly. Daddy helped if he was home in time, but that wasn't often the case, and he had to load them in the truck very early the next morning for delivery. There were other "bunch" vegetables as well as eggplant, peppers, both sweet and hot, sometimes cabbage. Occasionally we raised potatoes but had more luck with sweet potatoes than Irish. I was off in college when Daddy added tomatoes and asparagus, Mother's joy, to the crops. He always gave her the earlier stalks in the spring, but sold it when it was more plentiful. We had watermelons and cantaloupe some years, but I can also recall cantaloupe so rife that we had to feed it to the livestock. It's easy to see why we weren't always happy to rush home.

In spite of all that, we were permitted to stay after school for pep squad. We even stayed for the out of town games if we had a ride; and for activities having to do with math contests, rehearsals, workouts, and such. Daddy loved for us to compete in those activities. Lemar didn't indulge in football, but he ran. I can recall the hullabaloo when he ran a mile in under five minutes the first time. He was known as Rabbit in those days.

Dan was the actress in the family and in two successive years achieved success from a windfall role. The first year there was one black lady and a majority of Caucasians in the cast. Dan undertook to be "Niobe," which included wearing a black make-up and wig. As juniors in high school, the other girls had failed to see the many possibilities concealed in the role. Proud parents thronged in to watch even the dress rehearsal the night before production night. Dan was proud, and erect, but she unintentionally brought the house down by a nervous slip of the tongue, sending both audience and cast into explosive peals of laughter.

Instead of, "This is the end of poor little Niobe," Dan mourned, "This is the poor end of little Niobe!"

Her bruised pride was partially soothed later when many members of the audience sympathized with her. But the rest of the cast were so jealous that when casting time came for the senior play, they all clamored to be black characters, a regrettable mistake. They were plural in number, but there was only one white lady. Again Dan was the star attraction. Although she gives the teacher the credit for suggesting she should take the single white role, I can still hear Dan, on the day of casting, crowing that they had chosen their roles without thinking things through.

Dan always was keener about things like that. She had more maturity at any age than I did; and she had friends who even two years later would not have appealed to me much. I followed Dan, but I never quite came up to her standards in my own opinion.

Some summers Dan and I were allowed to spend a week or two with Aunt Edith and Uncle Will in Fort Worth. Uncle Will was a mechanic. In my memory, two unrelated bits of information about him stand out. First, he ate fried eggs at breakfast, but he peppered them until they were totally black before he took the first bite. Second, he added, to the soap suds all worked up on his hands, a teaspoon of sugar. It helped cut the black grease and stains from his hands.

They had two sons, several years older than us, Willie Payne and Douglas. I wasn't much interested in them, but we saw them at our house or theirs. Then came two daughters to round the family out. Edith Grace was a piano student, and she played superbly. To pay for the lessons, Aunt Edith did the teacher's laundry. She also did laundry for a few other people, and it was from her that Dan and I learned to finish ironing a shirt. We had ironed only work shirts before, and they didn't matter much. Last was Luella, happy-go-lucky, a shade spoiled, and lazy. Aunt Edith was good to us, and fun to be around. She also served bakery bread with every meal. It was a novelty we enjoyed in spite of missing our biscuit.

I believe it was Willie Payne who was visiting one year when Daddy wanted the roof repainted. He and Lemar thinned the paint and applied it with an old fly spray. Remember how thick the flies could get at times, and the spray sent hand pumped droplets of death over them. Of course some of them survived, but they were willing to leave the house. Anyway, the two teen-aged boys were transforming an aging roof to a new green, but a silly cat kept investigating. At last the painters latched on to the feline pest and sprayed it green. We never did know where the cat wound up after she ran off.

One of Daddy's extra money schemes paid off every time, and we all, with one exception, he himself, hated it. With so much space once filled with chickens, we had lot space to let; and meat producers were eager to hire it for fattening lots. For two weeks or more cattle which were accustomed to running the range milled around in quarters which were much too close to work off their rambunctious frustrations, lowed, day and night, and answered nature's call. From the first, we never dared to encourage even a close friend to visit us. It was not possible to enjoy a visit in that spicy air. We did have interims of peace, but none of us ever knew when to expect what, as the old saying went.

Chapter VII

Like many families, we used to gather around the piano and sing while Jessie accompanied us. Daddy loved to "Come, come, come..." to the "Little Brown Church in the Wildwood," and he like to "tramp to the vintage" in "The Battle Hymn of the Republic." There were others, but those I still hear him sing most frequently while I wash dishes or knit today. Nine out of ten of us could sing—and I was the tenth.

My lack of musical ability was evident in my voice. My biggest problem was that I was not aware of the fact, and my careless acceptance of an unlovely voice was roughly changed to disquiet one day in class. We were average teenagers in Olden, and the words of new songs were written down and passed around for everyone to copy and learn. "Wabash Moon" was the latest to be eagerly committed to memory when our music teacher asked us each to stand and sing a favorite song. Dan sang an old standby. She passed with flying colors. I was foolish and decided to follow the crowd. I tried to sing "Wabash Moon." I shouldn't have: it was so bad that no one even teased me.

In our teenage years we also began to notice that we had matured enough to be expected to keep silent in some circumstances. I remember the first time that I caught on to a little chicanery which I'm sure was common practice. The county road grader was parked on our farm, with permission, and would be put back into duty the next morning by the same operator. But this time I realized that Daddy was to syphon out some of the gas to "make up for the favor." At the same time, the operator would be credited with using the gasoline in doing more county road work than he had done; for he was paid for so many miles per gallon. To circumvent the truth in certain circumstances, I thought then, might be all right if it did not mean a loss to someone; but that driver should not cheat the county. I don't know whether Daddy accepted, then or ever, the invitation to help him. I prefer to think that he did not.

In either case the friendly machine operators continued to visit and share information. We saw them frequently when road work brought them to our door. The highway department bought water from Daddy. They filled their trucks from our well at a flat rate per truck. The splashes and the tracks left on the gravelly road from the well house, a few hundred feet from the house, to the exit from our place are lodged in my memory. The section of the road from the well through the gardens was sand and dirt, and more apt to be muddy walking in wet weather.

School picnics were not held so often that they became mundane, but neither were they extremely rare. Sometimes we walked to nearby spots; sometimes we went to a place called Butler's Springs. I could never have found it alone, but we had fun even on the way. Rigid wires moved back and forth near oil wells and sometimes our path led over them. We liked just to stand on them where, inevitably, we lost our balance; or we made sure they moved in front of our heels without moving us. A cable swing, made by climbing a tree and catching the cable when it was swung upwards, awaited us at the picnic ground. Holding tight with a death-defying grip, the brave one then stepped off the tree. Tough boys, like Lemar, rode it eagerly, and the rest of us watched enviously. Teachers and all, we enjoyed these outings.

After I began to cook, my contribution to picnics often was a cake, vanilla with chocolate icing. I recall the day that the picnic was cancelled because of sudden rain. The careless teacher had us eat and then dismissed us for the day, but she never had us share our contributions. We were not offered chips, or sandwiches, or fruit, but were prevailed on to share the cake. We did not capitulate until we were accused of being selfish. When we explained what had happened at home, Mother shocked us: she didn't offer us a meal! How utterly silly can teenagers be?

Helen Adams was valedictorian when we graduated at the end of seventh grade, and I was salutatorian. She bested me by less than a point. I was happy with her honor and mine. I was delighted too with the white organdy dress, gorgeously ruffled, which Mother and Daddy bought for me. Basically we wore dresses made by Mother.

That was the last time that Mother went shopping with any of us. She didn't like shopping, and one of us was old enough to take the lead if clothing must be bought. Usually Daddy supervised coat and shoe buying, and at times he even brought the percale our everyday dresses were made from.

High school was a whole new ball of wax. We had nearly an hour for each subject! And such math courses. Algebra, two years of it, and geometry. They were much more enticing than the four basics of math. I struggled some, but I never threatened to fail. But one day as we took an algebra test, a girl asked me for a particular problem. I hesitated, then nudged the wad of paper I'd solved it on off my desk. Though I had the correct answer, I had not properly arrived at the solution. Mr. Collins took ten points from my grade, but he took six from the other student's. Neither of us ever dared ask about it, and I have no idea why the discrepancy to this day.

Mr. Smith always liked me as a student and he always graded fairly. Also he rarely put a plus or minus sign by the letters given for grades on report cards. As high school graduation drew nearer, he saw that the committee to verify and announce the honor students was distinguishing between A's, A+'s, and A-'s. For fear they might not make an accurate selection, he found all his grade books for the last four years and added pluses or minuses where deserved in accordance with his records and listed the range covered by each symbol. I won by less than a point, besting Helen to the top spot by one-twenty-seventh of a point more than she had beat me in the seventh grade. That speech was harder to write in a way than the other had been, for I had sat in the Methodist Church the year before and watched while Dan got her diploma; I'd seen how many people crowded in for the ceremony; I had seen the candidates for diplomas seated on the platform facing the audience. Never again was I so grateful in my life as I was to Betty Gray Nix when she turned and sent me an encouraging smile just before I got up to speak. Somehow I survived it. After it was all over, my classmates and I could brag about our class of fourteen; for there had been only ten graduates in Dan's class. Of course the bragging was done tongue-in-cheek.

Daddy had had fifteen years as secretary of the Rotary Club in Eastland, and he decided that it was time he stepped down. As soon as the other members knew plans were made to make a big thing of it. What Daddy didn't know was that the others wanted a pin for him that didn't exist, for it was an unusual record. So on the big day he was touted and toasted and given sort of an official raincheck to be presented with his pin ceremonially when the especially ordered award came in. He was all smiles and fun when he told Mother about it, as proud as could be of the exclusiveness of his retirement from the position.

One day Daddy decided to take a gift of hot peppers to Miguel who ran either a cafe or a small neighborhood store, and was one of the many acquaintances and friends Daddy had. Miguel smiled brightly, sliced the peppers into a bowl, topped them off with salt, pepper, and vinegar, and began to eat. He demolished the lot, praising and thanking his benefactor all the while.

Daddy was amazed, having assumed that he would eat off the offering a week or more; but he continued taking peppers with little if any break in a day after day regularity. At last Miguel threw up his hands and told Daddy, "No more, no more, Mr. Whisenant. I've eaten all I can."

I shall never understand why the man didn't slow down instead of burning himself out.

Mother did many, many hours of routine and cooking in their nearly 64 years of married life, but essentially she was an outdoor person. Sometimes we children would attack a field with hoes and then rake up all the weeds before it was plowed a final time for replanting. I have known Mother to work with us and deliberately hoe around one mustard plant, because it was young and clean and would be good eating, in spite of knowing that the plow would turn it under. What the plow did was none of her concern.

One year Daddy gave Mother a dozen rose bushes and set them out for her on the south side of the house in one long row. But it was not Mother who was expected to carry twelve buckets of water to them from the hydrant in the back yard. Occasionally when everyone else was busy she slipped them a drink; but Daddy never liked it and reminded her again to wait for help.

Mother could raise anything she set her mind to, and we all grew up with a love of flowers and plants. As Dan and I were so close in age, we would have individual flower plots at the same time. I loved carnations and planted them until I went off to college. Dan favored nasturtiums, or zinnias. Lemar was still of an age to have a small space too. Once he raised peanuts, which he oh, so coolly, spoke of as "goobers." They fascinated me, their saucy flowers who hid their faces, buried themselves in the earth in obedience to God's command so their edible seeds would evolve. Dismay on my face at the first taste of that premature moist, pink, mouth-drawing kernel must have delighted Lemar. What relief I felt when I was assured that those seeds would mature into the nuts we liked, and so it proved to be.

With Daddy in the business he was in, avocados were not unusual to us, and Mother used to grow the plants until they were too large to bring in and protect over the winter. She enjoyed it and added to our education and outlook. We would never have tried some steps that she took. I have seen her seal in a jar, with water covering them, seeds that take two years to germinate. After the larger part of that time had passed, she planted the seeds in the earth. I wasn't smart enough to keep up with how the plants did because by then I was a teenager, a college student, and a beginning teacher.

Mother was an expert seamstress, the finishing touches mostly self-taught; and she taught us to sew. We never came up to her standards in buttonholes, though; and I never saw a machine-made buttonhole that was as pretty as hers. Later Daddy bought her a buttonholer, but I never learned to use it. It was fairly easy to get Mother to hand-work them, very, if we took over the cooking. She was a magnificent cook too, but preferred to let us cook while she tended her gladiolus, day lilies, altheas, and bridal wreath. She could do a set of buttonholes and get outside too while I got a meal.

On the other hand, her meatloaf was so tasty that after I was grown I would invite company for dinner and ask her to make one. Among other ingredients, she used an ample amount of Worcestershire sauce. We were taught to say wooster too, the proper English pronunciation; but we always said *Lea and Perrins*, because it was the only brand she used. Imagine my surprise after I was married when I realized that there were other brands of it. Mother, in the way of many good cooks, measured only by eye once she had cooked a dish; she knew by instinct if something needed a little more of an ingredient. We tired of red beans, but there was always *Lea and Perrins Worcestershire Sauce* for Mother. Daddy saw to that.

We had a variety of foods, of course, but the standard fare during the Depression was red beans and cornbread one day and fried chicken the next. During growing season, pots of luscious black-eyed peas supplanted the beans quite often and we raised eggplant, squash, spinach and other greens to add to the table. And corn. To this day I prefer the less sweet field corn for "roasting ears." Our standby? Rice or potatoes, white or sweet, cook's choice; and always biscuit with the chicken, cornbread with the vegetable dinners. Or both. The hot buttered biscuit with jam or jelly made our dessert.

I gave our parents problems about milk. I never liked it but was forced to drink it. After I was grown, I learned to like both milk and spinach. I expect Mother would have enjoyed paddling me when I told her. She drank only buttermilk, but Daddy drank both, plus coffee and iced tea.

Tea and coffee. As we came along, the health rage talked about how bad caffeine was for us. Mother nipped that problem in the bud while we were quite young: she gave us a teaspoon of strong, bitter, black coffee some once a week. I may be the only one of us who never learned to drink it. Over a tablespoon of coffee in my stomach was a proven emetic for years. Now once in a while I can down up to a quarter of a cup if I'm determined and trying not to embarrass a hostess. The caffeine in tea wasn't so heavily underlined, and we all drank tea after Jessie got old enough to ask Daddy to buy it so she could serve it. He readily obliged, and I became as heavy a tea drinker as coffee fiends are coffee drinkers.

We used to go to the show every Saturday evening. Lemar and Dan and I had all gone on occasion while we still lived in Eastland, and we were used to reading the subscript, for the movies were silent then. The dialogue was read all over the theater to the younger viewers causing a low hum to rise and fall. John was the last of us to be read to. Then came "talkies." What a miracle! We saw serial movies, and our favorite was Tarzan. The last time I remembered to mention it to John she still denied it; still I remember quite well when Tarzan was trying hard to break a chain with which the villian's enemy was restrained while the reprobate slipped silently up behind him, knife clutched and aimed, to stab the good man in the back. The tender-hearted John was sobbing loudly as the picture faded to the words "Continued next week." Of course next week the chain broke, the loose end flew over Tarzan's shoulder, and the villian received a knock-out blow in the opening seconds. But John denies what she was too young to store in her memory.

In 1928, when the Eastland courthouse was thirty-one years old, the proper authorities decided to raze it in order to build a new one on that same site. As the old red brick building was part of our childhood, we kept up with the events that followed. Every man, woman, and child in the state of Texas (and it spread much further than that) was stunned when the demolition crew found an adult horny toad in the cornerstone with the expected Bible and other memorabilia. For a few days, both speculation and imagination ran riot; but thirty years is a relatively short time, and several witnesses testified that one of the workmen when the building was built had placed a tiny horny toad in the stone with the other items as a joke in poor taste. The porous cement block had apparently been visited by enough small brown ants so prolific in that neck of the woods to nourish him; and small amounts of rain water probably had trickled in as well. Thus the animal survived. He had been picked up and held by one leg so that the crowd of people could see and attest that he was indeed alive.

The little fellow was dubbed "Old Rip" and given tender loving care for the rest of his life. However, his life had been first protected against change, then rudely disturbed. In January, 1929, he fought a losing battle with pneumonia, following which he was embalmed and placed in a glass coffin lined with blue velvet. He still can be seen in that newer courthouse. To me it is quite a memory-evoking sight. But that was sixty odd years ago, I've not been back in some years now.

Back in those years Lemar was involved in scouts, too, and their car racing. The boys made them and one sat in the driver's seat while the second pushed him in the race. Both he and Daddy enjoyed it immensely. They used to return from those evening races and entertain the rest of us, and make us envious. By the time our son was in scouts, the race cars were miniature, and I never got to ride in one!

Some years Lemar went to scout camp. He would pack in a wooden trunk that he had made and fasten it with a padlock. As long as it worked, its age didn't matter, for Lemar had learned to make keys for them. Indeed one year he accidentally locked his key in one. Even the scout master thought he should take a hinge off and fish the key out. Lemar refused: He could spend less time making another key from an old spoon handle, and then have a spare as well. The adult got a big kick out of telling Daddy that story after the troops were home again.

While I have Lemar cornered, I may as well tell how his lips used to sunburn and peel when he was out in the sun too much as an older teenager. Nothing in Mother's and Daddy's experience did them any good. *Vaseline* and lip balms, under any name, proved useless. Daddy had him see the doctor, who after making sure there was no other path to take, suggested that he use lipstick as it was heavier and had color to help block out the harmful rays.

Lemar's lips grew smooth and soft; and, more important, free from pain. Eminently kissable, we assured him.

Chapter VIII

Mable and Vickey started school after I was in high school. Because John and Luceille were there to guide them, I was little involved in their school life. Mable's hair was brown, not curly, but easily curled. Vickey's hair was bone white, shiny and straight, worn rather short. Family names of their friends were unfamiliar to me. As we spent so many hours laboring in the fields, that was not surprising. The Depression had been rough, Daddy had been scolded by church elders for working on the farm on Sundays, and had explained that he was little more than feeding us at that. They found that too hard to swallow and at last struck his name off the church roll. Daddy naturally was hurt and never spoke of it in our hearing, but continued to take us when we asked for a ride. As he took us to the big Baptist church in Eastland, we learned Bible but nothing to enlarge our knowledge of and familiarity with the families in and around Olden.

I didn't know then about Daddy's being ousted, but I've marveled for years that he took the time and gasoline to run us back and forth without one word to make us feel guilty or selfish. We began to go to church in Olden during the first year after we switched schools. Daddy encouraged us and was agreeable to the change of location when Jessie asked. She chose the Methodist as she contended, "That's where everyone goes."

Dan and I were not comfortable there. I believe it was because we recalled so much Mother had told us about her church life as a child. She preferred Church of Christ, or Christian, although she had had no final choice in Ashdown. There the two had met in one congregation. The prime topic of discord was whether or not to make use of musical instruments. Annually they voted on the issue. If there was one dissenting vote, there was no piano for the coming year. I'd been uncomfortable in the Baptist church in Eastland; but we had had no choice. Mother attended with Daddy, head of the household, wherever he went. Then on one of my last visits there I was old enough to be appalled when the congregation "voted" a young lady into the church. Angered, I asserted that Man had no authority to say yes or no to one of an age that he knows what he is doing. Not long after that we began to attend church in Olden. Dan and I decided to switch to the Church of Christ; but John chose to stay with the Baptist. Luceille, Mable, and Vickey then each followed the sister just older than herself. So we were scattered out in three congregations.

Vickey's first year of school was my senior year, and I was far too busy to give my sisters more than necessary time. At least I thought I was. I protected them, if need arose; and gave Vickey and Mable help dressing or study- ing, if help was called for, but that was all.

Oh, how Mable hated cooked onions; and how mulishly she scorned the foods she knew Mother had put them in. Cush, or dressing, for example. Mother wouldn't lie about it as some of us might have, and Mable made a thing of picking them out or, if there was adequate choice, turning the dish down. At Mable's home, when she was nearing sixty, I laughed when she served baked onions and other dishes with that vegetable in them. Half puzzled, half mildly derisive, I challenged her about the onions.

Mable snorted, inelegant, true, but she snorted. Then she declared, "Mother ought to have killed me!"

Again I laughed. But I also remembered Mother's return from a visit to her sister when we were all adults. By then Aunt Anna was Mrs. Bernard Chamberlain and had two children, Bernadette and Dan. Bernadette was still at home, working and came in for lunch. One day Aunt Anna opened canned stew for the meal, and cautioned Mother not to mention that fact. Bernadette sat down, eyed her lunch, and immediately queried its freshness. Aunt Anna, without turning a hair, said that she had made it that day. Bernadette sat down and ate with gusto. Thereby did she prove her mother right in saying she could not tell the difference. Mother was shocked. A slice of bread and jelly should have been proffered along with the truth to her way of thinking.

While we were still at home, Daddy always had to depend on hired help. Sometimes we children liked them, and other times we spurned them, though never to their faces. I think of Willy and Darlene. He was a good worker and honest, but he was without ambition. He hunted and he fished, and Lemar thought he was wonderful. They didn't have children, which was probably a mercy. I recall her sitting in our back yard counting the hoboes on the train and talking as if she were our age. One time, possibly while we were fishing, she was counting them on a long train. Her outstretched arm worked like a pump handle while she pointed and enumerated audibly. We were closer that day, and the men on the train could see clearly what she was doing. They waved at her, and during a short interval when a passing car had no illegal riders, she remarked on their waving at her. With shock I realized that she did not even understand that it was a mocking acceptance of her and her industriousness!

It was hard labor, but the pay was good for those days. They had vegetables off the place; a house, the one we first had lived in; their choice of an electric bill or lamps and oil to buy; and a dollar a day. The future stretched ahead end-lessly and monotonously before those who lived there. We had a procession of workers, only a few who did not live on the place at first. Snigglefritz was one of them. I'll call him George.

Inevitably Daddy took several days to get a new work-er's name fixed in his mind. Daddy said, "Be in in a minute, Mamma, got to tell Snigglefritz to water the new turnip patch and plow the onion field." We all tagged along, to be with Daddy that much more. We carefully called the new man George. All but Mable, that is. At five or six, she very precisely called him Snigglefritz. To his face! Frozen silence, and horrible embarrassment descend-ed on the family.

George burst out laughing immediately! He told us his name, but also said he didn't mind the nickname at all. He was never called anything else. I always felt that he liked children. I hope he had some. It was a child's assessment, but he was likely in his forties.

Vickey still had three years of high school left to do after Mable graduated. When I went home, she always wished for dresses made like some of mine. One year I had her try mine on; she was fourteen by then, and they fit her well. A standing fit and a wearing fit are two different things, as it turned out. Vickey was sway-backed, and the dresses just did not hang right. Mother had to rip and doctor them, and that ended my trying to fit her from 350 miles away. Denny never said anything, but I always knew he was relieved. I think he had mental visions of me spending hours sewing for her for years to come.

Jessie wasn't really in any position to go to work when she was out of school because of her health; but Lemar took a diesel engineering course by mail and worked at a pipe and steel yard. Dan planned to go to college about fifty miles from home, riding to school with a fellow worker of

Daddy's. The college town was part of his area. I was never sure why Daddy changed his mind in spite of the fact that it had been his idea. It could have been a thin pocketbook in 1936.

I graduated in 1937, and in the fall of the year, both Dan and I began classes at Denton, Texas, at what was called North Texas State Teachers College. We cooked, and we sewed but neither of us had had any professional training in home economics as Olden was not big enough for it until my senior year when I had other things to take; still we began with an eye to a degree in that subject. When the first term ended, we knew that it would be far too expensive as a major for us and quite time consuming for two students who were forced to work. Most of the students did work; some because they had to if they were to attend at all; some in order to take the more expensive majors; some just to have more spending money while they were there. So we decided to major in elementary education.

While we were there, we looked up Uncle Payne, Daddy's brother, his wife, Lois, and their adopted daughter, Mary, a very likeable four-year-old. Uncle Payne was very easy to know, and agreeable to furnishing rides home after church let out. Aunt Lois had led him to the Church of Christ. We visited, and dined with them occasionally, wholly for the Whisenants' sake as far as Aunt Lois was concerned. Of course she never said so, but she didn't care for Mother. Nor had she years earlier when our families had both lived in Eastland.

There were a doctor, a hospital, and nurses on campus. Treatment for routine ills, including needed hospitalization for contagious diseases—like my humiliating German measles when I was a senior; vaccinations, and iron shots were a part of the benefits. Dr. Howell generally referred us for more serious conditions. When my tonsils became infected, he told me to go to a throat specialist. We called Uncle

Payne for a reference. He took time off (he was president of the flour mill) to take me to his own doctor. I waited for the bill to come in. At last I questioned Uncle Payne. He casually said it may have come in with his own bill, and if so, he had paid it, forget it.

I felt a little resentful, like it was charity, but was not brash enough to resist Daddy's brother. I thanked him.

After Lemar finished his engineering course, he had to go to school headquarters in California and take the finals. That was in 1937 or 1938. He didn't return home afterward but called himself a traveling agriculturist, finding delight in following whatever harvest was beckoning. He helped gather various vegetables, picked plums, apples, lemons, whatever. Mr. Pullman had paid Lemar two dollars and fifty cents a day at the iron and steel yard and he made two dollars a day picking fruit in California. When he eventually went to work on the big Grand Coulee Dam up in Washington, he began at seventy-five cents an hour. In both '38 and '39 the men were laid off in December because of the weather. He wrote interestingly; his letters carried us right to his field of activity and we always pounced on them eagerly, Dan and I. The other girls in the home asked for his news too whenever we got a letter. Oddly, Daddy was more apt to write us than Mother was.

Before college began, I was offered a job assisting an English teacher in the demonstration school on campus. They also offered me tuition for my freshman year, both on the basis of my grades in high school. Immediately my boss put me to work grading eleventh grade English papers. It was a tough chore for one who was fresh out of the course, but my boss neither argued nor objected unless I took too much time to suit her.

One thing stunned me that year, though it was unrelated to either class or work per se. A student took strychnine, to frighten her boyfriend and make him jealous. She told a close friend that she had taken about four times the lethal dose. She lived several hours with her family knowing that she could not be saved. However far from a truth it may be, it was said that the overdose kept her alive longer than she would ordinarily have lived. I have to add that fact—that it was somewhat accidental—to retain my own peace of mind. I had seen her, and I had graded many of her papers. She was intelligent scholastically.

Dan applied for and was given a position waiting tables in the girls' dormitory. She set the tables, brought in the food, filled glasses, served desserts, and cleaned up after the meal. Each girl or boy was assigned two tables, accounting for sixteen students total. Once the routine was mastered, and the worker was well accepted, he might be paid extra to do "do specials"—dinner parties held in some rooms planned for that purpose. One worker might handle a party alone, or ten workers might be needed.

Lemar had worked his way north to Washington. There he was, picking apples, when one of the professors on campus in Denton finished her operetta and prepared to produce it. We had opera in Dallas and other cities large enough to support that entertainment; but for Denton, home of two colleges and little else, this was a first.

As was to be expected, Denton made a big thing of it. Surrounding cities carried the story in their papers; it spread and grew nation-wide. Reporters from many states attended the first production. Possibly some were too late to get seats by the time the editors assigned them to the story. Possibly they merely preferred the establishments that made their money on alcoholic drinks, anything which was intoxicating. I shall always believe that they knew how gullible their own people were concerning the myths about Texas and deliberately wrote their lying stories; for they were lies, obstreperous lies. The reporters would have questioned someone if they had been faking due to lack of entrance. They could have gotten some odd glimpses, and seen some lovely evening attire. Needless to say (but I will) Dan I were most indignant when Lemar sent us a clipping describing the farmers going to the opera clad in overalls with wives in poke bonnets, their barefoot children in tow. In that area farmers had sufficient money to buy evening clothes and did so. As a Texan by preference, Lemar had realized that the articles were slanderous.

Granted we were not supposed to, but students sometimes went by carload over into Oklahoma, just north of us; Denton County was dry, and the boys enjoyed a beer. We girls, many of us not realizing why they wanted to go at first, went for a lark. I was never with a group in which the boys overdid their drinking, but I'm sure it happened with some students. However, those trips quickly became boring and my conscience smote me. I finished my years with only a few visits and no drinking to mar my slate. The point in telling this was not to give a reason for going, but to relate another adventure.

North of Gainsville, at the Red River bridge, we girls became fascinated looking up or down river. The walk along the side called, and we felt that strolling across would be great fun. It nearly was. In broad daylight one time, when we were going nowhere special, Jane and I decided the moment was ripe. Traffic roared across, much of it heading for the cities, Dallas and Fort Worth. We realized when we stopped how busy it actually was and Jane backed out. So Tom and I struck out alone. I had not known until then what fierce suction was created by passing traffic, but I impulsively braced against it. Then I shifted my gaze from the water to the bridge and I saw that a bus coming from the north and a semi tank truck from the south would meet beside us! To this day, I'm sure there wasn't room for them to do so without destruction of the vehicles and the bridge. None of which happened. I wheeled and climbed up on the bridge; I hugged a huge girder for dear life. Tom slid both arms around me, and he held on for dear life too, mine. We went back to the car without completing our walk. I found out only then that he had thought I was going to jump off the bridge in an attempt (a rash one) to save my life. He had felt my fear with me.

Another incident in Denton that has remained phenomenal to me was finding Uncle Payne's house the first time Dan and I called on him. My psychology professor happened to remark that he lived on Congress Avenue; so I stayed late to ask if he knew Payne Whisenant. He did; he lived next door to him. When I asked for direction, Dr. Koenig gestured powerfully, and articulated expansively. I mentally noted his north and east correctly, but Dan and I did not find the street where it should have been. As we had crossed it once in a car, we knew it was not where Dr. Koenig pointed. At last we found it. The thing was that I knew north was south to me and east was west in Denton, and I had made the corrections. Mentally. It took other events for us to learn that, when I was three or more floors above ground level, the directions assumed their rightful positions for me. Such a topsy—turvy state of intelligence can make for an interesting life, or a hampered one. Dan never had that affliction and simply took the lead when we set out in new territory. She had taken me under her wing all my life; so why not then?

One incident of our college days will probably never be forgotten by any who were around that day. We were allowed to take Daddy's old Remington portable typewriter with us to type themes or reports. Fellow students latched onto it too when we were not pecking away on it. Ribbons never had held out so long before. Sometimes for short assignments we even held the typewriter on our laps, but more often we sat at a table, as we didn't have desks. Changing margins or the tab involved resetting some little sliding gadgets which were on the back of the machine. That in turn meant either turning it back to front or pulling it forward so that it was merely leaning on the desk and was at an angle.

One day a rather thin girl sat in her slip typing up a storm. When it was necessary to make a change, she pulled the instrument to the required angle and performed the operation. So far so good, but she found that she could not then return the typewriter to a usable position. A certain portion of her anatomy had moved, of its own accord, to nestle among the keys. With an audience of females help-lessly convulsed with laughter, she was forced to ooze her way out of her predicament alone. As she too was blessed with a good nature, she sweetly forgave us our reactions. She also ignored our crude adaption of an old cliché. Frequently one of us remarked that we hadn't had so much fun since _____ got her.... I shall leave the rest to your imagination.

After my first nine months, my scholarship was gone; my job handed to another needy applicant. I too began to work in the dining room. I also typed, starting at four cents a page, or proof read for students needing help.

We attended regular and summer sessions in 1938–1939. Then we were forced to quit. We worked in restaurants, and saved toward going back. It was slow; a quarter made a fair tip, a dime was more common.

Chapter IX

That summer, 1939, Lemar sent for Florence Edna Kidwell who lived in Ranger, and whom he had dated frequently before he left home. If they were already engaged, I was not aware of it; but she agreed to bring her mother's written consent to get married. They were married on July 6, some ten miles across the state line from Spokane, at Coeur D'Alene, Idaho.

In September, what we had viewed as a genial friendship between Luceille and Joy Duncan became a surprise marriage. Daddy was sick in bed with the flue; but most likely wouldn't have been given the chance to hinder the ceremony if he had been well. Although Luceille was only fifteen, she appeared older and had persuaded Joy that she was older. She did not like school, and now she had an out. They intended to live some fifty or so miles from us. John told our parents that as she and Wendell Hickerson were planning to be married at the end of the current school year anyway, they would marry then and move to the same town. John had graduated, and at eighteen could marry without permission. Wendell was three months older, but lacked half a year yet to graduation. Mr. and Mrs. Hickerson permitted the wedding. The young couple was married two days later.

Jessie was in love again also, and decided to join the gang. She came by my rooming house in Eastland and invited me to go and witness her marriage to Jimmy Simmons. I could hardly refuse, though I despaired of unheralded weddings. I had even more reason to despair when we came back home. The wedding had been read in Ranger, and when we stopped to tell Mother and Daddy that they were married, they refused to get out of the car, told me that Daddy would get me to town the next day in time for work, and sped away. I faced a totally dark house. I could not get out of it: I had to break the news to Mother and Daddy. Mother sighed, and told me to "go on to bed." If she cried, I couldn't hear her; and her eyes were not swollen the next day.

Although I didn't wholeheartedly approve of the manner in which Jessie conducted her affairs that evening (or even if Jimmy willing concurred—he obviously loved Jessie very much.) I later remembered an incident from at least ten years before; and I felt more kindly toward Jessie then: I had already retired when Daddy went to the living room and suggested to Jessie and the man whom she had dated that evening that it was time to call it a day. I can play my mental tape recorder and hear Jessie's every nuance as she replied, "But, Daddy, we're engaged."

Daddy sent the man on his way, and told him not to come back, ever. When I told Dan the next day and asked why, she did not know either. As it would have been cruel to drag it out in the open, we have never found any explanation for it. I know that at least one other time Jessie was engaged to a fine young man but saw little of him as his work carried him overseas frequently. Because she was young and lonesome for him, she dated other men and at last broke their engagement. Before that he sent her gifts at intervals. One was a train of ivory elephants in decreasing size from Thailand, when it still was known as Siam. After she died I brought them home with me, and most people assume that I bought them myself on my travels.

Luceille and John and Jessie all married within one week of each other. Lemar plus the three sisters, four weddings.

Jessie knew that she and Jimmy made it three in a week, but she didn't realize that evening that it also totalled four in three months. One half of Mother's and Daddy's children! Yes, the papers printed both records.

Joy got a local job after all; Luceille was happy. John and Wendell lived with his folks until Wendell had finished school. Jessie and Jimmy lived in Ranger. In a few months I went back to school. How different everything would be when next I came home.

Life seemed to accelerate. On September 5, 1940, Luceille and Joy's first child arrived, born in our back bedroom, across a tiny porch at the end of the hall which ran the length of the main part of the house. Some time in the past months Joy had come to work for Daddy, and the young couple lived in the small house. It had been suggested and accepted that they stay with us until Luceille was up on her feet again, usually nine to eleven days then. The doctor and his nurse came to the house.

I went in in the middle of the morning to change the baby Jerry Ruth Duncan and hand her to her mother for a ten o'clock snack. In those years, babies wore "bands," strips of material, pinned tight around their plump mid-sections to help protect against rupture, and we saw the stubby cord only at bath time. When I undressed Jerry, that time, the cord sprayed a line of tiny blood droplets across the bed. Mother had me call the doctor, who told me to boil a length of twine and retie it. He dropped by to check up later and assured us that the baby was strong and healthy, and they had had to tie the cord twice earlier. The episode was old hat to him, but it impressed me strongly—after all, I was the one who had seen the blood.

Lena Jim, John and Wendell's first baby, arrived a year later on September 12, 1941. Mother's sister Lena and her husband Jim were honored with the name. I very rarely saw John and her family, not because they were so far off but because I had no car.

In both 1938 and 1939 Lemar made trips to Texas during the winter shutdowns. In his diary he records that he drew seven Social Security checks at fifteen dollars. In November, 1940 he went to work for Wm. H. Owens in a welding shop for twelve dollars a week. In March 1941, he opened a welding school for Mr. Owens and worked in both the school and the shop, earning twenty-five dollars a week. In June he quit, and they came to Eastland, Texas. He worked first at Todd Galveston Dry Docks for seventy-nine cents an hour, missed some time in strike, went to another company, returned to Todd for about a month, and then went to Houston Ship Building Corp. Altogether he made less than 1,500 dollars that year.

Their first child, Jesse Lee, was born on July 20, 1942, in Houston. They gave him Lemar's initials, combining part of Daddy's name with part of Lemar's. Now we had the third J.L. Whisenant.

Jessie and Jimmy's first child was born in the fall of 1942. He lived about two months. The school where I taught had a fall break during which most of the students harvested cotton. I arrived home the day before the funeral, the first death of one in the family so close to me. Even when Grandma Fawcett died we were so far apart geographically that I didn't mourn as Mother did. Instead I helped her, dry-eyed, to prepare to leave after a call from her sister told us that Grandmother was dying. Mother knew she would not be home until after the funeral. She was holding her own sorrow bottled up to release later.

Before I could yield to my own empty and uncomprehended sensations, they left; and almost immediately Gilbert Clark, whom we had quite accidently stumbled onto at college, arrived. He was taking me back to Denton. Daddy had offered to take me too, but I felt that the side trip, while not very long, would be too much to ask of Mother at that time.

I had reentered college in January, 1940, with both Dan and Daddy contributing to my expenses. I lived further away from the campus and provided my own meals. Usually my breakfast was a glass of milk. I was on a route, and the milkman left a pint of milk every other day. It was simply a matter of drinking half the bottle on the day it was left, pushing to top back on, and leaving it in a shady spot. Tommie, my roommate, would take time to carry it up to our icebox before she left an hour later, and also would scold me those days I left it out. She never tested my assertion that it would not sour before I got home to do that chore myself.

I have the yearbooks of those years, as they were free; but my picture is not in all of them, for we had to pay for the photography, two dollars, which I didn't always have. As I was not enrolled for all of my junior year, I did not rate the annual that year. However, Mary Helen Wilson from Olden picked hers up and brought it to me.

Those were happy years; for we made new friendships and renewed old ones, as with Angelina Meredith. Her family had moved so many miles from Eastland that our family visits had become a thing of the past. Some of our friendships we gave up only after many years of separation. Modena Hewitt; Faydette Jones; Lena Hopkins; Frances Flanagan; Pauline Parker, whom the rest of us brazenly called "P.P."; Lillian Neale and her sister Myrtle; and Chlocelia Tonnita (Tonnie to me) Tunnell were probably my closest friends. I repented most the rift between Tonnie and me; and it was due to my own stupidity we lost touch. Although I loved her dearly, I was too cumbrous with my sympathy when her husband was killed in World War II.

Standing and having Lena Hopkins "hood" me at my commencement with my family there to watch was the fulfillment of my dearest dreams, and I think of Daddy's, that some of us would get our degrees. To him I was only the first.

We had sent many invitations—only because Dan would

have it so. I felt that I was asking for a gift, and didn't relish the feeling. Each student was given four tickets for guests. But I was lucky: Daddy brought a load of family; and Aunt Edith, with whom we had frequently spent enjoyable weekends while we were in college, was accompanied by a neighbor, Mrs. Schleimer, whom we had most outrageously nicknamed Mrs. Slick-And-Slimy. They had two children with them. They went to the auditorium when they arrived, early, and found seats just behind the roped off section. They were not challenged when officials arrived.

Dan was near to tears when I told her that Uncle Payne and Aunt Lois had given me a watch, for she had scrimped and saved in order to buy me a Gruen, which was a more expensive brand than the one they had given me. She could not see my wrist and didn't know that I was wearing her gift. I was and I gladly gave her the other one. Now it was her turn; and my pleasure for me to help her financially as she continued her education.

A few of the seniors had jobs lined up, but most of us registered with the college placement bureau, and bought the expensive photos that one photographer (the one who made the proverbial mud fence look attractive) made, and waited. My message came along with an application to teach in a town we had never heard of. Texas maps were useless, but Daddy went to the railway agent who located it easily. Allison, a tiny town on the railroad, north of Wheeler, in the Panhandle. I was hired to teach first grade and would be met at Wheeler, which could be reached by bus, by the superintendent on the date I chose to arrive.

Dan was left to prepare for the fall semester. I embarked. My birth was my first milestone; my survival my second; seventh grade graduation was a mild one; high school graduation was one; this was a special one.

The bus pulled into Wheeler, Texas, at eight thirty—one

in the morning. Mr. and Mrs. Peeples walked over and welcomed me. Unsure of myself, I had a hat along but was not wearing it. Oddly enough, perhaps for my encouragement, Gertrude Peeples also had a hat handy. I would have liked her in any event, but I appreciated that she was willing to follow my lead on that point. It was twenty-two miles to Allison. They first briefed me and then drew me out about myself. In Allison, I was delivered to Sam and Edna Begert, the couple with whom I would board. They were both a few years older than I; they had one child, Eldean, a boy of seven or eight. Edna worked at one of the two local stores, Allison Mercantile, where we could buy a wide variety of items. Sam was the principal of the school. The town also had a grocery store; a cafe; the post office, which was run by the Browns, but located in the Dillon's grocery; the bank; and the lumber yard.

I liked everyone and got along well, but one gentleman unintentionally ran me back into my shell of shyness when he brought a high school student over to me in public and told me that I would need a boyfriend. Not only was I at least five years older than this boy, but the school was all in one building and I was more or less exhibit number one at the time. Pile on top of that the fact that the first grade was the largest in the building. Think of hordes of parents with avid interest in the situation. As they had had a little problem with an earlier first grade teacher, he should have known better. I did date one or two young men; they reminded me of a college friend, Ewald Ramm, whom I'd dated off and on. He was fun, and he respected me. He used to say, "I'm a half breed: I have Roman hands and Russian ideas." He didn't try to prove it, however. Mostly I limited myself to ladies and couples for close friends.

It was a well known fact in Allison before I knew where that place was that I was a member of the Church of Christ. Blanche Begert, Sam's sister-in-law, sent me a message that she would pick me up on Sunday in time for church, sort of a royal command; and I was ready, glad to have someone to go with. I liked Blanche, but I attended church only twice. Their practices were so unlike many beliefs that I felt like an outsider. I reasoned that I needed the group study offered by Bible Classes on Sunday morning, for instance, and that congregation frowned on them. Here was a case of being "damned if I do, and damned if I don't," and I decided to try the Baptist Church.

Sam quite autocratically declared that I would do no such thing, that I would go with him and his family to the Methodist. I went along. Always the members asked questions about our differences with real interest, and took it for granted that my attendance was to be short term there. It was, and I was truly grateful when two years later I went to live where there was a real Church of Christ that coincided with my beliefs more closely.

I mailed my address home as soon as I reached Allison, and Dan and I scribbled notes to one another when we had the time to spare. She corresponded too with a dear friend whom she had dated, O.C. Barnhill. He was quite presentable, and had enlisted in the air force about the time Dan returned to her studies in Denton.

My hands were full too. The large group of first grade students would have kept me busy, but I had as well to turn five students who had passed "on condition" into our second grade. Beginning that year, Texas had twelve school years. It was up to the superintendents to insert the added year in the most strategic position. None of my five could be said to be a failure. In fact, one of them was an A+ student. I never figured out how my predecessor justified her placement of those children.

I made the princely salary of ninety—eight dollars and fifty cents a month for a nine month contract. Living on it at that time was not difficult, but I was determined to help Dan complete her education.

She went back to Denton with enthusiasm which decreased quite rapidly as O.C. was facing overseas duty and they were miles apart. Before I went home for Thanksgiving, she wrote warning me to bring my check book. She preferred married life with O.C. to education. Absence had, as we've been warned, indeed made her heart grow fonder.

I hadn't had time to amass a great fortune, but we did buy a lovely blue dress in Fort Worth before we went on home. They were married at the house and left immediately for the weekend together before he went to work. In a few months he went into the Air Force, and she soon followed him, first to Colorado, and again to Florida before he went overseas. She went to the Houston area then and into defense work. Tired out in the evenings and with no good news to impart, she let our correspondence trickle to a stop after a few months.

We did pool resources in order to afford nicer Christmas gifts that year, at her suggestion. Mother, bless her heart, felt that it was somehow faintly improper, a married woman and a single girl buying gifts together. She might have suggested it herself, in the years to come.

World War II was not a single event, nor even a series of events having to do with fighting. Nor was it a specific time. It was more like a malignant octopus, with injurious, tight-holding tentacles suppressing one moment; and evil writhing feelers boring their way in against all defense the next. Nor can we pass it off by merely saying we worked in defense for five years and saved for our new home. That way we merely list some bits and leave out all of the causes and heartaches and stifled opportunities.

Several times I started to tell some of the impact left in our lives by the war. I couldn't separate one year of it from the next.

Since my high school days things were tense. We probably couldn't always tell which tension was long lasting effects from the depression and which tension was due to the political situation in Europe. After Lemar and Florence's third child was born and they were living in Houston, his spiteful landlady turned him in for leaving his defense job—when all he did was move his home. He was promptly drafted into the Navy, but after boot camp and the checks to four dependents, Lemar was honorably discharged.

Wendell was in the Navy, in Norman, Oklahoma. Stanley called every man in a uniform similar to his father's "Daddy"; as a result John was horribly embarrassed over and over.

Morris tried to enlist four separate times and was four times turned down before he was rated 4F. He no longer hurt from the battles with rheumatism, but his feet couldn't have held out, and the doctors knew so at a glance. Friends who did not understand looked askance at his 4F, but non-friends sneered at it. I'm sure he was only one of thousands. They did not care that synthetic rubber was a wartime necessity.

In college students mourned missing or slain members of their own and each other's families. More than once we stood stock still in the serving rooms at being told of another death, the death of one of us who was never to come back to utilize his education; perhaps he was never allowed even to complete it. I hurt; and I can still remember that pain.

But Dan suffered agonies we were helpless to sooth. In 1943 or 1944, O.C.'s plane apparently was shot down. He was MIA. The plane at last contact was flying over Rumania. Thus the most devastating, all-pervading blow to the entire family began. We all hurt for Dan, despairing in our inability to help. I was having babies, moving, caring for husband and house; and Dan was still in Houston, working at a defense job. We just did not correspond often. Months or years passed, and he was declared dead.

Chapter X

One Sunday in late fall, I was waiting quietly between class and the sermon for the congregation to get seated. I wasn't consciously listening but I heard a voice behind me say, "I hit it lucky. I drove in home as Dad's last bale of cotton headed for the gin."

In horror I, who had not heard one word other than the quoted ones, heard a voice, my voice, drawl, "It sounds like someone is lazy to me." Even my grammar lacked the finesse that it should have shown. I swiveled my head and flashed a quick apologetic grin to two members and a total stranger.

The next time I saw the young man whom I had carelessly made my target, outside of an unavoidable hello in church a time or two, I was taking the tickets for a basketball game at the school gym. Sam had him in tow and introduced me to Morris Trayler. I had spoken to his father and stepmother in church, but wasn't well acquainted with them.

Four nights later he came to the house where the rules were "the one nearest the door answers." As his knuckles rattled the door, I obeyed; and was invited to the movie in Wheeler. We were all tired. Edna and I had spent the day, Saturday, sewing garments the Red Cross wanted for distribution to the armed forces overseas. Hoping that fresh air would ease my spent, tired feeling, I decided to go. I had no feeling at all toward Morris as a man at that time. Sam told me later that he sat holding his breath for fear I would refuse.

We saw *Mutiny on the Bounty;* and after the film we went to one of Wheeler's two drugstores for a malt. I was more cautious and drank a small *Dr Pepper*. A mistake. It was much too sweet. On the way home I rolled the window up and down, trying vainly to settle my stomach. Morris would stop and in a moment drive on. At last I knew the time had come. Morris knew the area well and pulled off on a nice grassy patch; but, humiliated by the situation, I dashed across to the other side of the road; I wanted no witnesses. He came and held my head. Next he placed a clean handkerchief in my hand. I felt much better, but still not normal on the rest of the trip. Morris was quite solicitous, offering to adjust air flow or speed, or to stop again. He did not try to draw out our "goodnights."

There was no way I could keep that incident to myself. I needed Edna's and Sam's sympathy and got it. The next two weeks were long ones, but at last Morris called again. Some months later, after a hot but amiable argument over the time lapse, I looked back in my diary, and found that it was less than a week!

Edna and I became fast friends; we even made one or two dresses alike. Eldean and I were good buddies too, but once in a while he would resent my authority when we were alone; however, Edna had delegated it to me and requested that I help keep an eye on him when she was at work. Edna and Sam and I all cooked, which gave us a wider variety of cuisine, for we had varied backgrounds. It also gave us a few laughs. For instance, I made cheese sauce to pour over the steamed cauliflower but poured it over the lima beans because Edna asked me a question and I looked up to answer her. We scooped most of the sauce off and I finished the dish while Sam stirred in the tasty coating which adhered to the beans. We enjoyed cheese and cauliflower a new dish to them, many times, and I increased my staple recipes too.

Next door to the Begerts was an elfin house occupied by two other teachers. Lorene Rhodes, my roommate when we began work on our Masters degrees in Denton the next summer, had dark brown hair and eyes. She was an excellent English teacher. Blonde-haired, blue-eyed Frances Dillon, the home economics teacher, was a lovely person except for one flaw that soon ceased to rate any attention. She was married to Morris's best friend, Neville Dillon, whose parents were the grocers. Neville was killed in the war before we had an opportunity to meet.

Most of my "parents" were happy with me. My principal, I soon learned, could hear every word spoken in my room unless I deliberately closed a door which I rarely noticed. It was in the entry to my room which had been a large cloakroom and had a second door between it and the main part of the room. One side of the entry was partitioned off with a flimsy wall that stood fifteen inches from the floor and ceased to climb fifteen inches short of the ceiling. It formed a tiny room used as a principal's office. Glenna Sue Elmore was an excellent student, but one day after a laugh we all enjoyed, she could not stop laughing. It took me forty-five minutes to get both the rest of the students and myself calmed down. Glenna Sue would try; but when she erupted, we all followed suit unfailingly, even those who hadn't found it so funny at first. Sam told me later than he and Johnny had enjoyed it with us but would like to know how it started.

Early in our dating life I found out that Morris's name was Maurice Denzil. His third grade teacher had ignored his request that she spell and pronounce his name correctly, and thus gave him the version of it that followed him about the rest of his life. I liked the Denzil of his name and in private began to call him Denny. On every date, Morris would say, "Let's get married, and have a little girl, and name her Fay."

We corresponded during the summer, and the fall sort of took up where summer left off. Denny, when a youngster, had

had some fierce struggles with rheumatism, and his feet were left hammertoed. It was for this reason that he was unable to serve in the military. It was earlier that he tried to enlist. In fact the last time, he faced the doctor with his shoes on and passed with flying colors until the doctor made him expose his feet. That rebuff was the last as he did not try again after we met.

Though I refused to marry him, Morris wanted to give me a ring; and one day we went to Amarillo, two to three hours to the southwest, where he bought me a ruby ring to replace one I had worn as a child. I had sprinted out of the house, hand flat on the screen door; and the latch hook had caught in the ring. It ripped my finger badly; and it severed and twisted my ring. I kept it for years, thinking we would one day have it reset, but it vanished while I was in Denton. I have often wondered which small sister took it; probably she intended to return it and lost it instead. At last I again wore my birthstone. I didn't mention it after we returned to Allison, but I held my hand in very awkward positions in order to draw attention to it. Of course a child first saw it: Kenneth Waldrip, a student, who told his mother, "Miss Whisenant has a wed diamond. She's going to ma'wy Maw'wis." Then he burst into tears. Mrs. Waldrip assured him that one must not assume too much and forbade him to tell the story to anyone else. He obligingly pointed out the ring and steered clear of his assumptions.

Kenneth and I had quite a relationship. It began on my first teaching day. Mr. Peeples brought a couple and their small son to my room. Kenneth had run and hid when the bus arrived, and his parents had brought him in. I took the students to the school ground to play games; in the midst of "Flying Dutchmen" the parents went home. We followed a like pattern the next two days; then Kenneth fell in love with me and began to enjoy the rest of the students. He boarded the bus without protest after that. Toward the end of the year he was victim of measles, just one of an epidemic; but quite different in as much as his parents had to catch him and put him back in bed at bus time each morning.

It was a February night and Denny was driving aimlessly down a country road; I sat without a conscious thought in my mind, enjoying the star-studded sky. It sounds silly, but I too was caught unaware when I heard myself say, "If I wasn't afraid I would break my promise, I'd say I would marry you."

He hadn't even asked me yet that evening, but he was no dumb bunny; he stopped the car, gathered me in his arms, and kissed me, either just before or just after saying, "I won't let you break it."

It's odd, but I cannot remember when we told our news. No one was surprised. With our engagement no longer a myth, Kenneth, who had been in my class for two years, saw that our marriage wouldn't be the catastrophe he had first envisioned and was happy for us. Kenneth I loved, but the hardest one to part with was D'aun McCoy, the lively and lovable daughter of some friends.

Our decision made, we saw no reason to tarry beyond the end of school. I suggested we get married on June 4, Mother and Daddy's anniversary. I also assured Denny that I didn't want an engagement ring because I liked a wedding band alone on the ring finger. We went home early in spring. I hadn't told my family that we were engaged, and Denny surprised me with a diamond ring, a white diamond set flat in a platinum setting on a gold band. Of course I accepted, and wore, it.

We met at the bus station to go down together and had barely time enough to slip off from the crowd of passengers for him to put the ring on my finger. It was late evening before we arrived, and I twisted my gloves around my left hand to hide the ring until the family traffic thinned out so I could let Mother and Daddy know first. I wanted to ask them if they minded our being married on their anniversary. I went into the kitchen to get a drink of water, and Vickey followed me in. She was leaving in a minute to spend the night at Luceille's.

"Fay, what are you doing with that ugly old thing?"

I informed her that Morris was six years older than I, and that he was a wonderful person. I mocked and smiled at her teenage reaction only later.

Mother and Daddy had suspected this outcome, but we had formed the habit of bringing friends of either sex home with us while we were in college. They wouldn't have been vastly surprised if they had been wrong. They liked Denny at once, and were pleased with our plans. They didn't even mind that I wanted to be married at home at twelve o'clock noon. And Vickey was most contrite the next morning. She came to love and admire Denny in a short time.

I was quite flattered by the attitude of the residents of Allison in general. I was pressured by one member of the school board to "talk Morris into farming." He wanted me to return to teach another year, but I felt it was up to Denny, as breadwinner, to choose; and he soon left for Borger with its heavy job market. He wrote often, and had our apartment rented before school was out. We rode the bus together from Wheeler to Eastland again. This time we bought our marriage license in Childress during a long stopover. We had yet to see the preacher, and finalize the last few details for our wedding ceremony. These things done, we chatted with Mother and Daddy and we took frequent walks around the countryside. To us this was a family time, and we had not invited anyone outside the immediate family to attend. With the war going on, tires almost unobtainable unless one "knew someone," and gasoline rationed, even Denny's family did not try to attend the brief ceremony.

I had always wished to be married at noon; that's where we struck the first snag. Dan was given exactly twenty-four hours off from her defence position and wired that she could not be home until five o'clock; We were married at six in the evening. The preacher, Brother A.T. Thurman who preached at the church next door to our old home, told us not to worry if he was a little late, not to go ahead without him. I am afraid we did not properly appreciate the joke, for the very nervousness he was trying to dissipate clogged up our senses of humor.

June 4, 1943. We roamed about, saw to our clothes one last time, picked some wild flowers, "torch flowers" we have always called them; they are a variety of wild cypress, I am told. These and some greenery decorated the living room. I think everyone else was busy at something or other. We were sure Dan would make it, but breathed a sigh of relief when she arrived all the same.

Denny and I stood holding hands so tightly our knuckles gleamed, we were told later. Denny wore an attractive light gray suit, and I wore the Bemburg sheer of slate-blue, with pale lovers knots on it, which I had spent many loving hours making. After the ceremony we had the wedding supper Mother had supervised. Then Denny and I boarded the bus to Wichita Falls. We had not made a reservation, our mistake for early June in an Army base city; but our taxi driver took us to a hotel, quite clean and somewhat quieter than the larger ones would have been.

When I woke up the next morning, I looked over at Denny asleep at my side and realized that I was no longer on my own.

We went on to Wheeler. Lawrence and Hazel Trayler, Denny's brother and his wife, came to meet us and take us to Allison in Mr. Trayler's car. The tires on the old car were so thin that we had two or three flats; then we ran the last several miles on two rims. Tire rationing truly held every citizen in its contemptible grip.

After a brief visit with Mr. and Mrs. Trayler, we moved to Borger. And again we rode with a friend.

Chapter XI

Our apartment was the north half of a "shotgun" house. Living-bedroom, kitchen-dining room, and bathroom. At the middle of the house was a porch and entry for both sets of tenants into identical apartments. Denny was gone all day, and I tried to make a home of the space he had been fortunate to find through a fellow who was moving out. The motto of the minds behind the outstretched, greedy palms in a boom town always was "First come, first served," and few if any of them would honor a waiting list. We were on-top-of-the-world happy and never doubted that we would eventually get better quarters.

In the meantime, our first neighbor was a near-deaf old lady, probably around eighty, who loved her soap operas and kept her radio so loud that it filled both her apartment and ours. I would have gone deaf too with it closer to me. One day I'd grit my teeth and bear it; the next I'd have to get out and window-shop. We were only about two blocks off Main Street where all the stores were in the bustling downtown. But it was June, and extremely hot during soap opera hours. It was a relief when that tenant moved to be nearer her family.

Our apartment was "furnished," but sparsely. We had to buy flatware as there were about eight pieces in the kitchen if one includes the bent and the rusty. Chores like that I tried to take care of during radio hours. The day I bought flatware, I was questioned spiritedly by the elderly man who owned the hardware store at that time and urged to become a genuine citizen of Borger and not just a resident. I didn't realize just how old he was until I unwrapped my purchases. There I found the entire box of forks in with the six knives and six spoons I had also bought. It wasn't the mistake of the very young or inexperienced; I had overlooked his years because he was so interested and interesting. Our stainless was not the dazzling tableware one can get today. Returning the extra forks gave me the excuse to leave the house again on a real errand. It also raised the eyebrows of the clerk who waited on me in the owner's absence. He too soon became a friend and was very kind to me in the years to come, even when he became the owner of the store. Oddly enough he had a very acid wife. I found that out several years later when we took college classes together.

For awhile our neighbors were Melvin and Fay Somebody. Mel used to yell, "Fay!" Time taught me that when the calls exceeded two or three he wanted an answer from me. They were congenial but not particularly honest. It was a relief rather than surprise or dismay when they moved. We had been to the carnival together a few nights before they left, and we took the loss of the small fortune, twenty dollars, which he had "borrowed" that night, philosophically. In ten years it was not quite so much, and today it would be a mere drop in the bucket compare to its value then.

On our first Sunday in Allison after we were married, the entire congregation visited, as was their wont, in the church grounds after services. During one lull between best wishes and congratulations, Denny wandered off and came back with Ralph Pugh. With the two of them facing me, Denny ordered, "Tell her."

I was dumbfounded, but not nearly so much as I was when Ralph obeyed him, a constant grin on his face.

"Morris asked me who you were that first day at church after he came home, and I told him Fay Whisenant. He asked if you were married or engaged. I told him no; and he said, 'I'm going to marry her.' It's the truth, Miss Whisenant—uh, Fay." His grin got bigger at the end of the story.

That day I marveled at anyone falling in love with one so lacking in beauty and poise as I. But he had, and today I think, "Denny and I could have been married a year earlier if I had been quicker to fall in love."

Denny's family belonged to the Church of Christ by preference, but they too had found it impossible to drive to a neighboring town (if twenty-odd miles away can be call a neighboring place) on little gasoline and thin tires getting thinner by the mile. They went to the Methodist Church while they lived in Allison. Lest religion should become a bone of contention in the days of his repetitious proposals, Denny underlined the fact that he would be baptized into the Church of Christ when we were married.

We went to the congregation on Second and Deahl Streets on our first Sunday in Borger. When the invitation song was sung, Denny answered immediately. James Reynolds was a fine preacher and glad to welcome us. The baptism over, the last song sung, and the last prayer uttered, people began to move about, many to welcome me.

Denny had just fastened his shorts, he explained later, when the door to the men's dressing room opened. I had just looked to see if he were coming out when the lady carrying a load of juice trays which are used in the communion service opened the door to gain access to storage space for them. I knew from her reaction that he wasn't yet fully clothed. We laughed off the incident at home, but we never mentioned it at church. If it was ever circulated, the story stopped shy of us. We never knew.

Morris was an employee of Manhattan Walco Construction Company, which was building both a synthetic rubber plant, and a butadiene gas plant five miles west of Borger. Butadiene was an ingredient of the copolymer rubber to be produced. Both products were used in the war, and the government had built housing for the employees of the two plants. But getting a house wasn't easy. The upper echelon came first, and a few years later were the first to move into better homes. The "copoly" plant (so it was affectionately dubbed) was finished and put on production on July 23, my birthday and the day Denny went to work for the company. We had originally planned to go on construction, travel with the building company, for a time. Although they paid very well, I was glad when Denny elected to stay put, more so as we wanted a family. We moved to one of the smaller houses on October 13, Mother's birthday.

Now we lived in Bunavista, but lo! someone had goofed. There was a Buena Vista in south Texas, and we wound up with Philrich Branch, Box whatever, Borger, Texas. Time elapsed; we went on home postal service as a Borger area even though we were not adopted by the city for many years, and our tiny post office was closed. "Philrich Branch" was dropped from our address; but just try to get it removed from an official document or an established company listing. One may as well butt his head against a brick wall.

In our house there were rods on closets so that we could hang curtains, either blended to match furnishings or made as near the color of the painted walls in the houses—a universal ivory in every room in every house—as it was possible. The only variation in the houses was quite basic: one, two, and three bedrooms with minimal changes otherwise, like smaller bedrooms in the largest house to leave room for a hall which gave access to the third bedroom. It was assumed that the rather slapdash erections would last for fifteen or twenty years in fair condition. Now almost fifty years have passed;

many have been enlarged; most are still occupied, as is 211 Estireno. I received from Spain a letter sent to 211—but no street name—one year. Faulty memory had produced "Estirend" for the city, and Texas, 79007, USA. The correct zip code saved the day. And only a few days ago Bill's wife forgot and mailed a thank you letter from their son to me at Bunavista, Texas. Again a zip code proved its worth in the prompt delivery of mail. Evidently she and Bill have had a recent session of reminiscence.

It was that fall that I met the McCluneys. Roy worked with Denny, and he and his wife, Billie, were near our age. We visited a great deal. Roy went to work at Lewis Hardware and stayed there until he retired. As our children arrived, Roy and Billie also wanted a family. Their first daughter was stillborn. They eventually adopted a baby boy and gave him Roy's mother's maiden name, Lundy. Lundy was very friendly, a year or so older than our son; they became quite good playmates.

During the winter we found that we were indeed going to start our family. Like most couples with their first child on the way, we had our early morning events. The one which I remember most lovingly reflected Denny's love for me: some of our cookware was of glass because metal was saved for war material. One morning Denny was shaving, and I was cooking breakfast plus a pork chop for his lunch. The chop was in a glass skillet which suddenly cracked quite audibly and fell apart. One of the pieces struck the floor; Denny threw down his razor and came running, assuming that I had fainted. I could laugh over the incident, but he never could. At last the doctor had me stay in bed until Denny had brought me a mild breakfast. That, my loved ones, was humiliating, for I should have been cooking for the man who shortly had to go off to work.

Now the time for our baby to be born loomed closer, we knew arrangements must be made, for we still had not managed to find a car. Used ones were as scarce as hen's teeth, and we were definitely in no financial bracket that would allow the purchase of a brand new one if it could be found. Tales of false labor abounded also. We were praying for guidance. Then a couple two doors up the street reserved the privilege of taking us to the hospital. So while I dressed, a little after four one morning, about two weeks before the earliest date on which our baby could possibly arrive, Morris went to their house and roused Lynn.

Though we'd heard those warnings, they hardly came into our minds that morning. Lynn took us in, and I, despite the assurance of the nurse that we would have hours to wait, did my share quickly. Meredith Fay arrived at about six fifteen on September 2, 1944. We had our little girl.

The dumb stunt which is attributed to all new parents, however, was actually done by our chauffeur. Later Claudia told me that Lynn stepped into his trousers, pulled them up, and dropped them before his fumbling fingers could get them buttoned. He yanked them up a second time; he dropped them a second time. Claudia declared she would have screamed had he fumbled them again, but he made it on that try.

Denny left no choice: we had our daughter; we had our Fay. I would have been content to leave it at that, for I had gone all my life with a single Christian name. Mother maintained that a child with two names easily forgot his Mother's family name, and I had not felt hampered. But Denny wanted her to have a middle name too. I had always loved the name Julia, and wanted to name a daughter that; but it was not to be. We had one unlovely neighbor with that name, and I was not risking her telling the whole world that our lovely baby was named for her. I liked Meredith and allowed it, but she was always called Merry Fay at home. Meredith came into play after she was an older student. She was a pretty, blue-eyed baby with light brown hair and a most infectious smile. She came home from the hospital with a black eye because one day she threw a crying fit, and kicked herself into the head of her crib. Claudia dashed down to the house and took her up. Merry Fay swiveled her head and seemed to study the room.

"Oh, look, she'd going to redecorate!" Claudia averred.

Texas school children must be six on or before September 1 of the year they are admitted. Merry Fay would be about six hours too young to enroll in school in a few years. Doctor Barksdale apologized to me the next day. He had not thought to certify that she was born shortly before midnight. I was not unhappy though, and assured him that the older students had an easier time as beginners. While that is true, I also could never have lived with that lie on my conscience; and I believe he was relieved. He was our medical stay for years. One of our children and one of his ran neck and neck through bronchitis and the so—called "childhood diseases." He went to Taos, New Mexico, when he retired. He then was called on by hippies and drop—out artists for some years, if rumor can be believed. I saw him occasionally in Borger, but we did not discuss that. Taos is now less infested with that specie of humanity, I am told.

Merry Fay was surprisingly good as a baby, and she was happy. I found one day when I waxed our bedroom floor that she could have her bad times as well. Nothing I did seemed to please her; she whimpered and would not be bright and smiling until I happened to move her crib back into its accustomed place. She greeted her old friend in the mirror happily. I had not realized that when she was conversing daily, largely with her own reflection.

Later, when another baby was on the way, I stumbled on the idea of putting a cookie and some toys at the end of her crib before Denny went off to work; then I lay back down for a short doze while she was still asleep. I'd wake and find her playing happily, my own churning insides at rest.

I too could face the rest of the day in good spirits. Soon those first queasy months were behind us; the rest of the waiting period was faced easily.

Normally I took Merry Fay with me wherever I went, but one day I gave in to a neighbor who insisted regularly that she would keep our toddler while I ran an errand. One of the first things she told me when I returned home was that when everything grew too quiet, she investigated. She found Merry Fay eating the dog's food from the dish that was kept filled for their Scotch terrier. I liked the dog well enough, for he was always welcoming with me—to their utter surprise—but I did not relish the thought of him and Merry Fay sharing the same dinner plate. Besides, what if it made her nasty tempered, like the Scottie was to Denny? I didn't leave her there again. But shortly after Merry Fay's birth, a young couple with a baby the same age as her had moved in at the other end of the block. Keeping two little girls was little more trouble than keeping one. Marie and I both took advantage of our exchange, and neither Beverly nor Merry Fay ever objected.

That was during the days of soap rationing. During the time I was in Allison, various items, including shoes, meat, tires, sugar, and many more, were rationed. When we signed up for ration stamps for those items, we had to vow that we were not hoarding sugar. I think farmers were the worst at doing so, perhaps because their big old kitchens adapted to it; but they and others made sugar syrup of it and saved it for canning. They argued that with all their fruit, it was a logical course. We had to use ration stamps for ours, and had no home canned fruit to fall back on. They also took a casual approach to butter and meat rationing. Occasionally we could buy a small roast which looked puny until women who had big families and/or their own meat supply bragged about smearing real butter on both sides of a roast, and browning it well before sliding it in a low oven to cook tender. We became proud of our legal ones then.

When we discussed such incidents one day, Marie raged against the practice. Knowing that she had her husband and her mother to stand in line for soap advertised for one to a family, Denny remarked that hording sugar was not any worse than hoarding soap. The young mother snatched up her child and stormed out of the house.

We neither saw nor heard from her for some time. Then one day the local grocer stewed over the fact that the lady who preceded me had not taken the small sack of tomatoes she had paid for, only the larger sack which bulged with heavier items. He didn't know the customer, but I went to the door and caught a glimpse of her. Marie. Had she been in a car, I would not have seen her. We were lucky to live that close anyway, for gasoline too was rationed. I assured him that I would take them by. Marie patently was tired of her privacy and began visiting again the next day.

I couldn't make up my mind whether I wanted a girl or a boy this time. I did decide whichever it was would be named for Dan. "For" in this context was a mania with me. I have always contended that I was named "after" Lincoln, Virginia Dare, Confucius, and many others, but I did not bear their names. A boy could be Dan or Daniel, but I decided to make it feminine if we were given a girl. Dana Maurice was born on February 10, 1956. She was two weeks early and in a last minute rush as well. I got up for a routine visit to the bathroom, and Denny had to carry me back to the bed. He dashed next door, intending to call a doctor who had his practice three blocks down the street. He received no answer when he hammered on the door, and hurried back to see about me. Then he hurried off again and didn't have to knock, for the neighbor was at her door with her robe around her shoulders. She let him in and donned her other garment on the way to our house. This time the doctor didn't answer; so Denny called the ambulance and rushed home again. Dana had wasted no time and was waiting to greet him. Mrs. Whozit had picked her up. He saw that I was all right and dashed back to the telephone again. This time he reached our doctor. We gathered soon after that at the hospital.

I had glanced at my watch a couple of minutes after it was all over. 1:30, on a Sunday morning. We left Merry Fay with the neighbor, but I never did know whether they stayed at our house or went to that blessed lady's home.

I was famous, briefly.

Dana slept in a bed we had borrowed from John, and was meant to be used in a trailer house. It was only thirty-five inches long, and had very low sides. When the time came to put her in a larger crib with higher sides, she bawled and squalled and refused to go to sleep. True to our predictions, she pulled up and fell out a few times, but still insisted on her own bed. At seven months she began to take steps when she wanted to but she didn't cut loose and really walk until she was nine months old. She walked then as well as she can now. In desperation, we took her out of that tiny crib and put her next to the wall and Merry Fay on the outside of a double bed. They both liked it at once and we returned the crib. The girls slept together until Merry Fay went off to college. If they had ever set up and hue and cry for twin beds we would have bought them, but double beds are handier for guests, and leave more floor space.

Dana was nothing at all like Merry Fay as a baby. She kept the hospital staff torn up that first week and a half, eating well one meal and almost nothing the next, which made her cry for Mamma before the third. I refused to fret about it, and put her on a four hour schedule when we could decide for ourselves. It worked beautifully, but a few weeks later she began to whimper and then to cry in pain about one a.m., night after weary night. Then I would push our aching baby, crib and all, to the living room, allowing Denny to get the rest he needed.

Quite accidentally I stumbled onto the cause of Dana's trouble. I forgot that I was out of orange juice. Without it, she slept peacefully until four or five o'clock. Sheer hunger woke her. I didn't give her any more juice until she grew up. Well, at least for some years. I had to keep her in bootees for an extended time as well, for even the size zero shoes proved too large until she was five months old.

Dan came to see us in April and brought a friend along, Felix Sawicki. We had a very pleasant visit. It's possible that our instant concord helped her to decide whether or not she wanted to marry Felix—who answered to the name of Phil. They were married soon after the visit and called to let us know. We were truly happy for them.

Dana came up with another problem; her stomach rejected all formula and canned milk. She could drink boiled skimmed milk. After she could walk she had both pneumonia and tonsillitis. Antibiotics were in use, but not on a one a day basis yet. She was entered into the hospital where she received shots every three hours; her little bottom looked like a rusty sieve. When the question of a tonsillectomy arose, her age prevented the doctor from performing one. When she attained that, three years, polio had reared its ugly head. Dr. Barksdale informed us that a child who took polio within months of having a tonsillectomy invariably had a very rough case. On the other hand, if she caught it while she was in the throes of tonsillitis, it was apt to be severe and hard for her body to fight, I pressured him to admit. We decided that to remove them gave her more chance of good health.

Waiting in her room for her return from the surgery was an ordeal. It took an extremely long time. In reality, the nurses had neglected to inform us that an emergency cesarean section had been rushed in before her! Everything was fine, and she woke up very indignant the next morning.

"Where's my breakfast?" she wanted to know.

I applied to the nurse, and she tried to assure me that tonsillectomy patients never, but never, ate breakfast; but I overruled her and ordered Dana's standard fare, a bowl of oats. To the nurses' amazement she ate every bite. She did not have polio, for which we thanked God fervently. Her health improved steadily.

While the girls were still pre-school age, I took them on their first train ride. We rode between Weatherford and Ranger; John and Daddy served as our dispatchers and greeting committees at the stations.

The girls loved Denny, and he them. His taking them to the drugstore five blocks away each afternoon after work for an ice cream cone became almost a ritual. A large number of our friends remarked on it. Denny was our daughters' best-loved playmate. That still held true in the summer of 1951. Then one day as he romped on the floor with them, he felt a tearing pain. He had had a tissue-thin looking place near the groin for years; while there was no outer tear, he had to have an immediate hernia repair. It proved to be quite extensive; the doctor would not take his appendix out, usually a routine matter, because the incision, already five inches long, would have to be increased in length too much.

When Denny came out of the anesthetic, he found himself so tightly bandaged that he could not straighten his body to get relief. Neither would the nurses loosen the bandage on one edge and replace it. We managed to trim it a little bit with my fingernail scissors, but it wasn't enough. I nearly passed out because of his pain; and bless his heart, he made me sit down and put my head between my knees. Sturdy me! Of course the doctor redressed it when he came again, mouthing maledictions against the nurses all the while.

Merry Fay started kindergarten when she was nearly six. I walked the few blocks to the highway crossing with her and Dana in tow. There was a crossing guard to make the journey safe when classes started and the children preferred to walk alone. Although Merry Fay was eager to stay, some children fought strongly and cried to return home with their mothers. Dana was four and a half and looked at the five year-olds in wonder. Then suddenly she too burst into tears.

"What in the world is the matter?" I demanded.

"I don't want to go home," she sobbed. "I want to stay at kindergarten." We had no trouble with her the next year.

It was that winter that I became pregnant again. I was agreeably surprised, and definitely wanted a boy this time. Dr. Barksdale assured me that I would never carry the baby. As I had trouble the whole time, I became a big baby myself. Denny remarked one day, to me only, that my tear glands must be connected to my bladder! But we made it.

In early summer we visited with Mother and Daddy in Bastrop. Mother took one look at me when I struggled out of the car and said, "Good Lord! You're just like all the rest of them!"

Our baby was due in September. Mable and Gray expected a child in October; and Dan and Phil expected one later, in the winter, in February. It was not all of us, but three at a whack was big numbers to Mother. Especially as it was the second time.

At a routine visit to the doctor one Friday in August, he told me that he was afraid I would be caught at home with the two girls and produce this baby as quickly as I had Dana. I was to come in the next morning about ten. We parked the girls with Roy and Billie McCluney and arrived at his office about ten after ten. A two minute examination was followed by a tiny shot of what looked like pure water. Then we went to the hospital. At noon we had our son. During the short interval that I managed to stay awake before I slept through his birth, we had reaffirmed Denny's earlier suggestion that if the baby was a boy, we would name him for Denny's father; and if it were a girl, we would name her for my mother.

Bill weighted between seven and half and eight pounds, and appeared even larger. Immediately he began to gain and grow. The doctor tied my tubes, at his insistence, in a day or so. I went to his office ten days later for the stitches to be removed. We stood in his waiting room, ignored by the comfortably seated patients and their escorts until a friend arrived, admired Bill, and asked how old he was. Suddenly I saw eight or ten people leap to their feet and stand ashamed beside their chairs, each insisting that I take his seat. I knew from their bizarre faces that they had thought Bill was much older than he was, and I could hardly restrain a laugh.

School had started again. Merry Fay had been briefed, and as a second grade student allowed to go alone. Dana was excited about beginning "real school," and needed no ride as it met a block from the house. Lists of students names were posted beside each door. She would find her name and enter the indicated room. Poor Dana! The lists were placed above her level for the parents' benefit; she roamed around rather forlornly, ignored by parents bent on only one thing—their own offspring. We had envisioned the lists placed lower on the walls, for the children to read. Providence took a hand and sent a neighbor, Elinora Argo, to the building, possibly to meet a friend. She saw Dana immediately and got her into the correct room.

Denny's folks still lived near Allison, in Wheeler now, about seventy-five miles from us. It was simple to go there more often than we went the three hundred and fifty miles to see my family. We bought a portable crib which we used as a playpen as well as a bed when we were away from home; it was a lifesaver when Bill was nine months old and we vacationed in Yellowstone National Park. He played happily in the crib by the side of the river while we fished but he preferred to be out of it in the cabin. I would stand him by a chair and place toys on the seat. However, he was already pulling up, and in a few minutes would drop to the floor and crawl over to anything that looked inviting. The rough, wooden floors had be scrubbed until they were quite splintery; hardly a safe play area even when they were apparently clean. So on the second attempt at freedom each time he was standing out of his bed, I plucked him up and deposited him back in. He played, but he resented it; and in sheer self-defense began to walk. Of course he continued to walk and was a healthy little boy with an inexhaustible supply of energy.

I did not do so well. The doctor prescribed medicines, and rest, determined to save my insides if he could, and at last he put me on a regular dosage of codeine. One Saturday morning I took my pill and we set out for town. Suddenly I was deathly sick. In fact, Denny thought I was going to die right then. I was utterly colorless, and he set out for the hospital, but the pain began to recede about the time we got there, and I refused to go in. I thought it over carefully, and remembered eating a cracker that lay on the table about ten minutes after I had taken the first codeine tablet. So confidently I ate a cracker after the next one. Again I was extremely ill. The next time I waited ten minutes then ate. I'd done it! No more medicine problem. We lost anyway, and I had a hysterectomy on Memorial Day, 1954.

What a holiday!

Chapter XII

Luceille will always have the distinction of presenting Mother and Daddy with their first grandchild, and John will have the same honor for the second. Lemar had the third one Jesse Lee, on July 20, 1942. When we began our family, they were adding on to theirs. Luceille, John, Lemar, and I had babies in 1944, in June, in August, and two in September. I do wish that I'd planned this family saga long ago. I might have been better at making lists and checking them twice. I didn't though, which was an undoubted error on my part. So let's bring the record up to date with the rest of Mother's and Daddy's grandchildren. (To be truthful, this idea first struck me when I decided to add Bill's arrival so soon after the girls' births.)

Jessie and Jimmy lost a second child, stillborn; and it seemed to hurt Mother and Daddy as much as it did the young parents. However, they then had two healthy sons; first Floyd Lemar, born June 7, 1947, at Dallas, Texas. We had only minimum letter writing time, but we kept up, to some extent, through visits home and seeing one another there. Of course the number of our visits home equalled in ratio the ratio of the miles we covered going home. Therefore I scarcely heard "Floyd Lemar" spoken, but heard him called "Happy." Mother declared frankly that he was the happiest baby she ever saw. Then in 1950, on January 29, Jessie and

Jimmy had their fourth and last child, another boy, whom they gave Daddy's name, or possibly Jessie's and Daddy's, Jesse Lafayette. They didn't call him Jesse or any portion of the unwieldy Lafayette. He was always J.L.

When both boys were of school age, Jessie and Luceille saw a good deal of one another, worked together, and walked together at times. It was through Ceal that we learned that Jessie had suddenly begun to fall—after walking only a very few blocks. Over a period of time her problem worsened, and doctors blamed it on a childhood fall, but that proved to be an erroneous diagnosis.

Happy married Patricia Jean Ballard. Patricia was born May 16, 1951, in Waco, Texas. They had Tammy Annette in 1969; James David was born in 1970; and Larry Lemar, a year later. Tammy has been married twice. She had two children: Andy C. Bloomer and Jessica Ashley Levesque.

As Jessie could not care for J.L. after a few years, he spent some time in Vickey's home and some in Mable's. There was no conflict among the children; but J.L., who was a whiz at mathematics and a poor reader, just never seemed to feel at home. By mutual consent he tried living at Christ Haven, a Christian home for children. He felt more one of the team and stayed there until Happy took him out.

A month after J.L. was born, Lemar had an appendectomy and the next April he had a tonsillectomy. Apparently he has had better health since. On October 22, 1943, he and Florence had their second child, Joyce Jean. They have always called her Jeannie. I was asked to come help and went to Ranger to be with them for a time. Florence cared for the baby; I cooked and kept house and corralled J.L. He was an intriguing imp, and just as agape as any other youngster over a tiny sister. We had to forbid him to go into the room, with her unless we invited him in; but he would walk up to the door, stand with his toe on the line where the rugs met—an eye fixed on us—and shove his foot in the room when we blinked. He drew it back out immediately. Of course he still dashed in as well the moment he thought he could get by with it. Diaper-clad, he never felt the swats we administered occasionally, but he resented the jar they gave him. Slaps on the leg were very little more effective. Lemar stayed in their trailer house in Pasadena, which would not have served for all of us; and Florence soon returned to Pasadena, a Houston suburb. There would now be two babies in their trailer.

Their third child, Carol Ann, was born September 13, 1944. A few days younger than Merry Fay, she became the fourth and last of the cluster of grandchildren who stunned Mother and Daddy that year. I've wondered: Did they look on them as a congregate blessing or a congregate blow? They loved all of them in either case.

Lemar and Florence continued to live near Houston, and he continued to work in the shipyards. There he was drafted into many hours of overtime. Eventually Florence became so tired of it that she began to run around. Then she left the children and Lemar; and in July 1947, a divorce was granted. The children remained with their father.

Lemar did everything for the children that he possibly could and had time to do. They had a new sewing machine, and he drew on his earlier experiences, gained when we were children making and playing with rag dolls, to help him make playsuits for his own children, which surely pleased them a great deal. He drew around them, added ample fabric to cover the thickness of the little bodies, and sewed up the simple garments.

He came back to Ranger for a time then. Since Wendell was off in the Navy, Lemar asked John for help. She moved in with them for awhile. Wendell returned home, and John moved out again. Lemar worked with Daddy for some time but quit and wound up in Fairhope, Alabama, operating a bulldozer for Joseph Schnieder early in 1948. They resided with a Mr. and Mrs. Anacker, and she cared for the children while he was at work. He met Grace Jeanette Childress there and they were married. She took the children to her heart. They lived in Fairhope, Eastland, and Weatherford, but then bought a farm at Cleveland, Texas, about fifty miles north of Houston. From then on Lemar farmed, and operated bulldozers or other heavy equipment.

They added two girls to their family. Martha Marie was born in 1953 and Nina Faye in 1959. One month after Martha was born, while he was clearing a section with a bulldozer, a tree top fell on Lemar; inflicting quite severe wounds. One result of many broken bones is his acute arthritis in later years. He jotted down in his diary that he settled for $1300. I wonder what it would be today!

J.L. lives near Austin. He and Shirley Turner were wed and have three grown children. Sherry is married and has a son, Matthew. Susan is married and has a daughter, Morgan. Glenn is now twenty. Vickey and I were made welcome when we stopped by one day while the children were still at home.

Jeannie and her husband, Jim Kulhman, have no children, but substitute an ill-natured, sleek black tom cat who does not get his disposition from his owners. They spent several years in Kuwait working for a U.S. oil company, and live now in Montrose, Colorado. Jim is retired. They travel down to south Texas to see family fairly often, sometimes on a route through Borger; then they make a very welcome visit with me.

Carol married John Wilson Borden. They have lived near or in Houston all their married life. They have raised four children. John III, born May 29, 1964, is single and finds it handy to live at home. Jeannie Lea, was born May 8, 1965 and lives at home with her baby girl, Kimberly Jean. Beverly Ann, born March 18, 1971, lives at home, is studying to be a paralegal, and working. Steven Wade was born November 24, 1975 and is a student living at home.

Carol has always been one of the friendliest, and happiest individuals I have ever known; I feel sure she would welcome me today as warmly as she did the day I dropped in at Houston unannounced, and called them to come and get me. Martha married Ron Scott (Scottie) in 1953. It was her second marriage. They live in Michigan and have no children.

Nina Faye and Kenneth Fridley were married, her second marriage, in 1988. They live in Arkansas and are childless.

John and Wendell's son Stanley was born on August 2, 1944, just a month before Merry Fay was born, and Butch—Wendell Jr.—was born March 31, 1954. They also lost two babies by miscarriage, babies they had already begun to love.

Lena Jim married Robert Wilson, and they have two sons, David and Robbie, both married. Robbie and Denise have one daughter, Rachael Mae.

Stanley was in our country's submarine service for some years. He married Elizabeth and they had one child, Debbie; then Elizabeth divorced him. He remarried, and for a while had a step daughter, Kirstin, for Debbie to play with. John and Wendell adopted Debbie because Stanley feared Elizabeth might try to take her away from him. They took her along as their own when Wendell was chosen by General Dynamic to go to England for a few months. Kirstin's mother took Kirstin back north when she decided that she could not adapt to life in Texas. Stanley married again, a Panamanian lady, Frances Maddox, who had four children. She was very attractive, and the one son that I met was one of the most thoughtful people I have ever Known.

Butch married Patricia "Tricia" Simmons. They have one delightful son whom they named Wendell Hickerson, III. They call him Chad. Tricia divorced Butch when Chad was three or four. Butch married Lisa (Luther) in 1990. It took me a few seconds to place Wendell and Lisa when near Christmas I received a card from them. A nice surprise.

Luceille and Joy's second child, Morris Ray, born June 14, 1944, in Ranger, is the only one to show the evidence of his father's French blood, in his dark hair and eyes and his volatile personality. J.D. (Jesse Dan) was born in September, 1945. Luceille also lost a daughter in premature birth. At a time when Luceille was suffering very poor health, she and Joy broke up. In 1955 she married Robert Maurice Thomas, a genial, happy man who strives to love all mankind. They had one son, Robin Eugene, born December 20, 1957.

Jerry Ruth married Jack Carroll Dollins shortly before her twenty-first birthday. She has four step children, of which the oldest is only nine years younger than she. To her they are as much her own as the one daughter she and Jack had. They are Jeanita Ann, who married Walter Hankins in 1968; Deborah Ruth, who married Ronald Ellis in 1979; Karen Lynn, married to Gary Anderson in 1973; and Jack Jr., who married Christy Sackman in 1979. Jere (a spelling adopted later in life and court approved) Ruth and Jack's daughter, Stephanie, was born January 2, 1967; she is currently finishing a college education that illness held at bay several times.

Morris Ray and Patricia Morgan, nee Lumpkin, married in 1972. She brought to their marriage Lonnie Ray, who married Cheryl Holden, and Kevin Lee, who married Stephanie Gerth. Morris and Pat have two children, Julie Elaine, who was born December 21, 1972; and Jeffery Scott, born May 6, 1974.

J.D. married Asuncion Perez, whom we called Terry and who was a trained vocational nurse, in 1968; she was born in Puerto Rico but reared and educated in New York. They had one child, Kimberly Lynn, on December 21, 1969. Terry never stayed a stranger to anyone. J.D. has long worked in the Fort Worth area selling and maintaining boats. He and Kim delighted in long motorcycle trips made together. Terry left J.D. while Kim was a young girl and married her boss. Then only a year or so later, she died following heart surgery.

Kim married Ross Helton; They have one child, Courtney Rochell, born in October , 1987. J.D. has recently remarried. Robin married Marianne Burggess in the early 1980's; and they had one child, Robert. He is a smart, good looking boy who has just come to live with his grandparents. His mother has divorced Robin and remarried. As a consequence, Robert is somewhat upset, but I firmly believe he will enjoy school and feel more settled in the fall if they are firm where it matters, but not nit-picking with him.

Luceille raised four children. She and Bob count their five and the six step-grandchildren as their own eleven, and they also consider twelve great-grandchildren theirs. Some of the grandchildren are not yet married; therefore the last figure likely will become larger in time.

During the time that Lemar's and Luceille's babies were on the bottle, they were at Mother's and Daddy's quite often and one of the youngest frequently set an unfinished bottle down, intending to pick it up and drink more after a pause.

The sibling just older usually would grab it and empty it to the loudly bawled objection of its rightful owner. One day when that nearly happened, Luceille absent-mindedly reached out to put it in the small hand that couldn't quite reach it but saw in the nick of time what was happening. Quickly she dragged the nipple through some Lea and Perrins on Mother's plate before she released it. The little thief repented of his ways and quit nursing a bottle then and there.

Dan and Phil (Felix) had three boys in a row, all born in Houston. Felix arrived on March 15, 1948; Richard, still called Ricky, was born July 29, 1949; Gary made his entry on February 23, 1953. Felix was a perfect gentleman who enjoyed life. Ricky was rather rebellious but got the most out of life. Gary was totally extroverted: he knew everyone, loved everyone, and did his own thing despite anyone. Today he's nearly forty and hasn't changed.

Phil was captain of a merchant ship and he was away for long stretches of time. When she could, Dan met him at port wherever he hit shore in the states—especially if he could not come home before embarking on the next trip. In Florida one November, while Phil worked at his job, Dan kept herself busy addressing Christmmas cards and inserting notes. Proud to be ahead of the task for a change, she mailed them off to friends and family—in a corner mailbox. At Christmas time, deluged with cards saying none of us had heard from her, she elucidated, very sure of her innocence. Doubt ran high when no one received even a late card. But in February the cards began to trickle in. We assumed that in an area devoted to satisfying tourists' needs during certain months and rather more than less ignored the rest of the time, some post boxes were bypassed out of peak season.

Dan and Phil lived in Houston at first but wanted more room and a homeplace. He also made good money on the ship, but missed too much time with his family. So they bought a ranch near Bastrop and built a two bedroom house there. As Mother and Daddy were now in their seventies, and had decided to retire, Daddy agreed to feed the cattle and horses that Phil hoped would keep them in a high income range. So Mother and Daddy moved into the small house which was furnished with some of their own pieces and some new furniture. Phil and Dan moved to Smithville, about thirty-five miles to the east, and made plans for their house.

They deliberately built a large basement which could be partitioned with curtains but had both kitchen and bathroom walled and finished. There they planned to live while they got on their feet and built their own house. Dan had little time left from being mother and father to the boys, patently not enough to oversee the erection of a house. The building plans changed and had to be agreed on a second time. Before they had the new house built, Phil had retired early.

Someone had given Bill a delightful one piece corduroy outfit which zippered down the front and in the crotch. I had taken scraps from outing dresses I had made the girls, a blue one and a red one, and sewed an outfit pattered after the corduroy one for Bill. It was so attractive that I used it for dresswear. When he outgrew it, I sent it along with some other pieces to Dan for Gary. She liked it and dressed Gary to go to town. At bedtime she could not remove it, for Gary was a huskier child than Bill. She had to cut it off. That was the only time that I ever sent any hand-me-downs to Dan. She didn't have to count pennies like I did. John and Vickey could make use of any hand-me-downs I had later.

Felix was studious, attended school at Bastrop, a town noted more for the lovely state park of the same name, and later, the man-made lake, than for its school system. So he taught himself calculus since it wasn't part of the school curriculum. He went on to get his degree from the University of Texas, in electrical engineering. He married Evelyn (often called Eve) White in 1987, and holds a position with IBM in Washington, D.C. He is still a rather quiet personality, and easily liked, genial, and helpful. their family consists of a daughter, Jennifer, three; and a baby son, Matt. They are at home in Great Falls, Virginia. Eve too is quite friendly and well-liked, and more outgoing than her husband.

Recently, when several of us were gathered at Dan's, tea and coffee flowed constantly and was frequently made by the one who had the yen for a cup. We rarely took time to make a full pot of either lest we should miss a spoken word, but just shoved a cup of water into the convenient microwave to heat for an instant drink. All of us but Eve, that is, who invariably brought her water to a rollicking boil in a small saucepan on the electric stove. When the young couple left the house to visit an old friend, we who stayed behind first agreed how well we liked them; then laughed as we endeavored to explain why Eve preferred to heat water on the stove over heating it in the newer appliance. All the conjectures that we once heard from those people who felt the need to explain away their burning desires to own the new ovens, plus any other wildly improbably and paradoxical ones which we could dream up, were aired. Dan was out of the room, seeing them on their way. She returned, and listened with mild interest before she asked what in the world we were talking about; we explained. She remarked that, shoot, she would ask Evelyn.

Lunch was underway when the young couple returned, but Dan soon remembered and asked Eve pointblank for the answer to the question which was uppermost in our minds. Her reply sent us off into paroxysms of laughter.

"I like my coffee very hot, and if I put a full cup of water in the microwave, the handle gets too hot to handle," she explained.

So much for modern technological knowledge.

Phil brought Dan myriads of exotic gifts from overseas, for more than she could display at one time, and wanted her to keep and cherish them; so she rarely gave them away until her supply was voluminous, and she felt certain he would not miss a few. Then we all enjoyed the fruits of his largesse. Eventually they got their house, but not on the old basement or even its site. First they lived in a huge trailer house, and then went on to have that long awaited and well-planned brick house built.

Ricky quit school and took a GED test which allowed him to go to college. He attended for three years and then went to work on a shrimp boat for two years before he returned to college. He was cited for his high grades when he turned to computer technology in junior college; and he tutored other students who had to struggle to learn the use of computers. He had taken most of his major courses toward his degree but twice has stepped down to work in areas necessary to keeping the armed forces well supplied. Presently he is mud-logging in the oil fields in order to help lest our domestic supply fall too low during the war with Iraq. He is determined to complete that degree in the future, however.

Gary did not like high school, felt that he was wasting his time, and joined the Air Force. After a year and a half he transferred into Texas Inter-nations Guard. He earned a captain's license for boats up to fifty tons during the year and a half he spent in the Virgin Islands. He was 32 at the time. He also began his college education some years ago in a community college, and though it wasn't his major, he also tutored other students in computer techniques. He earned a degree in geology at the university; but in his position, at Austin Community College, he has been promoted to the office of network administrator over the computer laboratory—which is comprised of about fifty work stations. Although he has an apartment in Austin, he comes home often to do the chores with which Dan needs assistance.

Mable attended some college classes, but being without money bothered her more at that age than it had Dan and me. For one thing, she felt that she alone didn't have the money to spend on the rest of us for Christmas. One Christmas she made and wrapped for each of us just one good-sized piece of fudge to hang in the branches of the tree. She didn't finish college; she went to work. Merry Fay and Dana were probably two and three when Mable and William Edward Gray of Houston invited us home for their wedding. It was in the Methodist Church in Olden. Morris and I were their attendants because we were there, not because it was planned that way.

Gray had been married, but his first wife had left him and taken their two daughters. I did not know that, and as luck would have it, he walked down the hall to find me down on my heels helping Dana get her sandals buckled just before we left for the church building. I looked up and teasingly advised, "Just wait 'til you're married and have a harem of your own." Gray never batted an eyelid. When I found out, I gave him a mental plus for diplomacy.

William E. Gray, II (Bill) was born on December 14, 1950; Keith Alan was born on October 17, 1952, both in Houston. Gray worked for Sinclair Oil, and the company transferred him to Kansas City, and Steven Lewis was born in North Kansas City, almost before we even found out that Mable was pregnant again. This time they worried more, the RH negative factor in mind; but Steven Lewis, born July 16, 1960, was alertly attended by a fatherly doctor who decided to forego any testing. He gave no blood transfusions, to their amazement, and all was well.

Bill was like a small adult by the time he was one year old. He looked like one, and he behaved like one, but still managed to make some small boy mistakes quite often. Keith used to hear his father at the telephone. Gray's invariable opener was, "This's Gray with Sinclair." Until his parents caught on, Keith reported that his name was "Keith Alan Gray with Sinclair." Smart kid, he was. As he was only six weeks younger than our Bill, they played together very happily at any given opportunity. Steven was like almost all children who are several years younger than their siblings: the nosy one, the helpful one in many ways; thus the one who was very rarely excluded from anything before he left the nest.

Bill married Nancy Schwartz in Utah. He and Nancy have four children: Alexis Lea, born in April 1979; Willie born in June 1981; Daniel born in June, 1984; and Kelly born December 1986. They now live in Minneapolis.

Keith married slim, attractive Susan Jacobs, who has a wealth of dark hair. They had one child, Laura, in August of 1978. They broke up less than ten years later. For several years Keith lived in Florida; then he returned to Nashville. Laura lives with her mother and stepfather a few miles from Mable and Gray, and they see one another fairly often.

Steven married a twice-divorced woman and mother of two children, who seemed to keep him very happy for a time. They had a daughter, Kelsey Meredith; but the mother is now suing for a third divorce. Steven lives in Durham, North Carolina.

On one visit home I found Vickey being courted by Jimmy Moak, a pleasant young man with dark hair. They went off to the woods to follow a course of instruction which obviously he had begun earlier—teaching Vickey to shoot a pistol, to shoot it properly and well. I wondered where they had lived to feel she needed that. I had always lived where one could leave doors unlocked but still feel assured that everything would be safe. Deep down, of course, I knew that it was not really as simple as that everywhere. Borger had been one of the "dens of iniquity" that we read of, but Bunavista was as peaceful as Eden at that time.

Vickey and Jimmy were married and settled in Bay City, which is north of the costal city of Matagorda. Later they moved to Waco. We saw one another at home, as ones parents' home can always be claimed as ones own in those conditions. In June, 1954 Vickey and Jimmy had a son, Kenneth. they had room in their hearts for more, but it wasn't to be. Several later pregnancies ended in spontaneous abortion. That meant that Kenneth was their only child for some sixteen years.

That was when it started, anyway. A lady with five or six children (her husband had walked off earlier) requested help when one of them was very ill and in the hospital. The person to whom she had applied, knowing how helpful members of the Church of Christ in Hurst were, asked the minister if the ladies there would help. They would; but after they had taken it turn about to care for the children for some time, Vickey suggested that the four or five most involved ladies each take one child home for the rest of the duration. The mother agreed, and Vickey took Tommy.

Mrs. Jones kept her house sparklingly clean, every toy carefully arranged on shelves, shelves too high for the toys to be played with often. She washed, cooked, took physical care of the children. But is it good for a child to be told to stay in bed until he is given permission to rise? Their wet sheets were washed without fuss on many mornings! Sent out to play, they came in only with permission. Imagine, if you can, having to knock at your own door and ask if you may go to the bathroom.

Tommy loved staying with Vickey's family, and was loved by them; but for some time he did not speak for himself. He merely repeated whatever was first said to him. If someone asked, "Tommy, would you like a glass of milk?", Tommy would reply with the very same words. This from a two and a half year old boy!

Eventually the children all went home. Tommy cried so for Vickey and Jimmy that Mrs. Jones feared he would be sick from it. She called Vickey, and they agreed for him to pay his adopted family a visit. This took place several times, but when asked, the mother refused to let them have the boy permanently. As Vickey and her family had come to love him, it was heart rending to give him up. She warned Mrs. Jones that she would not take him again. Mrs. Jones asked if they would keep him while the Joneses moved to Brownwood, but let them take him too on their final trip. Vickey agreed.

They didn't see hide nor hair of that woman for over a year! Later the tardy mother moved back to Fort Worth. She made no effort to take Tommy back. On the other hand, when the boys were nearly five, she brought Terry to visit Tommy, and then raved about how much Terry missed his brother. At last Vickey suggested that she bring him to visit for a few days in the future. Mrs. Jones went, there and then, to her car and brought in a paper sack of ragged clothes. That was on December 23, and Terry's visit never came to an end either. In fact he told her that, "I knew I was going to get to come live with you."

For fear of losing her allotment from the state for the children's upkeep, she continued to disallow adoption. Only when Tommy and Terry could feel sixteen looming did adoption become so important to them that they urged Vickey and Jimmy to adopt them in the face of possible unsavory publicity. But time had elapsed and the lawyer saw a way of avoiding it now. He decided they should sue for back payment for food, clothing, doctor bills, et cetera if Mrs. Jones persisted in holding out.

The last step was almost farcical. On the day the man of law said, "Let's go," the prospective parents, the quite wide-eyed boys, and four attorneys surged to the courthouse. Four attorneys? Yes: one for the Moaks, one for the boys, one for the biological mother, and one for their biological father. No one arrived to contravene anything. Vickey and Jimmy had hired all four lawyers (and had to pay their fees) for the proceedings to be legal. Their lawyer went from one courtroom to another scanning the dockets. He skipped those rooms that he deemed would take too long. He led them into one where uncontested divorces were being okayed at a rapid rate. They sat for about an hour, and then took their turn. No opposition; no problem.

Tommy and Terry Moak were wildly happy to have that name made legal and permanent. You see, in one sense it hadn't mattered until they learned that one's driver's license must be in his legal name. Tommy took his driver's education before Terry did, and he had a learner's permit in his legal name twenty-four hours before it was re-issued under Moak. During that time junk mail dispensers bought the current crop of new names and addresses from the state. Tommy gets (or at least did) two batches of usually useless mail to Terry's one.

During those years, Kenneth has added his natural flair for computers and his keen diving ability to his marketable talents. He bought a house, and moved into it. Through the years he has dated many girls, but is still single. He has spent many hours in college classrooms but has only recently taken possession of his B.S. degree. He's still part of the family, runs by and calls frequently, lends and accepts aid when he sees the need for it. He's a happy man. I hope he doesn't get lonely.

Tommy works for a company that builds and repairs fire trucks, but they are closing out their Fort Worth facility, and he must decide in the near future whether to set up his own business or find another position. Before Tommy was 21, the mother of a girlfriend asked him to help her move to the coast, and she stampeded him into marriage with her daughter before he knew what had hit him. Neither was ready for such a step, but Tommy did his best. Wifie went on buying sprees and ran around. It ended in divorce and a wiser Tommy.

Terry works in security. He has lived in an apartment with Tommy, and for a short time by himself. Today he is a Tarrant County deputy, living at home, and talking about an apartment of his own again.

Recently I flew into DFW Airport for a visit, toted my luggage the short distance to the sidewalk, and waited. For years now Vickey has checked with the airline and timed her arrival so that she has only to slide to a stop, wait for me to load my burden, and cruise for the exit. This time I had to wait a few minutes. As I stood watching for her to slide in from my left, a male voice spoke from my right.

"Pardon me, Ma'am."

At the same time, the speaker stepped just past me and reached for my luggage. My first foolish thought was that I hadn't noticed the area had been re-marked. Was I waiting in a restricted zone? My eyes fell as I sought to do eye-battle with what was obviously either a thief or an accuser. All I saw was a deputy sheriff's badge on a brown uniform sleeve. My eyes lifted immediately, and met the gaze of my suddenly, totally, adult nephew, Terry. He was grinning with all the assurance of a professional buffoon.

So! He obviously had a little bit of small boy left in him after all.

Chapter XIII

We were allowed to move into a two bedroom house when Dana was only a few months old. The rule read that a couple with one child could get a two bedroom house only when the baby attained the age of two. The rule-makers dismissed the fact that many couples prefer to have their children nearer in age. The reason for breaking the rule was the desire of one official—this was a federal housing unit—to give his friend our one bedroom house! He even heckled me to get moved before I cleaned the very dirty house we were allotted prior to our moving to it—as a convenience to him! I tied Dana in the little wooden "child cart" which had been all we could find when we needed a conveyance for Merry Fay. Under Dana's feet I put soap and cleaners, brushes and rags. Then carrying the mop and broom in my hands as I pushed the cart, I walked. Merry Fay, just over twenty months old, walked at my side. When Dana was that age, I would not have dared to strike out to walk a distance of several blocks without her hand in mine. She was taken to sudden darting away.

My parents visited us only rarely. One reason was that Daddy was a workaholic who believed his years of application to his business would amount to nothing if he took off for a few days. However we managed to see them and my brother and sisters from time to time. Mother and

Daddy did visit prior to moving to Dan's and Phil's ranch at Bastrop.

Morris's father and stepmother visited more frequently. They had invited me to call them by their given names while we were still dating, but I felt it would be disrespectful, and I fell into the habit of calling them Mr. Oscar and Miss Ione. Later I called them Gramps and Granny as the children addressed them. We saw Denny's brothers and sisters usually at their parents' home in Allison or Wheeler but did make an occasional visit to their homes.

Denny had aspired to teach, and firmly believed that he would; but, due to his carelessness about his grades, he was drafted instead to help his sister Mildred go to college. A gap in his school attendance, due partly to health problems, partly to a rural school which taught only through the tenth grade, had caused them to finish school together. She made the better grades that year, but she had no real interest in teaching. Her desire was to have a family and teach them in Sunday School, which is just what she accomplished after she began college only at her father's and the superintendent's insistence. She married Walter Cummings, and when no babies arrived, they adopted two children: Mike, near Dana's age, and Cheryl, close to Bill's age. They were happy and proud of their family. Now they have also five grandchildren whom they love as they did their own. Mildred writes or calls me quite frequently and I love her dearly.

By the time Mildred left college and refused to return, it was obvious that Morris couldn't help the family and also attend college. He was the oldest of five: in order of age, Morris; Mildred; Bill, actually Robert Barton; Lawrence, who was nicknamed Dump; and Lottie Belle, whom they called just that until she married Alfred Bell. It was difficult to do, but they shortened it to Lottie.

Bill and his wife, Mildred, lived in Perryton. They had two children, Grover and Roxana, before Denny and I married.

Grover was killed in a tragic farm accident before he was of school age. After a few years they adopted a baby, Richard. They now have a passel of grandchildren. They just recently marked the end of their first fifty years of happiness, and their children hosted their reception assisted by some of their grandchildren.

Lawrence and Hazel were married soon after I arrived in the Panhandle. They have four children, daughters Nelda and Sandra; and sons Phillip and Steven. I had not seen them in years until recently. Then when Merry Fay wanted to see all her Texas kinfolk we could get together, Mildred called from Levelland and had a telephone visit; she told us Dump lived in Weatherford. Bill and Mildred came down from Perryton, a good visit, and they too said he was in Weatherford. Mable and Dana met us at Vickey's, and we all went to Weatherford, to John's. By telephone we located part of the family there and the rest in Mineral Wells. Nelda lives in Weatherford, and she and Dump both met us for a good long visit. Hazel's heart was acting up, and she was resting. All four children are married, and have given Dump quite a few grandchildren. Nelda is about a year older than Merry Fay. Sandra is close to Dana's age.

Lottie and Alfred have one daughter, Lana Lynn, who was born after her father went overseas during World War II. She was several years old when Alfred came home. They planned a larger family, but Alfred had been very seriously injured in battle, and they never had more children. Alfred has passed sixty now, and has been unable to work full time for some years. Their home is in Long Beach, California. We seldom get together unless I can manage to stop by when I'm in that state; but we do love one another and write occasionally.

Soon Mr. Oscar began to have health problems; so Denny, along with his brother Bill, moved them to Tulia, to a house very near Mildred and Walter. Suddenly both sets of parents were further from us. We could still go on weekends to visit Denny's folks, but the 500 miles to Bastrop was much too far for a weekend trip. We went there, but we could sty only a few days at a time because of the heat. It hurt Morris much too badly. On other vacations we went to the mountains or a lakeside in a cooler area for the most part. We covered the northern half of New Mexico and the state of Colorado; then explored various places from here to Yellowstone.

We went yearly to the Trayler family reunions in either north Texas or Oklahoma on a hot summer weekend. Usually we camped out one night. One year it was at Lake McClellon and as usual cooked food was brought from home by old timers; we younger ones brought ice boxes, lunch meat, bacon and eggs. Something had spoiled, but not badly enough to get the full attention of people eating automatically and visiting rather more determinedly. Black-eyed peas? Roast? Pie? Between seventy-five and two hundred people usually gathered by noon the second day, but while there were a large number of us, a count had not been made. Getting up during the night was risky; another person might already be behind the bush one headed for; by daylight many of the clan were ready to head home, us included. Our children threw off the germs quickly. Denny did within just a few days. I lived on medicine for a month, fighting what the doctor diagnosed as a combination of intestinal flu and food poisoning. We had enjoyed the previous get togethers, but they'd gotten too big due to families with Trayler blood in them inviting their spouses's in-laws as well. That debacle seemed to prevent our working up any enthusiasm for another.

Oddly enough, we Whisenants staged a reunion a year or so later. But we never held them yearly. Wendell and John had a rented lakeside lot at Weatherford, and our family gathered there. Stanley had run into a pole the day before and cut his head severely. After hours of tears from him as he bawled and pled and watched others swimming and boating, John carefully coated the top of his head with half a jar of vaseline and let him join the fun. It worked, and there was never any sign of complications.

That reminds me of the time Vickey took us to the lake. We had no bathing suits with us; so John produced some clean underwear of Wendell's from their car, and Morris wore them. I was taking pictures. Morris deliberately asked aloud for our camera and pretended, to Vickey's consternation, that he could see deeper into the scrub oak than he could.

Mable and Gray vacationed at Sabinal in the San Antonio area several times, and found it green and pretty with good fishing. It was dry, hot, and dusty the year we went along. We were luckier the year they came here on a winter holiday. We went to Palo Duro Canyon, sightseeing, walking, climbing, in shirt sleeves. The next morning we put bread wrappers on over her boys' shoes in lieu of boots. Then we allowed them to bundle up and play in the snow. They hadn't needed boots for bad weather in sunny Houston.

Dried off and given a snack, they happily started home an hour later. Not knowing that they couldn't make it, that the highway was declared clogged, and closed, they drove the 350 miles to Abilene. They were glad to stop there for the night, however.

Going to the farm to visit my family meant a great deal to our children. They chased frogs and lightning bugs, eyed the hogs, did what they could to help or impede when the vegetables needed gathering. I've seen Bill lugging turnips as big as his head across to show someone, fondly believing that he was helping. And he had no hesitation at all about setting out to catch a sheep or a goat. Of course he mired down or got lots of grassburrs and skinned knees that way.

And the cacti. Huge clumps of prickly pear to avoid or wish one had. The girls proudly presented me with a prickly pear apple to eat a time or two. They are edible, and I ate them rather than let our side down, but frankly I find them vastly overrated, good only for when one is starving.

When Dan was married again, and lived near Bastrop, we saw her family more frequently. She always had fascinating souvenirs that Phil had brought her from overseas, and there was the great out of doors to explore. Bill and Gary became inseparable playmates; Felix and Ricky, older, had their own amusements. On their occasional visit north, they could not believe the vast wheat fields, the prodigious number of oil wells, nor the lack of trees.

Luceille, Jessie, and Vickey we saw around Fort Worth, and Mable too, later. The regiment of cousins enjoyed being together. Bill and Kenneth played together a great deal; it wasn't until later that I knew Bill was bullying Kenneth. I guess I thought he was perfect. Kenneth, though, could take apart, and reassemble so that they worked, clocks, cookers, cars, or whatevers long before the older cousins, including Bill, could.

Sometimes the children took friends when we visited kin folks. Merry Fay was prone to take Virginia Creager who was born the third day of September. She had many other friends of course, but through Virginia our families of six and five met and became friends. Sally, Jimmy, and Judy ranked high, but Virginia came first. Phyllis Vanlandingham, whose mother was a good friend of mine, was Dana's closest friend. Then Jerri Chisum first tied her and secondly outlasted her. Her parents, Elene and Herbert, were and are also friends of ours. Tom Cox was invariably Bill's favorite guest. We had known Bill and Betty Cox before even our girls were born. Bill Cox has died now, but I see Betty, who has remarried, occasionally.

During those times, Jessie's condition grew worse, and Denny developed an ulcer. More than once there was a strike at the plant, and he took them hard. He didn't complain, as he enjoyed working in the warehouse and as purchasing agent; but he also had to mop floors and check out supplies and the larger tools when his workers, both men and women, went out on strike.

Once he had iritis, and doctors said it was the result of another infection in his body. They found many abscessed teeth. As he had also two which were dead from a harsh blow suffered in a car wreck, it was decided to pull all of them. He wasn't yet forty. He chewed (mauled?) bubble gum to make his gums tough, and many people did not even realize he had lost his teeth. Another time, with the same affliction, the cause couldn't be found and he was sent to the hospital and given typhoid shots to run his temperature up in order that it could break up the infection. But he had such a terrible headache that Dr. Voet gave him two aspirin for the pain; it was too high a dose for that and dropped his temperature to normal within minutes. He had to wait twenty-four hours and then go through the process a second time. The eye healed.

Before all the tests were done, the iris of Denny's eye was shaped like the entire eye, the effect of adhesions. We had to put drops in the eye daily to keep it dilated, which prevented the adhesions from taking permanent form. One day Bill picked up the tiny bottle of drops and looked at it. He set it down with precise four-year-old care; but apparently the bottle had a drop of the fluid on it, for he rubbed his eyes soon after, and one of them became hugely dilated. Our poor Bill! He complained about too much light and fuzzy sight.

In addition to feeding cattle on the place in Bastrop, Daddy inevitably began to raise the crops he could and sell them to the local grocers. It made the place seem more like home when we went to visit.

Mother was having trouble with her eyes too. Doctors in

Houston and Austin helped but little. One even told her that she would be blind in only a few years. Daddy brought her here to have the doctor who had done so well with Morris check her eyes. Dr. Voet was a highly ranked ophthalmologist practicing in this town of 25,000 for the simple reason that her husband, an employee of J.H. Huber Corporation, had been sent here. She delved into the history and treatment of Mother's eyes before giving Mother a complete physical herself. She explained that the center vision of one eye was lost due to hardening of the arteries there, but declared that she need not lose more of her sight if she kept her blood pressure under control.

Daddy spent a great deal of time reading to Mother after that, stories or flower magazines or newspapers. Mother could see enough to cook, to work her flower beds, to clean house; but she sewed on an old treadle machine mainly by feel, too independent to give in altogether. She wrote letters because she knew what she wanted to say and how to write. She held her place with one finger at the left margin, moving it down when she began the next line. Though it overlapped only occasionally, she could read neither what she had written nor our responses.

Feeling that it would expedite things and give her more freedom, I sent her a tape recorder and tapes of news. She never enjoyed them. Every hesitation was a serious thing to her, a sign that I found it hard to communicate with her. A sister (I won't say which one, but she's the youngest of us) tried to explain: "To begin with you feel like a damn fool when you talk to a mechanical object. It's just like trying to think of the right word when you're writing." Mother was having none of that, though; and I had to go back to my pen. Dan inherited the recorder, and someone read our letters to Mother as usual.

There were numerous children in our neighborhood, which was typical of all Bunavista. On our side of our block were seven houses with a total of twenty children. Half or more of them were as old or older than our assortment. Fourteen of them were of an age to play with ours. Across the street in the same block were fourteen children with twelve of them in our children's playing range. Four of the twenty rarely visited on our side of the street, however. Seven houses on our block faced the street behind us; they housed twenty-one children, with some thirteen of them in the same age bracket as ours. Families were shifted frequently, and at times the statistics, changed while at others they remained static. A birthday party invariably overflowed the house of the hosts. Most of us usually had a child or two from other residential ares as well as the countless neighborhood ones.

In our local menagerie were four little girls of three whose birthdays were from May to September: Linda Argo; the daughter of our next door neighbors, Elnora and Warren Argo; the Tarbox twins, Lorene and Marline, from across the alley; and Merry Fay. Before Dana was old enough to follow along, Merry Fay had learned that her father came in for lunch just after the third plant whistle. She would listen for it, and aim herself at our driveway when it sounded. Then when the car came into sight, she would catapult herself home, a pace or so ahead of the other three, screeching at the top of her lungs, "Daddy! Daddy! Daddy!" The remainder of the regiment mimicked her faithfully in every respect. As it was always Denny whom they inundated, it was Denny, and occasionally I, who had to explain away the quadruplets.

Dana's first crony other than those same four girls was a boy from across the street, George, the son of Herman and Alice Ochs. His mother and I had to watch them scrupulously lest they stray; we also had to break them kindly but firmly of an innocent but potentially embarrassing bad habit—that of lying on their tummies in one of our sand-boxes, laughing and talking. And dressed just as they were at birth! Often one of us was apt to peep out and find them so.

We had hastily erected a red cedar paling fence before Dana was allowed out of the house alone. Warren and Elnora had twin boys a few months younger than Dana, and the three spent many happy hours together. We had replaced the paling fence with a heavy chainlink fence before Bill was born.

The Argos's moved, complete with their son who was almost a year older than Bill, and a young couple with a small girl and a baby boy moved in. The baby required home treatments four times a day to correct a problem with which he was born and his mother, Gloria, got highly excitable over it if even a single drop of blood appeared. Because her husband asked that I soothe her when she needed it, we were soon friendly. Thus Robin, their daughter, hale and hearty, and Bill became fast friends.

Bill at times appeared, especially to another neighbor, to be overbearing. That neighbor's son, the same age as they, wasn't allowed to learn that children sometimes misbehaved. She tattled to both of us on a regular schedule but Gloria never let me interfere abruptly, and soon we saw that they rarely got mad and never really hurt one another. But a few days before they were to begin kindergarten Robin and her family moved north. Bill stored and treasured many early memories, and at once became a tough little boy. One neighbor watched him trotting off to join a friend one day, and asked, "Doesn't Bill ever walk anywhere?" His son never seemed to get in a hurry to us. That same boy, George, son of Doyle and Clema Forrester, overcame that little habit in only a few years.

Before he and Kathleen started their family, Bill told Kathleen all about Robin and that, if he ever had a son, he wanted to name him Robin. And so it turned out to be.

Our children went to school in Bunavista through grade school. Junior high or middle school (we had some of both) met in town, at the end of a bus ride. Even though I taught in both, the advantage of making sixth-graders the top-most rank in a particular educational building was never clear to me. The little darlings seemed, if bent to snub or fight the lower classmen, to be worse about it than they were in grade school; and that includes the Trayler children. Actually I did not teach ours at any level other than as a substitute. I substituted for a year before I went to work full time again.

I didn't mind a party at the end of kindergarten, but I remember the first kindergarten graduation I heard of and how uttery ridiculous I thought it was. Graduations should belong to high school and college, to the end of elementary level at the lowest. It demeans graduation later on so that the students today demand the right to stay up all night and even drink far too much intoxicating beverage, trying to show distinction between aiming for and reaching real milestones in ones education.

So much for that sermon.

One of the biggest laughs I received from our children in kindergarten came after I had substituted for a few days for their teacher. I had carefully picked out melodies for songs they wanted to sing and I didn't know. Merry Fay told a group of people, with undeniable pride, that it took their teacher two hands to play the piano, but not so her mother: She could play with one! Such is fame.

Oh, yes, children definitely benefit from kindergarten, but the proudest I was of one of ours at that age was after Dana and her best friends reached the highway crossing just a minute too late and found the crossing guard gone. Dazed, they stared around. Then Dana went to a service station on the corner and asked the attendant if he would see that they got across safely. He did.

Bill's teacher, Mrs. Little, loved him; and I was never sure whether he and her son cruised through her classes at a dead heat, or if Bill led her son to be braver, perhaps more daring and prankish, than he was by nature. And it was just before kindergarten that Bill and Tom Cox met. They formed an immediate friendship which continued throughout school. They even called one another at times after Bill went from Texas to California. Time and space finally ended that. I should like to see them meet at nearly forty. I believe they would be much like those two little boys used to be.

We ran the gamut of scouts, both girl and boy, starting with Brownies and Cubs, going through day camp for the very young, and regular camp when they matured a little. We have had the burnt match picture frames, the hand prints, the den (or is it pack?) flags on the crooked tree branches, and the special recipes brought in from the various activities. We appreciated all of it. I grew with the children, clambering from Cub den mother and Brownie leader to scout leader. Yet I had never earned any badges of my own.

One year at camp, Merry Fay somehow managed to puncture a blood vessel in her forearm with a sliver of glass from a frame she was making. It wasn't serious, and certainly did not have to be stitched, but for four or five days it began to bleed again every time she took the Band-Aid off.

Bill was scrawny when he began swimming class with the Red Cross, and the instructor refused to believe that he had not touched the wall of the pool before he turned around to complete his continuous lap. Bill was refused admittance to intermediate instruction unless he repeated the course. He refused and went to scout camp. He earned his badge and the next year he received one for lifesaving.

Somewhere during those years Dow Stevens became his scout master. The two of them quickly became very close friends and scout work took on a new dimension. Bill also became Dow's right hand man as "odd-job" boy. He was shown how to get in the house without a key—which he did until I learned Dow's neighbor thought he was sneaking in. I insisted then that Dow give him a key or get himself a new boy. Otherwise there would always be a shadow over Bill. He fed the German Shepherds Dow and Sarah kept, and in the summer ate almost as many meals at their house as he did at home. He also became assistant scout master. He worked with the scouts into his college years.

Merry Fay took to sewing easily when she was of an age for me to start her on it. Neither one of the girls wanted to bother with it in school; they took chemistry and physics and courses aimed at helping them in college. Dana refused to try to sew until she found her last years' clothes rather too tight one summer. When she asked me if she was to have new ones, my answer was that she would when she was ready to make them. It cost at first, because she thought she had to have all the material called for, a new pattern for each set of togs, and every suggested extra as well.

We had a White Rotary sewing machine which held a small spool of thread in the shuttle, eliminating bobbin problems. I also had a nearly new Sears with zigzag stitch adjustment. It could make buttonholes, do fancy trim work, and embroider if we took the patience to guide it. Merry Fay and I sewed on it and enjoyed it. Dana's touch wasn't just right. She would in some way manage to foul up on it and return to the old rotary despite its heaviness and the fact that it had to be lifted to a table. Gradually she adjusted to the handier and newer machine. At last we sold the old one. I cannot recall whether we got three or five dollars for it.

Dana would not study typing either so I spent a great deal of time typing themes for her. During the summer after her sophomore year, therefore, I compelled her to take it at the junior college. For six weeks she rose and got to class before anyone else had to be up. Both girls had had drivers' education and received their licenses at fourteen, the legal age. When Dana was a senior, one course on her schedule was college English. Just before school began, there were only three or four students enrolled for the class; the counselor advised her to choose an alternative course to fall back on if necessary. Dana elected to take typing as her speed needed a boost, and business letter writing could come in handy. At that time Mrs. Bertell, who had been teaching typing at the college, decided to move to the high school. Now Dana began to stew and fret. She "knew" that Mrs. Bertell would expect her to be much more proficient than she was; but I realized that Mrs. Bertell would simply start her out with the others in the class and change speed later if it proved beneficial. Dana could not believe that. Before typing met on the first day of school, however, an office aide came to find out what Dana was taking in place of the non-existent college English; the counselor had misplaced her notes. Dana said sewing without even a twinge of conscience. By then she had made and lined a wool suit, but the teacher didn't know it. Dana received an A in the course.

Merry Fay lapped up chemistry like a thirsty dog would a bowl of water. Mr. Holmes thought she was marvelous. Then Dana received a B in the course at the end of the first reporting period the next year, and it haunted her. She could not understand Mr. Holmes's point since she had good grades on all her work done. Enough was enough, and at last I asked her if she wanted me to brave the lion in his den. Shock—she did!

Mr. Holmes knew she was a good student, but he was also convinced that she was not up to Meredith's standard.

"But you don't have anything to worry about—she's not a bad student." He flipped his grade book open and ran his finger down her row of grades. There was not one grade less than 93 on the list.

Quickly he shut it and talked ramblingly about her not being a bad student. He looked at his grade book from then on when he made out his reports, I assume. Dana had no more trouble.

During these years the doctors had eliminated first one and then another hypothesis as to what Jessie's trouble was. At last they diagnosed her condition as muscular atrophy; it differed from muscular dystrophy partly in that there was no pain in conjunction with it. There was growing inability to perform. Her muscles literally wasted away. She spent some time in a wheelchair, but could not right herself if she slumped uncomfortably. When she could no longer lift her own head, someone had to do so for her. The next phase was flat of her back, which was for the rest of her life. Mercifully she could both talk and swallow to the very last; and her attitude was marvelous. I'll always be grateful that she and Luceille had become members of the Lord's church before she became so ill.

Jimmy cared for her as much as he possibly could but at last had to put her in a home, which he left for our sisters who lived nearby to do. He wasn't ever seen by any of them, or by myself when I stopped on a rare visit, but he visited her at times when no one else was around. He could not afford the pay for her upkeep by then, and likely was ashamed for us to see him, but every of us would have lacked the funds in those circumstances.

Happy had a good mind and a healthy body, but could not find a position that would keep him in college. He enlisted in the Army. Our families were scattering more and more, it seemed.

Chapter XIV

In the summer of 1962 Morris did not feel wel a great deal of the time. He did only his work at the plant and any about the house which he considered too hard for a woman to do. He took far too many aspirin, and he refused to see the doctor. A vacation seemed not to rest him at all. Then on a Friday evening in September, he felt a searing pain which he could not hide or ignore. He knew he must see a doctor, and I called Dr. Barksdale who had me bring Morris to his office. He predicted kidney stones, and an X-ray showed him to be correct.

After the diagnosis, the doctor gave Morris a shot and I took him home knowing that he would most likely have surgery the next morning. However the doctor told me not to let him suffer but to call if he didn't rest well. I had to take him to the hospital, and after he was eased and went to sleep, I went home and told the children that he would have surgery early the next day. But he began to thrash around, and everything within arm's reach hit the floor. The nurses called me to come stay the night.

Morris's condition didn't improve, and Dr. Barksdale had him transferred to Northwest Texas Hospital in Amarillo on Sunday morning. I stopped by the house to report to the children again. Merry Fay stayed at home with Bill. Dana came with me. I called a friend, Dee Coleman, an electrician at the plant first; the weather had turned bad and the furnace was acting up. Dee promised to take care of it. Incidentally, although he was forced to make two trips, he never let me pay him.

The doctor warned me that Morris was quite unlikely to live. I called Delores and Jesse Kerr to come get Dana, and I got in touch with Mildred at Tulia. I left her to let the rest of the family know. She came up and stayed with me at the hospital. Morris died on Tuesday, of a ruptured ulcer. Whether he had a kidney stone was immaterial to me.

His family, my family, and friends were all good to us; but we had a tremendous amount of adjusting to do even while our grief was fresh and raw. Merry Fay, who had just had her eighteenth birthday on September 2, was a senior in high school. Dana was half past sixteen and was a junior in high school. Bill was ten, a fifth grader.

I sat down and told them that we would have to gird up our loins, for Morris's salary had been much more than mine. As all three of them were planning college in their futures, they agreed to cooperate. I didn't mean to frighten them in order to achieve some economy, but I did. Merry Fay stopped playing her flute in the band and sold it. Had I held out a little longer, she would have resumed playing; but, to quote her words, she had thought "that we were about to wind up in the poorhouse."

Bill and Roy McCluney were extremely good about coming out to visit, which I appreciated very much. Frankly, I was the biggest baby of all, and had to take tranquilizers for a period of time. It hurt my pride, but they straightened me out. I think one of the hardest things I had to face during the next few months was attending Merry Fay's baccalaureate sermon without her father. At least those people around me merely took it for granted that I was overly sentimental about someone's growing up.

Social Security reared its head. Merry Fay's allotment

began and ended with the September check as at age 18 she became too old. Then the rules changed, and Dana received hers all through high school. Next Social Security considered college students. It was decided they should have help until age 21. Merry Fay received two checks, maybe three; but Dana received help until she graduated from junior college and got married.

Merry Fay went to work at J.C. Penney's after school and into the summer while she attended junior college here in Borger. She applied for and earned a Phillips scholarship, which was paid out in eight payments at the beginning of the eight semesters most students attended.

After summer courses and a full year at junior college, she went to Oklahoma Christian College in Edmond just out of Oklahoma City. In 1967, after brief exposure to German, she went with a group of fellow O.C.C. students and faculty on a missionary trip to Germany. Because she worked at Penney's and went to school, she did not finish her quota of required hours for graduation with her classmates, but she went through the exercises and stayed in the city longer to finish elective work. She was head of the credit department in Shepherd Mall and often made my head spin when she dialed all over the states as casually as I would dial my next door neighbor. I think one reason that she stayed so long was a reluctance to leave her apartment and the friendly cardinals in the tall trees outside her second floor windows.

Merry Fay helped Dana move from Tennessee to California while she was still in college, and there met some folks who planned to open a Christian school. They asked her to come teach for them. So she headed to the west coast and was too early for the Christian school, but took a position with Kerman school district.

She fell madly in love with Fred Napier, her principal. He had a son and daughter, Dennis and Debbie, from his first marriage. Merry Fay and Fred were married in December

1969 and now have four children: Fred Morris, born April 4, 1971; Daniel, born September 26, 1973; Meredith Elise, born December 8, in 1975; and David, born October 19, 1978. Morris is in school at Lubbock (Texas) Christian College and a member of the a cappella choir. Daniel was prepared to enter the Navy early in April but fell twenty to thirty feet into a river the night before the Navy van was due to pick him up. As he said goodbye on a last visit with an older friend, a lawyer, the bank caved in. His anklebone was broken and had several pieces chipped off; his heel bone was broken; and, about four inches above the ankle, the fibula was broken. His triumphant induction into the Navy will be delayed until six months after surgery to remove the screws holding his ankle together.

Elise and David are still in school. Elise is studying sign language for the deaf and currently plans to continue working in that field after high school. David enjoys fishing and any chore which takes lots of strength to complete. They've lived all their lives near Fresno, California.

Merry Fay and Fred have been instructors for Christian as well as public schools; farmed, often raising grapes; and taught adult education. Fred is now a fully accredited and tenured teacher in a state prison, and Merry Fay is with the Lemoore School System, teaching mostly Navy personnel and their dependents on Lemoore Naval Air Base. She also teaches now and then at a community college. For several years she has capably spearheaded the graduation exercises on the base for both Lemoore students and students of other systems who have classes on the base.

Dana continued to play in the band until she graduated. She played clarinet, bells, cymbals, triangle, and bassoon, taking them up in that order. That meant that I, alone now, continued going to the football games to enjoy the music and the marching. I haven't forgotten the years that the Borger Bulldogs went almost to finals in the state. Every weekend the girls went to Wichita Falls to march at the games. Each time we went. At three or three-thirty were back on home soil, and I put Bill to bed while Morris went to the school building to pick up the girls. I was spared that when Dana was a senior.

All through high school Dana dated Albert. He was her mainstay when Morris died, and he had already adopted me as a second mother. Then Albert went off to college. He wanted Dana to wait for him. Dana wanted him to attend college at Borger before he went off. That was the beginning of the end of their association. They occasionally meet or have reason to speak on the telephone and still enjoy the visit. Once in a while he calls me, usually about alumni business; our visits are invariably gratifying to both of us.

Art Markart and Dana met here at college, he as a first year student and she as a sophomore. They missed very few soup and cracker lunches at our home before Art enrolled in the Navy. As soon as she finished junior college, they were married. They lived first in Millington, Tennessee, at the naval air base. Wherever he was, except at sea on a cruise, she went. Tara Lynn was born on February 9, 1967, in California while Art was based at Lemoore Naval Air Base; and Kelly was born January 10, 1968, in Borger, their only Texan. We have my insistence that Dana come home and pursue her studies on her degree when Art was aboard ship to thank for one Texan among the foreigners.

It was while Dana was at home that there was a blast on the *Enterprise,* Art's ship at that time; he had been on duty all night and was preparing for bed. He missed death by one minute, sixty seconds, according to the ship's bells when an elevator refused to operate and he went some distance to the next one. The first one was destroyed. It was long hours from the publicizing of the tragedy until his call that he was unharmed came in at three a.m. After due consideration, Art was sent from Hawaii, where they had limped to shore, to

California to help with the repairs. He came to Texas one weekend, and Dana flew out two weekends to visit him. That was when they decided on a larger family.

Dana received her coveted degree in the late summer of 1969, and Arthur was born in Millington in December; Art had been sent there again at the end of his cruise. William was born at Millington, too, on February 22, 1971.

As he felt he missed too much of the children's lives, Art did not continue to make the Navy his career. He taught at the base as a college employee. The children all went to Harding Academy, a Christian school in Memphis, through high school. Dana and Art bought a home in Memphis, making getting to school easier, and Art commuted to Millington to work on the base until May, 1988.

Then he went to work for Raytheon in Jedda, Saudi Arabia. Just before the "Saudi War" began, he finished a two year stint there. Now he is mulling over which of several positions he will accept—including the return to Saudi. Dana has taught at several private and church schools. She was happy to accept a place in the Harding High School mathematics department, sometimes teaching her own children. She has taught there now for six years.

Tara graduated from Freed Hardeman Christian University in Jackson, Tennessee, and now is with Staff Builders, Health Care Services in Memphis. Kelly went to college for a year and half, was not happy with her major, and dropped out temporarily. She has not gone back as she planned, but married Larry Brown in July, 1989. They live in Memphis. Both boys attend Harding, in Arkansas. Arthur, is an accounting major, ready to start his senior year there. William began college at Memphis State where he studied for one and a half years before transferring to Harding; he is a history major.

As Bill got older he spent some time at Paul McKinney's service station. There he learned to change tires, replace shocks, and do various other mechanical tasks. He also aided Morris McKinney, who lived a few doors down the street, with chores about his home and picked up skills which I could not handle or teach him. He went fishing with Jack Southern and learned a bit more, including cleaning fish and backing a car and trailer. Jack, our preacher, and Lorain were two of my best friends. Dow Stevens helped too. After Bill had driven for awhile, he went to work for C.M. Shearer who ran the drive-in movie. He was a good employer, liked Bill, and found him to be willing both to learn and to work.

Bill took his load at home. One spring he tied a heavy old rope around a large tree branch and asked me to keep it pulled taut while he sawed the limb off because it was very near the electric wires. Before he was through, he began to complain that I wasn't putting enough tension on it, that it would break the wire when it fell. He directed me carefully to a new position. The limb began to sway; he yelled for me to tighten the rope again, but it was too late.

He was unprepared for the limb to part company with the tree and grabbed it to regain his balance. At the same time I discovered, when the rope fell uselessly to the grass, that it was broken. I watched, my heart in my mouth, while Bill rode the limb to earth. He was unhurt because it was heavier than he and didn't turn over. Bill was furious with me for a minute. Then when he calmed down, and looked at the rope, he admitted his mistake. He waited only a few minutes before he climbed the tree again.

"If I don't," he said, "I might not have the nerve when I need to."

In spite of the friendly guidance, Bill still needed to be near a man much more often. He pleaded for me to allow him to go into the Navy. Instead, after talking it over with Merry Fay, I let him go to California and live with Fred during his senior year. After their marriage, he continued to live with them. He gave them some anxiety at times, but he finished and went on to college in Fresno.

Bill had become buddies with Toyaotaka Shitanishi, his high school math teacher, and they went fishing at Bass Lake one day. Shitanishi fell and hit his head on a hard rock. He was unconscious but roused to answer Bill (though not always lucidly) at times. Bill managed to drag him from the water to a ledge. He considered tying him there with his shoestrings but rejected the idea because the man might have rolled off and hung by his feet, possibly to strike his head again. So he took the car keys and went to a ranger station for help. He was highly excited, and whether Bill realized it or not, his pupils nearly covered his eyes when he was so worked up. (I'll always wonder if they thought he was doped up.) Anyway, the rangers didn't believe him; precious time elapsed while he persuaded them.

Shitanishi's car was left there, and Bill concentrated on finding the right place to climb up over a hump and down into the canyon. When he spotted their creel, the rangers refused to believe that they were in such a rough place, so Bill was sent back down alone to find him. But Shitanishi was not there. Obviously he had moved and must be found. Out Bill went for help again, but they said, "Find him."

Bill found him and reported back to the rangers again. The three men accompanied him that time, and found it too rough to use the litter. They had to radio for a helicopter. The pilot took one look at the exhausted and worried Bill and offered to come back for him. But all Bill wanted was to get out of there; he refused. The ranger was satisfied, but his two assistants spoke up and said they would appreciate the lift. The pilot refused on the grounds that it was too rugged and dangerous except in an emergency.

Two weeks later Shitanishi recognized Bill at last; his fractured skull was healing. His priorities were propounded when he asked, "Where's my fishing equipment?" All was well.

At some time Bill moved and lived with a young married couple and their four children. Ervie was an employee with some branch of the government, but was allowed to do most of his work in the small but well-equipped laboratory he owned. There Bill began to develop a deep interest in research.

Bill, with financial assistance from both me and Social Security, went to junior college and on to Fresno State. He took science classes with Kathleen Connolly. She was dark eyed, dark haired, intelligent, and amiable. They fell in love. They were married September 25, 1976. They have one son, Robin Brendan, who surprised them by arriving about six weeks prematurely on September 10, 1985. He overcame that handicap, and has finished kindergarten.

Robin has spent many hours on a college campus, some with Bill and some with other pupils in preschool classrooms. He has been on many field trips, of a higher level than most children of five have attended, with his eager, science—bent parents, and has learned much about the wildlife around him, both animal and vegetable. He is happy, and adaptable, always ready for new experience. And he often abashes his Grandma Trayler with knowledge which he has and she lacks!

Chapter XV

It had been a thorny year, that first one after Denny's death; but now I could smile when I walked up from the main building of the Bunavista School where I taught to the small primary building where my room was. I had missed two weeks of school last September, and my principal, Tom Hooper, who was so kind to me, insisted on escorting me all the way to my room on my return. As we toiled up the hill, which had never hampered me before, I remarked, "They've made the hill longer." Then I tucked my hand in the crook of his arm for a little assistance. He gave me the help gladly, but for just an instant he thought I actually believed the walk had been lengthened. He gave me a quick look of sheer consternation. It dissolved immediately, and he made a remark about something else. We walked on.

I had been thinking about something to do with my hands and my mind after the housework was more or less caught up—with a grade-schooler, a high school senior and band member, and a working college student in the house with one parent, how could it all ever be done? Then I opened a copy of the big, flat, lean magazine so helpful to elementary teachers, "The Instructor," and knew what I wanted to do.

Last summer Merry Fay, for freshman college art, had made a broken tile copy of a picture that had long hung in our living room; and I now decided to make a table top, using the same method, of the pictured Babylonian dragon on green bricks, a section of a fence. It was a full page picture; and although it wasn't pretty, it was very interesting.

I glanced at the clock. I had time to go to the school, closed for Christmas vacation, and copy the picture with the aid of a projector. I could adjust my distance until I had a likeness the exact size I wanted. The janitors always had the first week of that vacation in which to clean and wax in unhampered isolation, but they wouldn't mind my being there. Before the door closed behind me, the telephone rang, and I returned to answer it.

Jessie, unable to feel pain, had alarmed the home nurse by insisting that she was dying. Upset, the tender-hearted nurse had talked with the doctor. He had come to the home, expecting to reassure Jessie, and found her being permeated with a toxicity that could not be controlled. He predicted that she had an hour left. Not wanting to be alone dwelling on the circumstances, and knowing that I could not possibly reach her while she still lived, I went on down to copy the picture. There too I found a compassionate friend with whom I could safely let down my guard and talk. Within the hour I was back at the house. The next call came right on time: the doctor had been right.

That was Monday. We went to Eastland Wednesday for the funeral. Mother and Daddy were far more upset than the rest of us were. We were not uncaring, but we had wondered often what would happen if Jessie lost the ability to swallow and to talk. Could she have kept her joy in life then? During the last years of her life we had listened when she coughed, and her cough was little louder than a gasp. We had feared that she would strangle to death. We loved her. We were not glad she was gone; but we were glad it had been easy.

At times like that there's always someone who finds the answer to a question that has nagged at him, or learns about something that everyone in the family but him knew, and just assumed he did too. For instance, I learned that year what had made the front porch of the house on the farm become so weak. We didn't get many rains blown from the west or south; and the porch was protected by the house and roof on the north and east. Daddy was a firm believer in burning off the lawn every year or so. He didn't notice those messy black footprints that lasted "only a day or two." Ha!

Anyway, one year some of the flames slipped under the porch steps and got a bite on the porch. The younger children tried to tell the adults, but they didn't listen, and assured the children that they were only smelling the remains of the fire. However, Dan slipped out to check it out. It was true, and Daddy had already left for town. Luceille went to Lemar and asked for his keys so she could move his car, and he refused. But after a moment he came up to the house to check on her story and he too found it was so. He crawled under the length of the house. It terrified Mother at least, but the hose never had to cross the path of the fire, and Lemar totally routed every sign of the flames.

Two days after the funeral was Christmas. We did little Christmas mailing, just to Mother and Daddy, for there were far too many of us to give to everyone: sisters, brothers, in laws, and nieces and nephews. If we live close to one another, we might exchange gifts. Each year is due its own consideration.

The children remembered the vacations we had taken each summer and assumed they would go on. It was hard to go that first time after Jessie's death, but it proved to me that life went on. We took several trips before the children all left home. One that I remember quite frequently saw Dana, Bill and me at Monument Lake in Colorado. The cabins were constructed of logs; the heat was supplied by coal or wood in a fireplace; we carried our water in by the bucket-ful; bathroom facilities were out of doors and communal. There we sat, ghastly shadows dancing on the wall behind us. I knitted, barely able to make out my stitches, while we talked. Shades of the past!

In 1965 Grandma Trayler had a stroke. Mr. Trayler and Mildred spent many hours caring for her even though she had to spend some time in a nursing home. In July she died. I was grateful that all the children were at home. The funeral was held in Wheeler. A year later, the night after Dana and Art's wedding, Grandpa Trayler followed her. Knowing about our plans to leave town, when my brother-in-law Bill called to let us know, he insisted that we follow our schedule. As it affected so many people, we did. Art and Dana were on a trip, a honeymoon on the road to their home, just out of Memphis. We could not have reached them anyway. Since we had had one last pleasant visit from Grandpa a few months earlier, we had a heart-warming memory to hold onto in spite of having seen him ill during the last several months.

One year Vickey, Luceille, John, Jeanette and I decided to go to see Dana and Art in Memphis. We spent only a night or so with them and started home. Then remembering that on one visit Dana's family and I had gone on a riverboat trip, I suggested we do so this time. I didn't know where to find the harbor except it was in "that direction"—with the wave of an arm. We found it and enjoyed the morning tour. Studying a new map, we set about leaving Tennessee behind us. Except we couldn't. We had bought a map of such poor construction that the proposed route and the existing route blended into one and took Vickey in circles while I navigated. I yielded the map to her and took the wheel. She navigated us in the same old circles. Before we could find somewhere to ask for direc-tions, Jeanette caught on to what we were doing. Quite casu-ally she used her far better sense of direction to guide us to the highway. But she didn't enjoy all the frustration and laughs we got from it.

We went to Bastrop for holidays when we could. I could go for Thanksgiving but wouldn't even try at Christmas after I was alone because the Panhandle roads were too frequently icy. In 1966 we were all gathered and waiting for J.L. to arrive, when I gave Luceille a piece of gum that would kill the appetite. I had begun to use it after school because I was always starving by then as I had been moved to another building and given the early lunch hour. Snacking put food in my tummy without proper nutrition, which left me ready to dine at bedtime. Until I re-educated my insides, I kept the gum in my purse to chew on the way home.

We decided to go ahead and eat. J.L. would tell us why he was late when he came. Luceille whined and informed me more than once that she hated me: dinner smelled so good and she had no appetite at all after the gum. It wasn't long after we had eaten when the telephone rang. All desire for food fizzled for the weekend then: J.L had been killed in a wreck less than a hundred miles away. And Happy was in Germany. Grief for both of them swamped us.

I missed Merry Fay when she first left for college, and then to take up teaching; and I missed Dana when she married and moved out. But both occasions were natural progressions. When Bill went to California to finish school, I was left to live alone. Even that I accepted without too much struggle, I rarely saw Bill since he frequently came in late from work. Dana was in and out with her children, here one month and gone the next. In 1969 they ended their last stay with me.

I wound up with summers not totally full. I refused to make visits take up nearly three months. Time didn't have time to become a real problem anyway. Summers are heaven-sent opportunities meant for painting, sewing, and carpet laying. When I had to purchase a new refrigerator, I sawed the bottom of a cabinet off and refinished it for myself so that I would have adequate space for a refrigerator with an ice maker. I measured the cabinet carefully and took the door to a professional cabinet maker to be reshaped.

Then in 1971 or 1972 I stared at an ad in the Texas State Teacher's publication. A thirty-day tour was coming up, one which included parts of seven countries in Europe, for 978 dollars plus transportation to and from DFW Airport and one-third of our meals. I invited Wilma Gee to daydream with me, and to give it real consideration. She didn't, but she suggested that I try Marguerite Jackson, another very close friend. In June, 1972, after I had consulted with all three children, and received a full measure of encouragement from each one, Marguerite and I, chock full of madcap excitement, soared out of DFW. We would refuel in Bangor, Maine. Next stop: Amsterdam! Half of us on that trip must have touched earth with our fingers to be sure it was true when we landed on foreign soil.

In Amsterdam we traveled the streets of water by boat. We walked across parts of Paris and down the narrow streets to the Sorbonne. We visited the Vatican, the Coliseum, and, of course, Venice. We listened for the siren at the Lorelei Rock, and saw bomb-damaged Munich. We went by bus, tramway, rail, boat, and foot from hotel to mountaintop and back, in steep Switzerland. We ate bits of toast dipped in fondue in Austria, in spite of knowing that if we dropped the bread we would be kissed by one of the men at the table. We gaped in admiration at Monaco's castle, and shopped in Liechtenstein. We "oohed" our way through the Tower of London, tiptoed over the floors of Westminster Abbey, and ogled the new Shakespeare Theater. We bought a great many souvenirs, for this trip would surely be our only one. For Marguerite it was, for she remarried—for me it was the first step of a delightful and fascinating practice.

Later in the year I went down to see Mother and Daddy. I was shocked to learn that Daddy had been involved in a car accident shortly before I went overseas. Every other member of the family knew and conspired to remain silent about it; for, after the first few hours, it was decided that he would live and there would be no damaging results. Daddy insisted on the secrecy because he didn't want to spoil my trip! Not one sibling objected or complained that I was petted. Here Daddy was with great scabs still covering part of his scalp when I arrived over a month after the accident had occurred.

We had all long been worried because Daddy's reflexes were so slow, and none of us liked to ride with him anymore; but none of us tried to do anything about it. After he was well on his feet again, he was told that his car was totally demolished. Actually, with what his insurance paid and with each of us helping a bit, the car could have been repaired, but he didn't fuss. Dan, with my approval, contracted with a neighbor to drive him to town at least three times a week. I do not know if the neighbor fulfilled the bargain. I do know that during the next few years everyone of us was not commanded, but it may as well have been, to drive Daddy to one nearby city or the other when we were home on a visit. The towns Bastrop, Elgin, and Smithville were a snap, but Austin I dreaded. However, we made it successfully when it fell my due.

On one trip to Austin, a self-made gentleman (God does a better job) was showing Daddy pumps. After the first few didn't suit, the clerk eyed Daddy and asked, superciliously, what "crick" was to be pumped from. Daddy didn't even deign to look at the man, but answered smoothly that it wasn't the "creek" but the lake; that he had permission because his own holding tank had been destroyed by the lake. The pretentious clerk managed to refer one more time to a "creek" before he gave up. He was likely fifty. Daddy was eighty-five or eighty-six.

We had started gathering on the weekend nearest October 13 for Mother's birthday. It was harder to make it for Daddy's as there wasn't the equal of Columbus Day near it to help out. Lemar wasn't too interested in running around. Also he had younger children than most of us. So he worked long and hard hours and went fishing at every opportunity. Dan swept off full sail to meet Phil here and there and was content to stay at home and work the rest of the time. I dashed off to California or Tennessee and made an overseas trip each year. Johnny married off their older children and relished in the youngest one and the grandchildren. Luceille faced the ugly trauma of divorce; then she remarried and had another child. Mable set up a home wherever Gray was sent. They still had Steven at home. Vickey went through the throes of "now you have him—now you don't" with Tommy. And time passed.

Occasionally a few of us would get together and make a mad dash to see some other family member. One year Bill stayed behind after a visit to my parents to spend a couple of weeks with Gary, Dan's youngest. The boys all but lived in the creek and Bill stepped on broken beer bottle and cut his foot badly. So much blood flowed that Gary went to Daddy for help, but Daddy assumed that the boys were needlessly alarmed and didn't go quickly. He met Bill on the way. It may have made no difference; since the glass may already have been embedded; but it was at best a painful trek. I removed two half-inch wide pieces of glass from his foot.

This happened the day before Dana and Art's wedding, and we retrieved only one of the pieces that day. We could not hold the last piece with the tweezers long enough to extract it. Still he gave Dana away without anyone except family being the wiser, very skillfully setting his foot down with no weight on that poor sore heel.

As Dana and Art were leaving later that evening, I had agreed that we would go to California with Dan to meet Phil's ship. I bought peroxide and poured some in the gash at least twice daily while the two weeks passed. Quite late the evening that we returned home, the day before we were to make our delayed trip to the doctor, I gave it one last try. That time I retrieved the glass.

Dan and Gary spent little more time with Phil than Bill and I did, for Phil didn't have that much time off. But his first mate's wife gave us a deluxe tour of San Francisco. It was their home, and they knew it well. Chinatown enthralled us, especially me. Never before had I visited a place with such magic charm as San Francisco. Neither Dallas nor Fort Worth were in that class at all. To Dan and Gary, of course, the sparkle was not so rare and fascinating. They viewed it much more calmly than we did, although they still enjoyed it.

Chapter XVI

When Mother and Daddy sold the farm and moved onto Phil and Dan's place, we thought Daddy would feed cattle and keep an eye on things. Generally, help not too arduous for a seventy plus manly—but not him–not Daddy. As we should have known, he was soon dabbling in minnows and he had worm beds; he was also gardening and raising vegetables in rather limited quantities compared to back on the farm.

Who was it? The Greeks? The old warning springs into my mind, "Beware of Greeks bearing gifts." Ancient warriors had nothing on Daddy in the line of chicanery. First he had something to show us, his newest pursuits. Come see my new minnow tank, or how well my turnips are growing, or the neat worm beds I don't have to bend over.

The worm beds were wooden troughs on tall legs so that one didn't have to crawl or bend over. As we eyed them he would suddenly recall that he had an order for a thousand worms, or five thousand. There we were, middle aged or more, carefully cramming fifty juicy fishing worms into little round cardboard cartons. About halfway through the stack of cartons we stretched our necks, thrust out our chests, and flexed our shoulders to curb the menacing fatigue. Into a sudden calm fell John's commanding voice.

"Here, Mable." She held her loosely folded hand out to drop something.

Mable obediently held her hand out to receive whatever it might be, felt a light weight in her hand, and bowed her head for a look. Immediately she retrogressed to her former dignity, squawked, and threw an object from her. We laughed until we hurt when we saw that it was one lone worm.

Sometimes we helped count minnows for wholesale. Daddy could put us to shame. He had learned to come out within a minnow or two by just glancing at a handful as he took them from one container to another. One or two too many gained a little more in time and made for less stress. All the time the rest of us were counting those wiggly fish one by one.

The vegetable work Daddy reserved for himself: plowing with a hand plow; fertilizing; watering by ditch method; and gathering his crops alone, each one perhaps his last. There was a ready market for them in Long's Grocery, run by Adren and Ruth Long, in Bastrop. They puzzled me when I met them just last spring, but we threshed out hidden familiarity between us.

While we worked at those things, Mother cultivated her flowers, adding more each season until she had beds on every side of the house and circling most of the trees. Then she moved out a few feet and circled plots of lilies and irises, with smaller flowers. One day when she was in her eighties, I commandeered her own spade and dug the rest of a bed she had begun. The job done, I turned to put away the spade; but she smiled at my work—I had not squared the corners properly. She turned over every dab of soil left unturned. She never criticized our kitchen work or sweeping or bed-making though.

Mother never let her mind grow slack. All our lives we listened to her say the alphabet backwards, to her stories of the presidents' families, and to handy hints that she picked up from newspapers, books, and acquaintances. If she thought respect for Daddy was wearing thin, she knew the exact right moment to say, rather baldly but still casually, "Did you know that Mehitable Saxton hit her father?" Always the impact was sure and effective. If we had struck Daddy, he would have slapped us sideways, somehow without injurious results, and we would have learned our lesson. With no pain whatever for anyone, she produced equal results.

That was a part of Mother's make-up that we lived with when we were young, but which we appreciated for science and art only after we were grown.

Luceille and Bob found, and bought, a home which suited them in Fort Worth. Bob worked for years for the city water department; but he wasn't lured by four walls and a suit and tie. Nor did days of extreme heat, bitter cold, or constant rain ever seem to faze him. He enjoyed his job.

For years they had insisted that they wanted Mother and Daddy to move in with them when Daddy could bring himself to leave his agricultural pursuits behind. Their enlarging the house to be prepared for them guaranteed that neither Mother nor Daddy doubted them. Still our parents weren't convinced it was what they themselves wanted. So they gave it a short trial and went back to the ranch to give it more thought.

Vickey and Jimmy told themselves that retirement would find them in Mississippi, raising cattle. Jimmy was machinist for Bell Helicopter, made good wages, and loved it. Vickey worked at a variety of places, usually revolving around the feeding of the human animal. And she began to express doubt that the old family place in Mississippi would be productive enough to feed them, let alone dress and entertain them. At first Jimmy ignored her idea; then he opposed it; finally he decided to test it for a year. But he left the testing up to Vickey—at his instruction.

Vickey took Tommy and Terry, along with plenty of supplies and good bookkeeping equipment, to reside in

Mississippi. They lived in a trailer on what she called their hot, dry, unproductive acres. The boys were in school and Vickey fed the cattle Jimmy had stocked the place with. In just a few months, Jimmy called it quits. The boys were back in Texas for the next semester of school, and Jimmy began his search for a retirement place in Texas.

At last he found a peach orchard, or what could become one. His weekdays weren't home owned; they were bought and paid for by Bell Helicopter. Weekends did belong to him and to the forty acres he found near Mexia. Vickey took a position as manager of the huge cafeteria on the Northeast Campus of Tarrant County Junior College for a food concern.

Mable and Gray had quit being sent from pillar to post by Sinclair, which had become Atlantic-Richfield, and bought a home in Brentwood, a Nashville suburb. There they had the benefits of a large city and the pleasures of a lovely home on an acre plot in a small town. The two older boys joined a boys' choir that even made overseas trips. Mable took on a secretarial position and they educated the children and made a myriad of friends. They played bridge often (as they had done for years) and enjoyed bridge tournaments. Frequently Mable went to tournaments out of town, or state, too. When she had extra time on hand, she became a workaholic, cooking dinners for special occasions; making cakes for sale, and taking children in her home for evening baby-sitting are examples of her pursuits. Gray, on the other hand, found delight in the opportunity to play golf for hours on end day after day. Of course, distance insured that Mable and I managed to go home at less frequent intervals than Lemar and our sisters.

In 1974 Daddy began to have what I strongly suspect are called mild strokes today. They were just a bit worse than mini-strokes. Lemar helped Mother at first, then took both of them to Cleveland. There he admitted Daddy into a nursing home. We all contributed money until Lemar told us to stop. After one visit to Daddy, I came away with the feeling that he was unhappy with his religious standing, so I contacted Vickey at her Mississippi residence.

We made plans, met at Lemar's, and went together to see Daddy after a week or two. We talked a bit and then asked bluntly if he would like for a preacher to call on him. He stated quite positively that he would. Out we went right then to locate one whom we felt we could trust. After several visits, we succeeded. I do not recall his name, but he seemed eager to visit with Daddy on Monday—we were there on a weekend. We didn't tell Daddy that he was a Church of Christ preacher; and we never knew whether the man showed up, for soon Daddy was extremely ill again.

He died in March 1975, a few days before he would have been eighty-nine. Lemar and Jeanette chose a preacher to hold the service which, with Mother's consent, was held in Cleveland. If we do not come face to face with Daddy in eternity, it won't be their fault. That preacher talked him right into heaven. I never allowed myself to insinuate that to Mother.

Someone packed Mother's suitcase, and she was taken to Luceille and Bob's house without even a goodbye look at her home of the last several years.

It was very rough on Mother, eighty-eight years old and having lived with Daddy for over sixty of them. I realize as well as anyone that it would have been tough after only six months, but there is a keen difference. Mother was bound to be bewildered and wishing she could have gone with him.

She lived with Luceille, but it was Vickey who selected a doctor for her and took her for appointments. He was a kind practitioner who would not be gushy nor so friendly at their first meeting as to call her Luceille. His nurse, however, found out how mother felt when Mother admitted that she did not care whether she lived or died. Concerned, she told the doctor that Mother wished she were dead. Vickey sort of sat in the background and listened for Mother to come out on top of whatever might be said next.

Dr. Pafford asked Mother a few questions and found what might be a winning idea. "Mrs. Whisenant, live for me. Be my grandmother. I haven't a grandmother left," he pleaded.

By then Vickey had seen the writing on the wall before the hand appeared. She all but rolled in the floor between that suggestion and the (it wasn't a retort, but it had the same effect) answer.

"Well, one more wouldn't make any difference one way or the other, I suppose," Mother said, somewhat disconsolately. No, rather with a mixture of dejection and spirit.

Remember the old tag: you can't keep a good man down? Mother rallied and decided that she would like to live to be ninety, and then she would be ready to die.

I don't know who first took her with them on a visit to a friend in a nursing home. Whoever it was has my blessing. The home was clean and singularly devoid of the odors often associated with such places. Also we could have put four or five that size into the one Daddy had been in. But the fall that she was ninety she decided to move into the home until spring came, when she would move back in with one of us. This move was her reaction to how cold she felt we kept our houses. When warm weather arrived, she found her place. She was the spine that held some of the others together, the spriest of residents, and well liked by the nurses as well. She would visit out of that big house, but she was ready to go "home" at dark on most occasions.

During the past few years there had been various other changes too. Wendell had turned in a suggestion that saved his employers two million dollars a year. He was given an award, five thousand dollars. He and John had paid off their mortgage and were free to invest in a farm and grow pecan trees. Every few years they would have a fire set off by the sparks from a train. The railroad company would pay for the trees but no compensation for the loss of growth—and their corporate lawyers kept it that way.

John and Wendell bought an Appaloosa mare for Butch one year. She had a lovely colt for which they were offered two thousand dollars when he was barely a week old. They refused to sell, and the colt's coat changed rapidly during the next few months, and he was worth only a fraction of that price.

Dan and Phil built a lovely home near the shore of Lake Bastrop. Phil, disenchanted with his boss, decided the time had come to retire. He had the promise of an extremely good retirement. His boss twisted strings so that he received a good retirement but not what he should have. But Phil never intended to remain idle. He bought and sold machinery parts and expensive items salvaged from wrecked planes, expensive equipment up for sale after bankruptcy, or other odd lots of sophisticated instruments.

Lemar and Jeannette decided on the style for a new home and had it built in brick on the farm. They raised feed and food crops; and Lemar was constantly in demand for jobs that required a big equipment operator behind the wheel. It was when he replaced his old barn that he followed up on his notion of a family reunion. The new barn with no hay or equipment, no animals or containers of paint or poison, and no slithery squeaking pests or birdnests was an ideal protected area for sleeping out. They extended the invitation to us. Pleased, we descended on them in hoards.

There Mother, who of course had a bedroom in the house, enjoyed her seven children and many of her grandchildren and great-grandchildren. There we got acquainted all over again with nieces and nephews, and made friends with great-nieces and nephews we hardly knew existed. There we played endless games of Forty-two and relived hundreds of hours and events—some sad, some happy—while the younger generations struck up acquaintances with second cousins whom they had forgotten they had even heard mentioned.

Vickey told a story of her thwarted high school shenanigans. She had never played hooky in the lower grades, but she and three other brand new freshmen hit on that step to show their new adulthood. Unfortunately the principal saw them walk across the schoolyard and chose to investigate. He in turn was seen; and the girls dashed into the nearby Church of Christ. Calmly he followed them. Here they played it differently. Vickey led the quartet right to the front of the auditorium, put pious hands together, knelt in supposed prayer. There they knelt, and knelt, and knelt, until they heard the dismissal bell ring at school. Without a word the principal rose and went back to his duties.

Then the girls rose, painfully. Still not fully erect, they hobbled home. Never again were they tempted to truancy by either lovely weather or circumstances.

The reunion flew by. We took walks for exercise, but took them either early in the morning or in the evening to escape the heat of the day. It couldn't have been so sudden as it seemed when it was time to hand out any too big or too small clothing; exchange any old books for some other person's old books; take up another last minute roll of film; swap one or two more recipes; make sure of the neglected addresses; cry down the last shirt front; and drive off with hands waving.

1977 was the year that I went on a tour of the British Isles. Mother had listened eagerly to my itinerary; and she sparkled at the idea of my visiting Loch Lomand, Tipperary, and other places she had heard and dreamed of all her life. She reminded me that we had connection with the Hardies and the Sims families.

At last the conversation turned to other topics, but as she readied herself to go home, Mother said, "Now, Fay, when you get to Ireland, remember you've got Irish blood in you." She knew that our overseas flight landed in Limerick.

"All right; I will," I answered.

The conversation continued after a slight pause. "Now, Fay, when you get to England remember you have English blood in you."

"Okay, I will," I promised again.

The next pause was noticeably longer before she pursued her thoughts. "Now, Fay, when you get to Scotland, remember you have Scotch blood in you."

"All right, Mother, I'll remember." My heart went out to one so avid for her blood to go to the places of her forefathers. That was all she said. She was positive that my conduct would be impeccable as befitted a Fawcett in the land of her origin.

I brought Mother records from Ireland and Scotland, and Jimmy Moak made tapes for her to listen to. I brought her a scarf of the Sims plaid without thinking that I should have bought one of the Hardie plaid too. As we are also eligible to wear the Mackintosh plaid, it would have been appropriate to bring samples of all three. Wales she ignored, although we went there as well. I can't recall what I brought her as a symbol of England, but I think the thought that I traipsed about on those sacred soils meant more to her than all else.

Mother loved avocados and seedless white grapes, and as they would not keep indefinitely in her room, it was rather easy to take her a small gift. Luceille also took her a few tomato plants in the spring, and, with the authorities' full blessings, helped her to set them out on the banks of a road that circled the back yard. As the tomatoes ripened, Mother shared them with friends, other patients or staff.

When she was ninety-one, Mother broke out with shingles on her right side and arm. She turned purple-black there in a large area. Not only was it very painful, but she nearly starved. When she was ill, she wanted nothing but soup for her meals, and only chicken noodle soup at that; but she was unable to handle a spoon with her right hand. She had never found it easy to supplant her right hand with her left; and as she abhorred being fed by anyone other than herself, she now quit eating almost altogether. It was Vickey who summed up the situation and pulled her through. She made visits at meal times and spooned up the noodles. Mother then managed to transport the skittery potion to her mouth with her left hand. After she regained her health, she was given therapy to help her recover the use of her right arm.

One year Mother set out to learn Morse code. With real reluctance she gave up when she couldn't find anyone willing to share the experience with her. In lieu of that, she had us print the states and capitals with black, felt-tipped pens large enough for her to see, and relearned them. When I went down, she usually had a list of words she had gleaned from broadcasts for me to define for her. Many times I had to look them up before I could answer. Occasionally she had Luceille to do that chore too.

It was the day after her ninety-third birthday on which Mother informed us that she wanted to go for a walk, not an unusual thing, and wanted two of us to go along. Two was unusual but as three of us were with her, we didn't mind. Still we asked why. She announced that she wanted to see how far she could walk, and knew a guess at a halfway point to begin her return would leave her unsure. She wanted the second escort to drive a car in readiness to pick us up for the trip back.

Luceille drove, and Vickey and I walked beside Mother. A cold wind was blowing down the street; our flimsy sweaters were no match for it, we soon discovered. We gave thanks for Mother's coat and went on. But after a bit,

Vickey remarked that she wished Luceille would drive in front of us. Mother queried that, and I explained. Then foolishly for one sixty years of age, I scooted up in front of them where I swayed my body from side to side to protect them from that blast. But at fifty Vickey was little smarter than I. She declared she would let no one protect her, and she dashed in front of me and began to protect Mother and me. Mother momentarily lost sight of her goal and joined in the fun. She stepped right out and got in front of her daughters to shelter them. That extra flurry of energy and haste was probably why she had to stop just a tiny bit shy of half a mile. Ninety-three, and couldn't do better than that? We were very proud of her.

Chapter XVII

It was in the 1970s that John discovered a suspicious area on her anatomy and called on her doctor; he sent her to a cancer specialist. Following anxious weeks and many tests, she underwent a colostomy. She determined that being in her fifties and having a permanent inconvenience would not mean that life was nearly over; and she did all she could to keep her health otherwise good and to overcome any handicap. She was quite successful; and the doctors and the Cancer Society made a role model of her. She counseled many other patients before and after surgery at their behest. That she got sick is a drawback, but not the tragedy her death would have been.

More than five years had passed before she again faced cancer–this time she had a mastectomy; and again she made a remarkable recovery. Except the lymph glands were very disturbed and could no longer drain fluid from her arm. The severely swollen arm obstinately refused to return to its former size, and it took hours of deliberate use and struggle to overcome the pain and to regain control of it. It will always be larger than the other arm. Vickey suggested that she and I make John some casual dresses with one sleeve two or three inches larger than the other. John only had a few garments she could wear for a long period of time, and was so happy that she cried.

That cancer too is a thing of the past. However, tests

have proved that all of her natural cancer-killing cells are dead, and she will be on preventative medicine for the rest of her life.

While she was going through those experiences, Doris, a friend since first grade also was facing hard times. Extremely nervous and unsure of herself, she actually was in the early stage of Alzheimer's disease. John visited Doris's family as often as possible, and from her visits gained a keen insight into the ravages of the disease. Thus when we found Wendell growing strangely absent-minded, John realized that he was suffering the same pattern of affliction that Doris had. How she kept it to herself for several years while we pondered what could be wrong, I'll never know.

She had driven but little since her mastectomy because Wendell was so intent on protecting her. Now he refused her the right to drive their car, thinking it was for that purpose. However when we were going to Kentucky to visit Mammoth Caverns, we insisted that she drive. For a very few minutes she felt awkward at it, and then in a little while, from our passenger seats in Vickey's car, we had to warn her that she was courting a speeding ticket. We enjoyed the trip. Mable had Steven take her route and went with us through those dark chilly caverns. John was used to lopping some journeys short and waiting for Vickey and me to return. Mable, however, refused to leave John behind, even though we met again not far ahead or retraced our steps a wee distance. Vickey and I were made of sterner stuff, I guess. Anyway, Mable was good to her.

After that John tricked Wendell into letting her take a share of the driving. It was hard, for he had always been a good driver. He could still go directly to any place he had ever been in the metropolitan center; but as the rest of his family would not ride with him, she was compelled to do more and more of the driving.

In the fall of 1976 we received upsetting phone calls. On September 18, Stanley Hickerson was killed in an industrial accident. Just days earlier he had been joyfully advising Wendell to look up, to trust in God, to look on the brighter side of life. "Wasn't that a wonderful message for our son to leave us with?" John asked.

Now it could only be assumed that his hypoglycemia had overcome him, had been the actual cause of his fall onto the conveyer belt of the rock crusher he was manning at Clute, a town on the coast south of Houston. We all gathered at that Weatherford home where he had grown up to try to comfort his family and help to bear their sorrow. Stanley was buried in Eastland.

Several of us did not know Stanley's wife at that time. She was likeable; and she was with her son from a previous marriage. He gathered up some of us whose husbands were not along and took us in his car to the church. I was impressed with his grave courtesy, and his attentiveness to us. Stanley had matured and apparently had chosen well for this marriage, I thought.

As always at such occasions the "do you remembers" took up much of the conversation time. Stanley had loved a good joke, and some of his pranks were retold more than one time. So were some which had been played on him. Naturally Mother was very upset, and wondered how we could laugh at anything at such a time. The answer, of course, is that it keeps one from crying constantly.

None of Aunt Edith's family showed up at all. We could not but feel rather snubbed. I do not know whether anybody in our immediate family ever talked it over with her family. I was merely informed by Vickey that Aunt Edith had died the night following the services for Stanley, but some of us who lived nearer to Aunt Edith had known that she was ill. I'd already reached home, and had begun to catch up at school. All of my classes at that time were made up of children who had very serious problems in reading, and our substitutes rarely understood well enough to press forward unless they had been given specific instructions. I had no time in which to make detailed plans before Aunt Edith's funeral.

It was the spring of 1978 that I contacted Ruby Caffey, a friend who lived in Albuquerque, and invited her to go to Egypt with me. She refused. They had a rather new preacher who was going to Aukland, New Zealand, on a missionary trip, and several of the congregation were going, including Ruby. Why didn't I go along, she asked.

I was fearful of my ability to be much help, but I was assured that everyone has to begin somewhere. As Wilma Gee became envious of my impending trip, she was enlisted as well. Joe Gray was the head of the missionary department of David Lipscomb University. He was the chief preacher, the first activator of the trips. Ancil Jenkins, the preacher in the University Church of Christ in Albuquerque, was the tour manager; John Payne, preaching in Alabama then, was personnel director.

Over ninety of us left from the west coast in June. We stayed in the Railton Hotel, and worked with a friendly crew of local preachers and other members, as well as a number of university students who whole-heartedly devoted at least two years of their lives to assisting, in any required capacity, the minister of a local church of Christ in any country who wanted to accept and work with a young assistant. The eager students were paid an existence stipend and travel funds by a sponsoring congregation.

They became hard-working interns who came to missionary-staffed meetings any place in their country of work if it was possible. This was a tremendously happy time, the effort of doing something worthwhile, the thrill of seeing new converts baptized, the meetings most evenings all a part of it. Here baptisms were performed in portable basins made for that purpose. Aukland was not only the site of the first of the seven trips which I enjoyed with the group Project Good News, it was also the only city so large that trips to the baptistery were so long as to be inconvenient and frequently foregone.

PGN went only to congregations who asked for help, and only after Joe Gray, at least one elder from the sponsoring congregation for the trips, a secretary, and an eager parcel of workers to survey the field had brought back a favorable report as to the advisability of proceeding. From 1975 through 1990, there were only two sponsors. It was a position to be desired.

One church which we were fortunate enough to work with actually lacked a baptistery. We were some miles away from it, at Eight Mile Rock, assisting local workers who were beginning a new congregation. The building in which we met was not fully converted; and as it had been a bar, the baptistery hadn't been installed. It mattered not at all, for it was common practice to go to the seashore for baptisms. Workers waded right into the warm, rolling waves with the happy convert. The baptism frequently took place a matter of only minutes after the desire was made known. When a hard working student (or vacationer) had helped study with the one to be baptized, the worker performed the rite. There is no other glow that so impresses the watcher as the one on the faces of the baptizer and the new member. The latter is elated and has a look unique to new Christians who have come home and intend living up to their new position. Few of us have never seen it. That man who has experienced baptizing another, perhaps while he still is only eighteen or nineteen years old, looks as if he has just taken a step that he had previously approached only in his wildest dreams.

Sometime during those same years Dan began going on bus tours. The bank in Bastrop sponsors the tours for the local citizens, one in the spring and one in the fall, each year. They are geared to the senior citizen, and their clients are naturally first choice. I do not know if there is an actual eligibility age or not. Any historical or appealing scenic route or area they wish to see may be their next goal.

Lemar and Jeanette continued to spend many days fishing off the coast of Texas; but as Martha had moved to Michigan, and Jeanne and Jim had settled in Colorado, they would make a trip to see them every year or so. A few times they made a short visit with me as well. I knew that Lemar would not appreciate a stir-fried meal as much as most of do, but I also knew Jeannette would. Thinking that she would make her meals along that line when Lemar was not with her, I put one before them one day. I hope that their failure to visit me again was not due to that one slip-up! They also went frequently to see Jeannette's family in Alabama. From there a group sometimes made trips to Las Vegas, Nevada. Some folks insist that they go to Las Vegas only to see the lights and shows and country; I've not asked Lemar and Jeannette if that's all they enjoy.

In 1980 Luceille and Bob decided to take Mother to Arkansas to see her sisters again. Mary, Lena, and Ruth all lived there, and it was reasonable to assume that Mother would not be able to take that lengthy a road trip many more years. They all enjoyed the visit, but we knew that our aunts had lived so close together for so long that they surely would have less and less in common with Mother each time they were together. Still Mother was grateful for the opportunity. I think probably her personality and those of her sisters had always been quite different; but she stored more memories on each visit just the same. This last visit was no different in that respect.

Even before Daddy died, Mother wanted me to give up our home and my position, and go to live near them. She thought only of having me close and could not truly understand that

I stood to lose a great deal financially. To her, it would have been so easy to sell a house and buy one corresponding in size, value, arrangement, and suitability. I doubted that I could have found anything I could afford without mortgaging my very soul. She saw no problem. That we had rented for years before we were permitted to buy the house, and that we still had to lease the land the house sat on was of little consequence to her. We had signed the purchase agreement, but I had to pay most of the price after Denny died. It was years later that the company decided to sell us the land.

The house suits me; it has three bedrooms and living room, dining room, kitchen, bathroom, and a half bath. The asbestos siding is painted white. It would bring only a relatively few thousand if I sold it, unquestionably too few to buy another. Besides, I had no desire to pull up stakes and take on monthly payments for years on end. Also, the chances of getting a decent teaching position near her were thin.

For years I had wanted to write. As I got older I felt the opportunity slipping away from me. Thus in 1981 I began to look at early retirement. Would it be feasible? I would have my teacher retirement check and a much smaller one from Social Security. But anyone whose account in the latter had had nothing added to it since 1962 would not receive a huge amount out of it. In spite of that, I decided that I should be able to live on the total; I set the machinery in motion. Until I was past the point of no return without a tremendous upheaval, I kept my mouth shut. I realized that I must tell Mother myself, that she would be terribly upset if she heard it second-hand.

In a way I waited too long. After the hurt feelings at my refusal to move to the Fort Worth area, Mother would have looked forward to seeing me more frequently. But before the opportunity to tell her face to face arrived, she became ill and went into a coma. Vickey called me but strongly advised that I not come down. Mother had vomited and inadvertently had aspirated some of the ejected fluid into her lungs. It had seared them, and she had lapsed unconscious. If she rallied and grew restless, Dr. Pafford said, then someone would need to be with her all the time; but at present he advised that we not do so. The more family who poured in, the more those who lived there had to bed down and feed; then if Mother did revive, everyone would already be tired out. His prediction was that pneumonia would develop as usual in such cases, and she would not linger long, or even regain consciousness. He was right; she died two weeks later, unconscious all the way. At ninety-five years and seven months one isn't strong enough to fight it.

It was somehow a relief not to see her during those two weeks. To have seen her would have been good; to watch her suffer, no. We gathered at Vickey's. While John offered beds, she was too far out for a gathering center unless one had a car. Luceille's house was smaller and harder to find; still she kept a few of us. Across the street from Mother's final home was a funeral home; it was there, about a fifteen minute drive from Vickey's, that the funeral was held. John and Ceal and vickey had hardly had time to tell anyone about Mother's illness; so there were few friends there. The most notable were the parcel of nurses and workers from the home. To me their attendance was rather heartening.

Is there ever a funeral that does not have laughter in the background somewhere? We were early, and visited in the yard and the family sitting room. One of my brothers-in-law carelessly leaned on a water fountain—and gradually ooched up until he was half sitting on it. His son warned him that he was not in an advisable position, but he scoffed and went on talking. Inevitably he activated the fountain. Then the icy water flowed into his hip pocket, which had been pulled open by his position. Numb, or nervous? He felt nothing at all until the moisture seeped through the pocket and finally began to run down his leg. He hopped, and he dried. And he went out into the sunshine and strolled about.

When we were summoned to our seats for the service, he and my sister sat on the back row of the family area. I sat further forward, between Vickey and Luceille. The talk went on and on; and I began to feel that it would never come to an end; but it did.

Mother had made only one demand through the last seven years: She must be buried by Daddy. As there were so many descendants who wanted to come to the funeral but could not, we decided to have a service at the cemetery in Cleveland. This meant that to return to Vickey's was the next logical step for the time being. The clock proved that when Vickey said the preacher couldn't have talked more than fifteen minutes, she was correct.

There I'm afraid we laughed a great deal, some truly at the wet trousers and some in release. Inevitably we stood remembering why we were gathered. Our expressions did not lend themselves well for pictures to be cherished or shown off. Realizing that, a sister's eight-month pregnant daughter-in-law mischievously cried, "Oh, my water broke!"

It hadn't, but we broke up. The picture-taking resumed with less stiff and sad subjects facing the cameras.

It was only after a great many more trips to Hurst that I could accept, without wavering, that Mother was not waiting in her clustered little room at the home on Weiler Street, just across the line in Fort Worth, to welcome me.

I knuckled down to writing with a vengeance, but failed to find a market for my stories. Perhaps I didn't send them to enough publishers, but they are good clean stories which neighbors, grandchildren, and my sisters read eagerly. Some publishers would not accept them because they do not have a strong Baptist or Lutheran flavor. When this saga goes to a printer, I shall pursue the sale of my novels; but this true story which we can pass down to those who wonder in years to come what went on before them is our first goal; but not for genealogy. It's to relate what those who preceded them did, and what they thought.

Some day a young man may boast that his great-grandfather used to ride the coupling pole on his daddy's wagon right through the water in stock tanks and drainage ditches.—Lemar did. He said it was fun. Or a child might say that her great-grandmother wore one slipper with a big hole in the upper all one winter—while she was teaching school—so her stubbed and broken toes would have space in which to ache and heal in peace. I did. Or one may tell the tale of her great-great-aunt who used to take the farm census for the government. Once she got the basic data 'bout the size of the farm from a neighbor, and truthfully marked it third hand information. After an exhausting day was over and she (John) was resting up for the next one, the woman who lived on that place called. She ranted and raved, said the canvasser was falsifying her records. As she became more irate, John cut in and calmly informed the taxpayer (so she had bragged) that she was "very sorry that you have had a bad day, and perhaps have a headache; you will feel better if you will take a couple of aspirin and then lie down for a short time." Stanley and Lena Jim heard John's side of that conversation. They whooped and hollered.

Said Lena Jim, "Mother very seldom answered anyone back but she certainly took care of that problem in a firm though very gentile manner." That's important.

Chapter XVIII

Mable too has had a bout with cancer. She'd undergone a mastectomy with flying colors and left on a trip while she convalesced before most of us knew it was to be. Bill Gray lived in either Minnesota or Utah at the time, and Mable and Ed went there and on their way back south came by to see me. Mable had worked out her plans, reviewed my likely reactions and excuses, and finally conceived the rebuttals that would overcome them. I was invited to sweep on down through Texas with them, seeing all possible members of both the Whisenant and the Gray clans at various stops. I went.

Gray and Mable did all the driving, but they stopped as frequently as the driver desired. Considering that they were inveterate drinkers on the road, mostly diet cold drinks, we made many stops that are the "other hand" to such traveling. Mable glowed with good health; we were incalculably grateful for that. Ed was obviously slowing down now, sleeping more, and forgetting more; but his indomitable spirit didn't allow him to believe it.

We wound up at Liberty, which sprawls along the Trinity River east of Houston. We visited in the lovely home of one of Ed's brothers on the shore of the lake there. Now south Texas has been flooded by much more than their usual amount of rain; and the number of families left either homeless or with greatly damaged homes is astronomical percentage-wise. I haven't heard if the Grays have suffered badly.

When Mable went to Mammoth Caves with us, she had given age no chance to work its worst in her life. She enjoys her courier route, and getting out and about keeps her young; so she had had a face lift. Although I would have denied that she needed one, she looked smooth and lovely. When the cave tour ended, John, Vickey and I took Mable home and began our trip. We were determined to see as much new territory as we could between there and home, but also to stop whenever any one of us particularly wanted to. We drove across the boot heel of Missouri and enjoyed the back road route to Texas.

Twice we chose to go where the crowds were in Arkansas, once at Hot Springs to walk about and see the treatment centers; the second time at Murfreesboro. I was not about to bypass probably the only chance I'll ever have to dig for diamonds. We were not lucky enough to find one, but, for a short span of time, we tried. We saw some behind glass in the display rooms. It was one more enjoyable step in acquiring all the knowledge and experience that we possibly could about God's world. Some fondest memories are the views from the bridges that allow one to see both up and down the lush countryside.

In January, 1988, Phil was forced to admit to a health problem that he had long insisted did not exist: he suffered from congestive heart disease. He had denied even to Dan—who knew something was wrong—that he was unwell. It meant immediate hospitalization; and before many of us knew he was seeing a doctor he had died once and been resuscitated. The family had been warned then that his body could not survive another such toll, and it did not.

To make matters worse, Ricky and Gary had been severely injured in a car wreck while Phil was ill; but the guilty motorist, between lies and little insurance, wormed his way out of most of his responsibilities. Dan had to assist with the financial problems which arose. However, the young men have regained most, if not all of their health and abilities, and had done so before Phil died.

The funeral was held on a Saturday, on a bitterly cold day for that section of the state. The wind was furious and blowing a gale. The cemetery, which we had often considered a beautiful spot, lies exposed to all weathers on a hillside. A shelter erected for the protection of the family was unable to hold the wind at bay, but Phil and Dan's own children and one of his sisters had been gathered, visiting and watching with him in the hospital for days, all knowing that the end was inevitable; and now Dan felt it would be asking too much of them to put those final rites off until Monday while they waited about in numb and helpless agony. After all, Monday's weather might not be any better. The most warmly dressed of us took the outside seats—those unprotected from the blasts of the wind which howled through—while the retired Lutheran preacher made his last few remarks. It was a bleak farewell from heavy hearts.

Phil had been reared in the Catholic church; and their marriage had been blessed by a priest, but Felix rarely went to church. Because he requested it, Dan made sure that the boys attended mass, but only sporadically. She never became a member of that faith herself. Therefore, when the priest could not hold the funeral service for Phil until some days had passed, Dan had located the other man. Of late Dan has attended the Church of Christ. We fervently hope and pray that she finds both peace and love there.

When Phil died most of us first met Eve; we liked her immediately. Jennifer was due in a few months and the prospective parents were very happy. Jests were fielded with good humor, and a little of the anguish of the occasion was eased by the knowledge that a part of Phil would live on in his children and grandchildren.

Dan has worked for Maynard's Real Estate in Bastrop for

years. She was both saleslady and secretary for the owner over a long period of time. She retained her position there after Phil died, thus forcing herself to get up and get out of the house daily. She also continues to take the bus tour twice a year. Last year the group took a trip to Fort Davis and Big Bend country. Dan was allowed to invite me to go along. We reminisced a great deal, and I began to realize how much we view many incidents in our mutual past from antithetic angles. But it was so good to be together.

Ricky and Gary now live either at home or nearby. They help Dan with her heavier work. She has the place listed for sale now, as she would prefer to live nearer town, and plans to retire fully. She will keep busy we know. She works well on local projects such as driving for Meals on Wheels, scooting here and there with the hot meals some unfortunates find they can no longer prepare for themselves.

She too likes to walk around and look at new territory, and gladly went with us to take the San Antonia river walk. Of course it goes for miles, and we didn't try to walk from one end to the other. Having a riverside drink and watching others stroll by makes a nice break before one goes back to his transportation.

Vickey and I had identical car trouble over a period of time—cruise controls that had minds of their own. When we slowed to wait as a car passed along a thoroughfare we were prepared to enter, our cars would decide to try to beat it. Not us. I, for instance, felt sure that it was my gas pedal sticking. How? I'm no mechanic. I'm sure I have much less ability along that line than anyone else in the world; but I did have ample presence of mind to keep a foot on the brake. It worked and I wasn't unduly perturbed. We would drive down a lane with no one in sight for miles, and feel our wayward cars take to their heels.

One day while he was out in Vickey's Chevy, Terry found himself with two options: gain uncontrollable speed or cut the motor off. Frightened, he wrenched the wires to the control out. As I drive less, I wasn't yet so terrified and took mine to the combination station/garage that has kept my car in good shape for some years. The owner-mechanic drove it off, but returned for me. It wasn't acting up at the traffic lights, but on the highway every time I slowed down to thirty or so the gas guzzling monster mulishly went into a gallop. Doug sat there with a fascinated grin on his face. It was a new twist for him. Of course he found that some insulation had worn off strategic wires, allowing a short circuit to engage the control regardless of my intention. Equally of course a surprising number of other drivers were having identical problems, but we didn't know it until later.

I have a new cruise control. Vickey's car is newer than mine, and we knew the part was more expensive. When the mechanic (to save face for his lack of know-how, Vickey thinks) said that he couldn't get one, she decided to do without until time to trade her car in.

On August 25, 1988, Keith Gray suffered a fatal injury. He had moved from Florida back to Nashville and lived in his own apartment. Apparently he had an evening appointment and decided to go get some cash before he prepared for it. His clean jeans were on the bed along with most of the papers we routinely carry, including a small book containing telephone numbers. His cash card was in his pocket.

One wheel of his car slipped off the street in an area where the streets were being repaired. Keith tried to swing back into the lane but succeeded only in turning sideways; a car close behind could not miss him. He was loaded into an ambulance and taken to the hospital. He "came to" long enough to tell an ambulance driver that he was Keith Gray, however, he was taken to a hospital without a trauma unit and then on to one equipped for trauma treatment. It was not soon enough. His aorta had ruptured at the impact.

His address on his driver's license was his old Florida residence. Officials called Florida, were given his current address, and went to his apartment. They called an uncle in Texas, the only Gray listed in the book. Only then did they know to call Mable and Gray.

Vickey and Luceille and Bob all drove up together, and Vickey suggested I go along. By the time all the plans had been made, it was too late for me to cancel the Sunday Bible School class I was to teach. I flew to Memphis, was met by Dana and Art. Vickey called from West Memphis and we met at a highway junction where I joined them. We found a motel in Nashville, for Jeannette and Lemar had also come with them; and we were aware that Mable and Gray rented out one or two bedrooms. Then we went at once to the house.

Soon the flurry of fresh tears and grief was over, and I looked around for a cup. I'm familiar with Mable's house, and I knew Mable would not mind my having a cup of tea. But I was not sure how all the attending friends, Mormon as are Mable and Gray, would react. They didn't censure—I should have known, but my thinking cap was tired.

Immediately one of the ladies jumped up, grabbed the first cup she saw, and filled it with water. Into the microwave oven it went. Her brain was tired too. Never before or since have I seen fire sitting with the jagged precision of comic strip fire on top of a container. The matching saucer with its metallic bands of silver or platinum sat nearby. After one single shocked gasp, I jerked the door open. That incident broke down all the little unintentional barriers between us. It was a time of loving one another and sharing grief.

The funeral was held after lunch the next day following a specified few hours of viewing time, a new practice to us from small towns. Then for the first time we heard a family member give a memorial. Some of us assumed it a difference spawned by religious customs. In that, too, we were wrong. It was a loving funeral.

Someone in the car had to report to work at eight o'clock the next morning. We had early dinner and took to the road. My eyes had not adjusted enough following cataract surgery for me to drive at night, and Lemar had not yet had his surgery. The others took it in one hundred mile shifts, and we all stretched energetically when the car stopped. Little sound sleep was snatched; indeed mine disappeared in mental pictures of Bill and the very blonde Keith as little boys playing so happily together on the farm out of Olden. Before daylight arrived, all stops were made where some sort of snack and coffee were to be had. Lemar and I made the effort to accept the front, middle seat and its biting seat belt sockets more often than the rest of the passengers. If you have never ridden long hours there, your education is still incomplete.

John had finally been compelled to take over all the driving, but she could never compel herself to be harsh with Wendell. When they struck out, she would send him back into the house for something which she had supposedly left behind accidentally. He would resist when he got to the car and saw her behind the wheel, but not for long.

In 1989 John and Wendell reached their fiftieth wedding anniversary. Had it been left to John, she would have asked the family members nearest to them over for cake and coffee, followed by Forty-two and a "bull-session"; accepted all their best wishes; made sure someone played dominoes with Wendell; and called it a day.

That wasn't the celebration the children felt it rated. So they cleaned the house, washed half a century's cherished curios, and sent out far more invitations than John allowed. Many preachers and teacher, neighbors and friends, kin and in-laws showed up. John loved them all. Wendell recognized most of them, but couldn't call them by name. Instead, very diplomatically he told us all, "I love you." Somehow we all knew that he meant it.

They both were exhausted by the end of the day, but far more important, they were happy. It was the first fiftieth anniversary to be celebrated in the family since Mother and Daddy had reached their's. Mable and Gray had lived in Fort Worth then and had hosted that one in their home.

Wendell has deteriorated at a rather steady pace; still he was often a delightful companion. He fed the horse, even using a pole to drag a trough or pan closer to the fence if it was out of reach. He entertained us by playing the piano–which he had never learned to do. Effortlessly it seemed, he would play a series of chords, causing a pleasant harmony to echo about the room, and smile gratefully at our applause and praise. He was like an appealing youngster when he held back a five count in dominoes until he would score with it. He would nudge the score keeper, and then point at the score pad until it was written down.

For a relatively short span of time, which surely loomed almost unending to John, he fought being undressed, which he had not faced since early childhood, or being cleaned up, if for a food-smeared face, or something much worse. Then when he quit fighting he was, by the very nature of the disease, much more withdrawn from his family. He has been ill with a bleeding ulcer, hospitalized with a blood clot, and suffered the flu in the last few months. John has gamely weathered all that and at last is considering placing him in a nursing home. The rest of us all feel that she should.

It was 1990. Vickey at sixty-one and I at seventy-one were out to view new sights. Vickey had never been to Carlsbad Caverns, and was about to fulfill a long-standing ambition. Also it had been almost forty years since I'd been there, and I enjoyed them as much as she did. But we got icing on our cake too, for I routed us through Monahans. And just out of the town is Monahans State Sandhills Park. Sand dunes at last. Both of us knew we had really climbed when we made it to the top of one. The down-hill drag of the very fine and almost pure white sand saw to that. Naturally we stood at the bottom of that one and took pictures of one another up on the top, and we are hardly recognizable. Dan and John and Luceille have not accompanied us the last few years; but Luceille and Bob both will go if we don't get too far from home. They almost believe that I'm younger than they are.

Many a day when I was teaching, I put things in my chair until the chair was hidden. (No, perhaps not a good precedence to set before school children.) As a result, I had to stand in the school room all day. I would sit through the brief lunch time, and sometimes during the one period we had for our planning and grading. Because I read books to my students, between five and ten minutes spent daily on one, I frequently leaned back against the front of my desk. I preferred those days to the ones when I sat too much.

Just as Dan retained her job for a part of the day to be sure she got up and about, I now have volunteer work to take up part of my time. After retirement I began to help cook for meals served by the church members to bereaved families—I had helped with it only rarely while I still taught. Now the ladies who headed this activity saw fit to invite me to join them. Happily I did so, but I felt that I could surely do more than that to help others, and at the same time keep myself away from my typewriter for more hours.

When one of the nursing homes in Borger asked at our ladies Bible class for help to keep the residents engaged in pleasurable activity, I offered to show my slides once a week. I could entertain the residents for an hour a week for several months, I calculated; and my offer was snatched up immediately.

The residents did enjoy them; they asked questions; and compared places to localities they had visited or lived in, and items to those used for the same purposes in the

United States. Putting the slides in order; loading and unloading the reels; hauling the whole to and from the home took time, but at last we had a routine well-established. When they'd seen them all and wanted me to start over, I could not deny them. Now I have friends I'd never have made otherwise.

After some time, I went to the second home and asked if they would like to give it a try as well. I do not know how many years I've now shown slides. The residents at one of the two complain almost bitterly if I have to miss, but stay careful not to anger me. At the other there is a far bigger percentage of helpless residents. I have less watchers; but I feel if only one person shows up, that one feels the need worse than ten or twenty who can talk together. Rarely do I have only one, but it has happened once or twice. My ladies (I have more feminine watchers than masculine, but the males are just as enthusiastic) want to see my slides after a trip almost as soon as I unpack my bag, even before I receive all the slides from the developers. Between those activities and my writing I have limited time to wish for something to do. However, I am by no means indispensable.

Chapter XIX

Many of our memories are special, but we lose track of whom we have and whom we haven't shared them with. With this thought in mind, I invited the rest of the clan to reminisce with us in this portion of our saga. As John's contribution came in first, it will lead the chapter.

When Lena Jim was three and a half, her daddy joined the U.S. Navy. We made sailor outfits for her and Stanley. At the base in Norman, Oklahoma, we had to hold tight to her when she was dressed for the part, or she would try to join the marching sailors. As a very young child, she played house, wanted to cook, and did her share of caring for Stanley. She learned the alphabet, to read a little, and to add—basic kindergarten skills. Texas had few public kindergartens, and she was bored in the early part of first grade. She wanted to help others, which displeased the teacher. Her hair was long and blond, but she begged to have a Toni Home Permanent until I gave in. Frustrated, she cried at the difference. Years later, she confided that what she really wanted was the paper dolls which were a part of the purchase.

We had a gravel driveway with a steep slope at the edge of the street. Lena, in the second grade, started to school three times with her hard-boiled Easter eggs. Each time she fell on the slope and grazed her knees. She also managed to break the eggs. After I patched her up for the final fall, I gave her the least broken eggs and sent her on her way.

Lena was part of a clique that lasted from first grade through high school. On the way home as third-graders, they discussed a child not of the group and got downright catty. Lena summed it up, "Well, Linda just isn't as manure as all of us are." She spoke more truth than she meant to.

Lena taught pre-schoolers in Sunday School when she was twelve. Both teacher and pupils loved the class. She quit when Butch was born. She had had her heart set on a sister, but loved Butch so much it soon ceased to matter. She spent hours caring for him, and slipped him from his crib into her bed when he was only a week old so she could cuddle him. We worried that she might hinder the healing of his little arm.

Lena was active in the Order of the Rainbow for Girls, and was elected Worthy Advisor at seventeen. She went into Eastern Star too, when Wendell was Worthy Patron locally and he conducted her initiation, making it doubly special.

As a senior in school, she was homecoming princess, won the bookkeeping award, played offensive guard in the junior-senior powderpuff football game, attended some conventions, and was an honor graduate. She was finalist in the "General Dynamics' Sons" scholarship program, but was disqualified at the insistence of one board member that she was not a "son." The rules changed the next year, but Lena Jim had spent a year in secretarial classes and was interested in Robert—and marriage.

When Stanley was just one he pulled a pan of hot grease off the stove. It hit a chair and splashed on his hips. We were three blocks from a doctor. I wrapped him in a quilt, and we hurried, but all the burned skin was off on the quilt when we arrived. For years after even wind hurt when he was wet.

Stanley gave us many laughs. One day Daddy missed just one minnow in the bottom of the bucket. Stanley pointed out the fish in the "tip bottom" of the pail. Daddy frequently failed to find things we laughed at funny; but he liked that and repeated it often. As he had been badly burned too, he truly sympathized with Stanley. We lived at home some while Wendell was in the Navy, and Stanley wasn't timid around his grandfather like some of the children were.

When Stanley was three, he wired the inside knob on the screen door to the living room door. Wendell had to take it off the hinges to undo it. In the first grade, Stanley dragged some long, slender venetian blind boxes to the terrace wall and managed to pull them on his legs. They were his stilts, and he was broken-hearted when they finally tore.

Stanley was small for his age. To make him grow he had Vitamin B-12 injections. He was on top of the world or down in the depths. When he began school, he fought frequently, and alibied, "I was just running with my fist out. He'uz in my way!" Later he had an old air rifle to be used only in a nearby vacant lot. One day Butch ran by just as Stanley was pulling the trigger. The B.B. hit him in the temple but was not forceful enough to break the skin. They picked it off, but Wendell broke the gun anyway.

Stanley loved animals, was active in Future Farmer in school; he went to the national convention in Kansas City as representative of the local chapter. An hour before he was to give his report, he found a skunk in the lamb pen. Alas, the skunk "found" him too. Soap, milk, tomato juice—not a thing helped. He sat alone at his table but he did give his report. He had an old donkey that all the kids rode, goats, steers, and chickens, like all F.A.A'ers have. He chose to raise Araucian chickens because they lay colored eggs.

As a high school cheerleader, Stanley went to SMU cheer school. He took a tumble while trying to do a pyramid, and X-rays showed a socket and a half in his shoulders. He had torn the ligaments that held the arm in place. They put him in a brace with big padded circle on his shoulder blades, and straps across his chest and over his shoulders. He went shirtless the rest of the week so his backwards "bra" would show. He got lots of attention and teasing about it.

Stanley loved puzzles and studied magic for a while. He enjoyed entertaining with his tricks, and became proficient enough to join a club and go to some magicians' conventions. He suffered from hypoglycemia which caused his ups and downs. On top, he kept us all laughing, but in the dumps he was stubborn, opinionated, and exceedingly hard to get along with. We believe the hypoglycemia caused his fall into the rock crusher, and death, at the age of thirty-three.

But God tempered our grief. When we last saw Stanley, Wendell was depressed and uncomfortable from a back injury. We stood watching him drive off, and he stopped the car and walked back to us. He threw his arm around Wendell and counseled, "Daddy, put your problems in God's hands and don't worry about them. I don't mean not to try to solve them, but don't worry. You taught me to love a living and merciful God. Now you need to lean on Him. I do." Wasn't that a wonderful message for our son to leave us with!

Wendell, Jr. was born after we had lost a little boy in miscarriage, and so was a double joy to us. Lena was 13 and took much of the work load for me. Wendell's lungs were not well developed, and he had a broken arm. It was so hard to thump that little bruised foot to make him cry, but it was a must every two hours to exercise his lungs. He screamed so when the splints were taken off his arm that his lungs never gave any more trouble. Stanley nicknamed him Butch, and it stuck.

Butch was four when I had surgery. Wendell's mother came to help out. The day she cooked chicken and dumplings, he would not eat. He cried himself to sleep and cried when he woke. At last he said, "Me'll just eat me dog." The dog was named Dumps, and he had though the obvious.

Butch alighted from his tricycle on the back porch one day and stumbled backward across the floor until he hit the pressure cooker and sat down forcefully. As the cooker was full of cooked chicken cooling to be ladled into containers for canning, he was well burned. Though it took some time to heal, the skin did not slough off.

Once Stanley and Butch were left at the ice cream store to drink sodas before they went on to the grocer's. Stanley whispered to Butch that he had lost their money, and that he must run for Mama and not look back. Stanley watched him go and then paid the bill.

Another time he helped Butch onto a freight train, climbed on with him, rode down the line, and hitched a return ride. He didn't tell us that for many years. Butch also streaked Lena's white bedspread and the skirt of her dressing table with lipstick. When she remonstrated, he put the blame on her for leaving the lipstick where he could reach it! Butch was five and not used to sliding screens when we moved into a new home. He hit one so hard that though it fell onto the porch he rebounded across the room. Leery, he gave the screen wide berth for some time.

When Lena and Robert left for California, Butch took it surprisingly well. They returned at Christmas to visit, and at their leaving time he hugged her and reported, "This time I know enough to cry!" Butch played saxophone in the band, and loved the trips to games. but he only knew by whether or not they did a victory march who won the game.

All our children on their own now, our household began to revolve around Debbie, our grandchild and yet our child. We had held a birthday party for her while her age group was still about us before taking her to England when Wendell was sent there temporarily. So first crack out of the box, in a nation where threes ride buses free but fours must pay, she piped up and insisted she was four. The bus driver believed we were trying for an unfair free ride. Our neighbors were impressed with the tot who singled out the U.S. flag in the display and pledged allegiance to it every day.

Debbie was a good child but an odd one. She was rather like her father but more even tempered. She learned to say the alphabet backwards because Mother did, and once when she was daydreaming in school, the teacher scolded her and asked what was on her mind. Debbie confessed; the teacher doubted her, and demanded that she say them to the class, who hardly knew them at all. She calmly obliged.

As a senior in high school, she was a third year French student. A neighbor with five children, ages four to nine, wanted her to tutor them a half hour daily before school.

Last but not least, is an item I stumbled onto through Lena Jim. Mother was in her nineties when she told someone that she found herself plopping down into a chair without so much as a pretense of grace. She felt she had let her side down. She began to practice sitting down gracefully when no one was about. Lena Jim went by to see her and confided in me because she was amazed at Mother's actions. Knowing what Mother had said, I knew what she was doing. I watched when I had a chance, and Mother did sit down like a graceful girl until she died.

Luceille started her reminiscing with a delightful tale of Jerry's (well, she was Jerry then) young outlook: no one goes around looking on top of houses for people, and surely she would be safe there. So she filled her pockets full of green apples and hid. I came out into the bright sunlight, and had to look down at the ground to adjust my sight. What an odd shadow the house made. I looked up, and spotted her immediately, much to her chagrin.

At two she loved music, and used to stand on the arm of Daddy's rocker and hold her ear against the fabric covering the speaker of the radio which held place of honor on the sewing machine nearby. When she was three, I picked her up about two one afternoon and aimed her gaze toward the moon. Amazing me, she announced that she knew what was wrong with it. I stared at the full moon overhead and asked what could be wrong. She replied, matter of factly, "It's turned off."

When we lived on the farm, we frequently used the truck for transportation, and sometimes there were five or six of us in the cab. There were no seat belts and no rules about the number in the cab. Little ones stood on the floor, the seat, or our laps—the driver's as well. They vied for space with the stick gear shift which, necessarily, was in the floor and had no cover at all around it. The roads were more gravelly than muddy, but there were always chug holes to keep us entertained. Once after a rain when we weltered through one of them, Morris Ray indignantly declared, "That spluttered on me!" And he wiped (smeared) his legs more energetically then gracefully.

Morris was accident prone as a youth. His hip received a load of shot one day when an unloaded gun and a loaded one juggled for position in a car just before he stepped inside it. With myriad stitches still in place, he fell over a gym basket and had to have more added, right in the same hip.

Our boys and Stanley were great buddies, but somehow it seemed one of them got hurt nearly every time they gathered to play. It was Morris who managed to suck a cashew so deep into his lung when they pitched them high and caught them in the time honored way. After all other efforts to counteract his encroaching ill health failed, he had to have one lobe of the lung removed. It was Stanley who wrecked his car. John and I tried to separate them when we could; but they neither truly understood nor appreciated our effort. Although J.D. was a year younger, he was involved as the other two.

When J.D. was learning his ABCs, a chore to him, he was forever leaving out the F. I would say, "Wait a minute; you left something out."

Over and over he said, "I tergotten." After many false starts he suddenly "forgot" things and returned the F to the alphabet. At the age of seven he seemed to be determined to put out his left eye. He hurt it in a fall against a coffee table; and he walked into a pan Morris was slinging around. It sliced a slice of eyebrow like a slice of bacon, complete with hair. He also had double pneumonia that year.

Robin was years younger, and when he climbed a trellis not designed for his weight, he fell. It took six stitches to repair him. Morris, mindful of his own recent stitches, burst out, "Can't you just stick it together with bubble gum or something?" Morris was in the Navy when Robin stepped on a broken bottle and had to have two stitches in his foot; so J.D. sympathized.

There are other memories too; as when I warned him that he was putting his shoes on the wrong feet. "But these are only feet I have!" And at one of the popular Tupperware parties, the hostess invited Robin to enter the drawing for a gift. He drew a number and remarked that he wouldn't win. The hostess admonished that he must be positive. Five-year-old Robin replied, "Okay, I'm positive I won't win."

Robin's son spent the past summer with us, and he quite capped his father. We had bought a load of groceries aimed at tempting his appetite with proper foods, and he indicated one of his own choices. "That's one of my favorites, but I haven't got to taste it yet."

My last memory is rather new: Courtney (Kimberly's four year old) was bitten by a dog recently. She had twenty-six stitches. Some were above, some below her left eye, others elsewhere on her face. But J.D. says it isn't as bad as it sounds. I haven't seen it yet.

Vickey started her reminiscence with Kenneth: When he was two to two and a half, Luceille kept him for me whenever I worked. She left small pieces of candy, gum, cookies, or some such enticing edibles on the porch, a Hansel and Gretel trail to follow into the house. One day he came in crying, and said, "Aunt Ceal, I can't bite this." Ceal had put out a fine big ball in the place of the tidbits!

Kenneth peeled all the bark off a nice big limb on our neighbor's trees. She had a fit, of course; so I spanked him to make her feel better. I did not believe he knew it would hurt the tree. I also made him apologize to her. He added to the apology, "It looked so pretty. Some things are worth a spanking."

Kenneth was always helpful. He painted a strip of four boards almost the length of the side of a man's house, using the paint he found in the yard there. The house was white. The paint was red. (Vickey didn't catalogue any outcomes of his youthful folly.)

Our son went through elementary and high school in the required number of years. It took fifteen years for him to finish junior college and attain his associate degree. Then in two more years he gained his B.A. He has worked another year on his masters. He now has two hundred plus accredited college hours. I've always said he could tell time; he just didn't know what to do with it. Currently, he teaches scuba for a living and earns a little jam for his crusts by doing computer programming and repairs.

Terry always was, and still is, the son whom the girls chased. He was quite a bit larger than Tommy and without a doubt would never lack for admirers. He was a first-grader when I was at school, walking down the hall. I saw him with two girls walking along, twelve to fourteen feet behind him, calling out, "Terry! Terry!, we love you." And one field day a teacher rescued him from a ditch. Some older girls were holding him and kissing him.

I knew he had a sense of humor and would get along with people well when he dropped a paper, stooped to grab it, and missed when the wind whisked it out of his reach. Terry ran to get it, laughing a little. The scene, and Terry's laugh, were repeated several times. Most of us would be miffed if we had to chase an object several times.

Terry had learned to play the guitar; once he played, and
sang a solo, for the entire student body of his school. He is the
most thoughtful and loving of our sons. His ambition
throughout his boyhood was "to be a cop." He is a student in
the police academy at this time and a deputy sheriff.

Tommy, who at first repeated our words exactly, was as
bright as a button and chattered like a magpie. He was very
small as a young boy, and we still were carrying him around
when he was five. When he was in the second grade, he went
to a bad behavior class—if the kids were not too bad, they got
a coke and could drink it in the hall, something none of the
other students could do. Tommy slyly asked the teacher just
how bad he would have to be to get a coke. Then one of the
boys in the bad behavior class really beat Tommy up; he got a
steak while Tommy got a sandwich. Even at that Tommy
liked to fight for several years. He and his brother seemed to
wrestle constantly, and as they both were quite ticklish, their
bouts usually ended in laughter.

When Tommy was in the first grade, he took a part in a
play. Right in the middle of it, he saw me in the audience. He
walked up to the edge of the stage and spoke: "Hi, Mommy;
I love you." Then he trotted back to his place.

Tommy weighed eighty-six pounds when he started to
high school. We had been to the doctor four times to see why
he did not grow. At twenty-five he has outgrown Terry, has a
small business of his own, and works as well for the city of
Fort Worth.

Much of Merry Fay's baby beauty came from an infectious
friendliness. At the age to sit up on our laps and smile at
strangers, she often attracted their attention. Service men
would ask her age, even query her development, and then
say, "I have a five month old daughter whom I have never
seen; I hope she is like yours."

Baby-sitters? She and Dana loved them all, and wanted us
to get new ones too—"cause we have more friends then." Bill didn't.

He preferred his tested and proved by himself. He didn't throw too bad a tantrum if the girls were also at home, but he and a stranger alone always meant a struggle we tried never to go through. He bawled loud and long even if he was left with a neighbor he knew and liked. After a few years he did quit sobbing when I was well out of sight and sound.

Dana had a tough time on her first accident which ended in a medical call. We were buying paint at the lumberyard, and the girls began to run to and from the end of a counter, out of harm's way and ours. Dana misjudged and hit a corner finished with metal edging. She had bounced some three feet back, and I scooped her up. My heart plummeted to my feet. Blood was running from one eye. We tore out to the doctor's office. He had to put a stitch between the eye and the brow and doctor the puncture below the eye. The blood had had to run into the eye before it could run out!

The next morning when Dana woke up, the eye was swollen shut, and she began to scream in terror. On Monday I had to see an ophthalmologist in Amarillo. Patients were money on the hoof. We were given appointments for certain dates and then had to sit around until called to the inner sanctum; we joined the masses. After Dana told her story to one or two ladies, she had had enough; still she was queried many times about her injury. She would swell up rather like a poisoned pup and say, "I'm not gonna tell you!" Her mother soon saw that it was best not to hear these sessions. She explained only if the questioner pursued her.

Another time, we had been to the farm and just arrived home. The girls stayed around well when forbidden to leave the yard, and they played hopscotch on the walk from the car to the house while we rested. As Dana hopped along beside a nearby flower bed, she dragged her right foot along a wooden retainer so that a splinter entered her little toe from its inside surface, pierced the toe, and protruded on the outer surface but left the skin unbroken. The wood, blackened by the ever-present carbon in the air, became a bluish knob the size of a match head.

Both Denny and I tried to remove it. It wasn't hard to get a good grip on it, but it resisted strongly. Obviously it had gone through the tendon. I scrubbed off a good layer of the carbon black; and off we went to the hospital. There the emergency room nurse pooh-poohed our assertions that it had clung too tenaciously for us to remove it. But she also found it impossible to extract, and paged the doctor on call before she snatched up a can of powdered cleanser, remarked that that was what she used on her own children's feet, and proceeded to remove more of the carbon black. Permit me to explain here that this took place before most cleansers had been "improved" until they were virtually useless.

Enter Dr. Smith. Repeat roughly the same scene, except he used that violent-looking green surgical soap. Before he deadened the toe and began to cut into it, he apologized for doubting us. It took a little longer than he had figured on and Dana began to whimper before he was through. From then on he kept an anxious eye on me as well as Dana. He asked, "Are you all right, Mother?" more than once. I assured him I was, but when we left the room, my purse was much too heavy for me. I told Denny to catch it.

He told me later that I kept saying, "Catch my purse," over and over, my voice successively lower in tone until it died away completely. We had been headed toward the desk to pay our bill; but when I came to I was in a chair and Denny was waving something under my nose. Dana was walking up and down, drinking a Coke. It was about half gone.

She had accepted the whole affair stoically, until Dr. Smith impressed on us that her foot must be soaked at least four times a day for not less than 15 minutes each time for the next several days. Her complaint was that she wouldn't have any friends left. Not so: the living room was the only room large enough to hold the circle of children who came in and sat foot to foot until it became foot against pan with the last one. There was no lasting damage.

One of Merry Fay's most traumatic moments came when she was in the alley with other children. Some unthinking soul had dumped his unwanted lengths of lumber in the incinerator without sawing them into short pieces. We, neighbors and I, heard Merry Fay scream and went dashing out of our houses to investigate. One burning two by four had fallen out as the children walked by. Her hair was singed, her face very red. I trimmed the hair, and the red faded in a day or so, but it left behind one tiny blister on the tip of her nose. It was years before anyone again failed to shorten lengthy material before dumping it.

Bill once had blood poisoning in a knee from what began as a routine skinned place. He was old enough then to clean his own knees, but one night he cried with pain and told me, quite seriously, that he was dying. I hadn't seen the knee until then. He did have blood poisoning and had to take some high-powered medicine. He had to stay in bed for weeks, ending in "walk to bathroom and dining table and back to bed" for the last two. My sister thought I was pampering him, and I had to overrule her orders to him when we visited her just before a trip to Six Flags Over Texas.

Oh, how our children loved to go there. We would stay with Mable or Vickey and go in a party. Merry Fay and Dana went to the top of the tree ride one day and Dana refused to turn loose. Her sister pried her fingers up; and from some distance away we heard her voice, "Merry Fa-a-a-ay" until she reached the end of the ride.

We learned to dump Bill at the gate with Kenneth, their telephone money separated from spending money, and to return to the gate only at the set time. Always they had to "check-in" a predetermined number of times. Bill didn't make it once; he looked under Moke for Moak and gave up but returned the dime which was the cost of a call then.

Bill's biggest triumph over a teacher was inadvertent, and the result of a bicycle wreck. He broke a tooth but the stitches under his chin were more serious. He was forbidden to get them wet for a week. That meant he had to have a doctor's written excuse from PE for a week; for a shower after that class was a must.

I used to take the children to see puppet shows, and they loved them. They turned the corner of the yard into a stage and put on their own productions with quite admirable ingenuity. Clothing, towels, and old bedspreads draped over lawn chairs and picket fences can make many rooms.

Dana would not sty at home, but persisted in trailing after Merry Fay when she was nine months old. We had no choice but to erect a fence. Merry Fay had not been a problem to restrict to the yard. I poured lines of bright nail polish across the sidewalk to mark her boundaries, and she cheerfully observed them. I feel sure we were lucky to have a fence when Bill began to walk. He had two sisters to follow...after all, going gadding just can't be compared to staying with a baby-sitter.

One day Bill came in as white as a sheet. Frightened, I ran to him. When I heard his story, I was grateful: while pedaling down the farm to market highway, he had an urge to see how fast he could go. When he passed the twenty mile per hour sign for the zone that connects with the main highway, he ignored it. The highway patrolman didn't. Instead he stopped Bill and read him the riot act. His points concerned safety, but also obedience to the law; however he evidently made more of the law than he did of safety. Twenty, point one, miles per hour, Bill was convinced, would mean a fine from then on.

Generally speaking, Dana was struck harder blows by the contagious diseases of childhood than the other two. Merry

Fay had them and that was that. A playmate a bit older than Merry Fay brought mumps to the neighborhood and Dana brought them home. She had them, one jaw one weekend, the other the next. Merry Fay then had them. She had to miss a few days of kindergarten, and that was that. Ten days later Dana had them in one jaw, and the next week in the other. The doctor was neither surprise nor worried. It happens.

And the chicken pox. One of them brought those in when Bill was only four months old. Dana had the highest number of pocks. Bill still retained enough natural resistance to put up a good fight. It took him eight days of fever to get all his breaking-out done—all four pocks, and two of them left scars. He was a very sick little boy. Again Merry Fay sailed through her share of it all.

Then came the age of the stomach virus. More than once I had to take her to the hospital in the middle of the night for shots to calm her insides down. It's a rather degrading feeling to be in that shape; and a doctor told our neighbor that it took seven years to rid one's system of it completely when one was truly struck down with it. Both Merry Fay and the neighbor were, and it did. But I cannot vouch for the ultimate truth of his statement.

Dana was the first to have to lose her tonsils. Merry Fay did at ten, and ate cabbage slaw at dinner the next day. Bill still has his. Denny's dwindled away as is fitting and proper before he was forty. I'm seventy-one, and mine are nearly if not all gone.

Chapter XX—Whisenant Bloopers

We've all suffered the giggles, shame, indifference, or woe of bloopers. Those herein recorded (and revealed) have been enacted by either an unwary native-born Whisenant or by the spouse of one. Also there will be no divulging of names either before or after printing.

One day a well-dressed lady went to work wearing a new half-slip and feeling good. During the day she was situated at a cash register. About noon she felt a sensuous slithery impression which alarmed her. She looked down; there around her feet lay that new item of clothing. Quickly, cleverly, she grabbed another employee to stand beside her. She told all approaching customers to go to another register as hers was being closed down. Other employees had seen it all, and collapsed with laughter. One subordinate worker, male, even told her later that he sat there wishing that she could see the expression on her own face.

By and large—whoops, I'll have to start all over. That idiom would surely be a blooper in this instance.

As a family, we run to neither huge bosoms nor utterly—I swear, word of honor; neither of those was premeditated—small bosoms.

The Whisenant daughters had just average-sized bosoms, but one of them, possibly after slimming down, decided that nature needed some assistance. After a shopping expedition with another of us, she laid her new falsies on a table but had to answer the door before she could put things away. On hearing the voice of a male friend, the second lady grabbed the new acquisitions, which had just been taken from a paper sack, and quickly placed them out of sight. There was little time and only a few hiding spots; so she laid them on top of a lamp, just hidden by the shade. Soon the man was looking about the room, sniffing suspiciously. Clearly something was burning. Desperately the hostess detracted their visitor's attention, and the helper managed to whisk the secret items out of the room.

One man of the family gave some trousers to another man of the family—through the two wives involved. The receiver tried on a pair and decided to wear them; he had to shop and run errands. He went by his wife's place of employment when he started home. She had him pose for her admiration of the blue trousers and matching blue shirt, and then suggested at once that they leave. She had to admit that her usual hours were not up when he questioned her. Then, of course, reason had to be given for the sudden urge to leave. Down the back of the trousers, in white thread that leaped to the eye, the wife of the original wearer of the trousers had taken pleats in an attempt to figure out how to take the trousers up; but she had forgotten to mention that fact. Said the wearer, "I thought they felt a little airy!"

One young mother who ordinarily had a passable feminine figure found herself quite flat after nursing a baby. After a futile search for falsies near home, she and her husband, accompanied by the small girl who had apparently caused the situation, went to a nearby town and found some appropriate assistance for nature. As they were getting seated in their car to make the return trip, an old and valued friend hailed the husband. Then he came and leaned on the window to visit for a while. Imagine the wife's amazement—and chagrin—when she realized why their child was so quiet and well behaved: she was clutching one of the delightful objects in each hand and flipping one toward her own self and the other away. As they drew even, she sideswiped them on one another.

All of the above was mailed to my sibling, and my mail and phone calls have divulged the following incidents. Some have indeed come in twice, and I have added to the first one any additional information that enhances the story. Thanks, Whisenants! That reminds me: once in Houston at a reading teachers' convention, I remembered that I had not written my niece's address down. I studied the telephone directory and called the most promising number. A male voice answered. I hadn't expected that, but I quickly asked, "Is this the John Borden that belongs to the Whisenant family?"

John Borden, bless his heart, didn't hesitate. "It sure is!" he replied as if delighted, and we went on from there.

Now on to the results of my plea.

This blooper is about Daddy, and he told it on himself to too many people to mind who knows it was him. After years of working for West Texas Produce Company, but only a short period of freedom in retirement, he walked out of one of the business establishments in Ranger and saw the company truck which he had driven for so long. Habit took over, and he climbed into the seat and drove home. Failing to see the pickup that should have sat there, he took stock and almost immediately realized what he had done, and what he must do. He went in and explained to Mother and drove back to Ranger.

The new man on Daddy's old route was standing near the curb, scratching his head and staring at the vacant parking slot where his vehicle should have been. He saw Daddy, and knew what had happened. They laughed together and then went away, each to his own pursuit.

Luceille told this blooper about me, but I can't recall either the incident or ever dating a man of that name.

Will the unfortunate victim forgive me if I relate this in first person? Thank you.

Ned arrived to take me to a party; and all decked out in my white ruffled dress I went to report to Mother that I was leaving. Mother acknowledged my intent; she also mentioned that I was too thin. A sister some years younger watched me go put on a half slip to remedy the situation, which didn't help at all as Mother was referring to my total lack of body fat. That same sister then dashed out to encourage, "Guess what, Ned! Fay's got on two slips!" Mother managed to drag the young culprit away, but she was a trifle late. The unmentionable, to Mother, had been mentioned.

This was turned in as a blooper, but as the perpetrator got by with it, it's just an incident which left some of us bare-faced and Lemar happy. We were preparing for a picnic. If we "blooped," it was in allowing Lemar to know that when the ice cream was properly set he would not be partaking of it. He swiped freezer and all. Even the sister who brought the tale back to our memories knew where Lemar and the cold dessert were and got her share. Should I now say, "Shame on you!" or "Congratulations!" The latter, I think.

The snitcher of that story also mentioned the time that I poured just a tad bit of syrup on their pillows as Lemar and cousin Willy Payne slept one night. It hampered them when they arose at 5 A.M. to go deliver the order. They came home and went for a swim in the stock tank before they ate breakfast.

Revenge was simple. An alarm clock was set for 2 A.M. and slipped behind the curtain of our dressing table (orange crates have their uses). I woke up down on my knees trying to fight my way through the curtains to get at the source of the unholy racket. Fair enough.

Next may we mention that a sister dated a young man who went by the improbable name of E.D. As young girls do, this individual did: she raved incessantly about E.D. and all of his manly characteristics. The sister just older presumably got tired of it. She wrote E.D. a hundred or so times, cut the paper into small pieces, and tucked the young man's name into every conceivable spot. The victim sat down to eat and E.D. was staring up from her spoon. As she went to dress, he peeped out from the dresser drawer where her socks found lodging. He even made dressing uncomfortable when scraps of paper prodded her in totally unexpected moments because she had not seen the mischievous reminders while assembling her clothes; she went to brush her teeth, and E.D. had first to be vanquished; her book covers sported his name. He haunted her endlessly, she comments—or is it whines?—to this day. The perpetrator sent in the final touch, either admitting or bragging of, her own guilt.

To understand fully, the reader must realize that just above the bathtub there was a window, four feet tall, which gave us a bit of natural light, though filtered through curtains. The bathroom wall was shared by a tiny screened in kitchen porch. The letter writer thrust her hand through the curtains, and in record time she dribbled some of the little bulletins into ___'s bathwater. Then she hollered, Momma! E.D.'s in the bathtub with ___. E.D. was quoted no more; and the young lover didn't speak to her nemesis for days afterward.

One of the favorite places to garner one's own Christmas tree without charge was Strawn Hill. This year, half of the Whisenant children went together with a young man who was in love with one of them to view the possibilities. They found and reaped a lovely tree; but on the return trip the car ran out of gas. No one had any money, not even the owner-driver of the car. He however prevailed on a station attendant to put in two costly gallons of gas—ten cents a gallon—with his vow to pay up the next day. They did return to pay up, and the attendant told them frankly that he had never expected to be repaid.

This blooper is hereby repeated just as the unfortunate perpetrator expressed it in answer to my plea: remember the cable we had stretched out over the big tank? We would hold on to the pulley and ride out and drop into the water. One day Bill G——— and I were in the tree and had a disagreement. I got mad, grabbed the pulley, and shouted, "Never speak to me again!" Alas, my bathing suit snagged itself on a limb. Bill had to unhook it before I could go down the cable—and he made me beg!

Rather delightful, huh? Some of the family watched—and refused to help.

Two sisters-in-law and their families went shopping one day in the Montgomery Ward store in Ranger. Totally pooped, they at last began to straggle out to the car. The lady who was leading the way heard giggling issue from a nearby car, and turned to see what was that funny behind her. Imagine, if you can, her chagrin when she saw her young son relieving himself at the curb. Her sister-in-law was just behind the child; and the guilty one strolled nonchalantly on, leaving her to bring the miscreant child along.

The mother involved in this story was a Brownie leader. She allowed the Brownies' dues to amass until she deemed it worthwhile to take the money to the bank. She kept records and hit on the idea of leaving the money in a bowl nearby to provide change and wrote a check for the deposit. Her first time to go to the bowl for change ended in stunned disbelief. Her small son, it turned out, needed change for candy every day after school and had helped himself.

Another time one of the men of the family and a nearby neighbor named Bill wanted to go fishing, but Daddy issued a command that the radishes must be hoed first. So the worker (who received a dollar a day wages) hired Bill as a helper at fifty cents. Bill felt quite flush and hired himself a helper for twenty-five cents. The worker wouldn't let the donor of the story explain to Bill that they were hired not by the job, but by the day.

One day after a visit to Dan, Mother, and Daddy, one of us started home with a Christmas tree. It was rolled in a burlap sack and fastened to the back of the car. As luck would have it, the car met a skunk on the highway while the traffic was too thick to dodge it. They felt a low tire and pulled into a station for air. A watching attendant thought he was seeing a deer, dashed out, grabbed the air hose, and eagerly asked, "How many points?" as he knelt to the tire.

That's when he got a whiff of the skunk. "I still laugh when I recall how quickly he backed up—still in a squatting position—to get away from that tire. It was really strong!" the informant wrote.

Once a Brownie troop were getting their jollies running down an absent member. Our blooper tried to shame them, and told them to say something nice for everything ugly they had said. They all sat silent for a few minutes; then one said she couldn't think of anything to say. The others followed suit.

Without thinking before she spoke, the leader indicated her own guilt—in spite of being guiltless—by saying, "Well I can't either. Everyone get busy." I wonder how long the girls laughed before they obeyed that command.

Family, do you know who said that Jimmy worked at "Hell Belicopter?"

When Dana was in high school, she lost a ring belonging to a male friend, a heavy class ring made to stay on a slim finger by the usual bulky wrapping of adhesive tape. It is one of the lesser understood facts of life that when a young girl loses such a heavy ring, the relief at the loss of that heaviness is so great that the wearer never thinks of trying to explain it until too late. But when cars, homes, tons of garbage, school and church buildings had been searched, most fruitlessly, the elusive ring was still missing. There was only one slim chance left as we saw it.

Dana took that chance. She dragged the hose out to the alley and carefully put out the fire in the incinerator. At last she deemed it cool enough to continue with her search, and she climbed on a kitchen stool and jumped down into the ashes and unburnable debris. There were no cooling breezes, no cushions. Occasionally one had to rise to his feet in an attempt to relieve his aching muscles. Dana stood up at the very moment that the driver of a car on nearly deserted ways looked down the alley. Poor thing—he almost drove a brand new car into our neighbors' house.

The teller of this story mentioned that Mother usually had just one piece of chicken for each of us on the days we had chicken. That was true to some extent, for at times one chicken yielded just enough to go around; but when time and finances allowed, we cooked two chickens and received two or more pieces each. This day the "bloopist" had eaten either one piece of chicken or a half of one and picked up the rest of her due only to drop it as her boyfriend walked into the room. She retrieved it and asked the narrator to put it up for her to eat later. The tale teller obeyed and the couple went on an undisclosed errand. They returned after a short absence; and perpetrator, without thought, requested the helpful hand to, "Go get my other breast for me." Not even in those days could the listeners have kept straight faces. Or managed to suppress their blushes!

Jessie used to keep our little neighbor boy at our home while his mother shopped. One day he dashed into the house shouting, "Aunt Jessie! Aunt Jessie! The mailman came, and he left you a mail."

One of the braver of us, figured that at fourteen she was grown enough to escape scot-free when she dared to voice an opinion that clashed heavily with Daddy's concerning the behavior of his children. Unflinching, on her feet, and eye to eye, she remarked, "Just because you are my daddy doesn't make you always right." She says she was wrong.

Then there were the days of "dollar perfumes." Essences copied from the most expensive scents were made and sold for one dollar per bottle. Those who wore it knew that it would soon evaporate, taking most of the odor with it. The trick, it seems, was to put on too much and allow time to take care of the excess. With skill one became proficient at having just the right aromatic aura fifteen minutes after applying those chemical bluffs.

This day Sister X had an appointment at which she meant to present herself ostensibly flawless. Within a few miles of her destination, she was stopped for a periodic check of driver's license. She smiled, at her best, and rolled down her window. Inexplicably the over-heated August air rushed in and intensified the odor wafting to their nostrils. The lady sat there fighting the urge to cough and fan the strong scent away. To this day she is convinced that that officer would never believe that she had not deliberately set out to catch herself a man.

A sister tells this story about her brother: He kept a can some eight inches in diameter and about two feet tall in his room and stored nuts in it. The sister failed to admit whether she was snooping or intending to "borrow" some nuts to graze on; but she looked in the can. Well hidden in the depths of the delectables she discovered a small magazine, a magazine which she didn't totally understand. She mentioned that the pictures didn't make any sense. Quite naturally Mother investigated. Of course she found a cache of naughty reading. Neither could the girl understand why she wound up in the doghouse! The grown lady does.

Chapter XXI

Writing fiction taught me that the closing pages of any story are the hardest to write. It isn't that we don't know how we want a particular story to end, but rather that we've become so close to our characters that we don't want them to more or less disappear. They are friends, and in some cases alter-egos. As novices we must compel ourselves to realize that these friends will live indefinitely just as we created them, that only we can alter their inner selves.

This is a different situation. I did not create these dear people; and although I certainly do not wish any one of them dead, I hate to skip any of their escapades, triumphs, sorrows or new beginnings. It has just occurred to me that I do not see myself in that same light: I suppose I think I shall go on. Oh, I realize that I shall die one day; still, "That's different."

Lemar is back running heavy equipment somewhere in the general area of Houston. He and Jeannette spent many winter hours fishing in the Gulf of Mexico.

Dan is currently out of her Meals on Wheels work as new management has taken over. She has lots of friends and runs around with other ladies, plays Forty-two frequently with a group of other domino enthusiasts; and she continues to weed and sort their belongings so that she can get the house on a realtor's listing.

Once she is settled in an apartment, she would like to enter into part-time library work or volunteer work, such as aiding hospital patients. She and some friends love flea markets, and may well drive a hundred or so miles to take in the huge ones that build up names for themselves. She continues to enjoy her trips twice each year.

John has put Wendell in a nursing home. He smiles when he's awake and she is there and holds her hand; but now will turn just as eagerly to the male attendant who exercises his arms and legs for him and bathes him. He has also developed another blood clot which will keep the doctors on their toes for the next several months if it makes the same progression as the others have. It will slow her down in attaining her goal of selling her home and moving to Fort Worth, nearer the family and the better medical facilities.

It's January 1993, now, and Wendell's release has come. Late one raw, bitter evening recently the home called John— at an hour too late for her to be expected to drive so many miles alone. She had already answered the same call several times, but this was the last call; nor was there sufficient time before he was gone for her to make it. Since John had earlier donated Wendell's body to a laboratory for research on Alzheimer's disease, it was imperative that they pick him up immediately. A memorial service was held early the next week. This isn't necessary to the story, but I felt doubly outraged that we had a rare smothering fog in the Panhandle, and I could not fly down to be with the rest of the family.

Luceille and Bob, insofar as I know, have no plans to move. They will take their trailer outings, continue their church activities, and assist both family and friends at every opportunity—especially if means going somewhere!

Mable and Gray also stay busy. But Gray is hampered by his multi-infarct dementia. He is a good driver, but a few months ago he let his license lapse. He could not think and get the answers down fast enough to pass the written part of the test to get another. As he sometimes took far longer to reach his goal of the moment than he did a few years ago, it is probably just as well.

Mable runs her courier business: Couriers Plus. She has quit working at cooking for so many people. The concern for whom she formerly made so many rich desserts (in addition to other dishes) dubbed her "our diet devastator." On the telephone this morning she reminded me of a time that she was visiting with Morris beside a flight of outdoor stairs going down to a department in a bank. The cut by the stairs was marked by a tiled ledge, approximately a foot wide, which led to the main floor of the building. A child was walking the ledge, and Mable feared that he might fall.

She explained to Morris, "Those steps go down."

And Morris obviously enjoyed answering her, "Don't they all?" She admits she felt gauche and silly.

Vickey and Jimmy both are on the road a great deal just now. Jimmy has finished building the house beside his peach orchards at Mexia, and is now furnishing it. Vickey prefers to work a few more years. One or the other of them stays on the road to share something with the other almost constantly it seems to the observer. She plans a family reunion at the new home Labor Day weekend. We're all eager for it.

I've not chosen my next project. Oh, there's painting, varnishing, getting new linoleum laid, and a few pieces of furniture to buy beside the weekly mowing and the flowers to be planted and tended; but there still must be more to life than that. I contemplate trying to sort through my poetry and see if it might be published along the lines a friend—a minister—thinks would be beneficial to himself as well as others in the ministry.

Or perhaps I will write other stories and articles that I've shelved for lack of time, I will feel pilotless as I was one morning in New Zealand. Brian Davis, a novice at preaching, nineteen years old, was my partner on that unusually icy day for Dunedin in the far south. With care we made our way over the black ice and the patches of snow that dotted the already green grass.

Suddenly I was not in control, I was sailing rather than walking. I followed the well-known steps to regain my equilibrium. First, you wave your arms in imitation of a windmill, you know. Second you pray. Whereas the next step is usually to fall, my ride was still too smooth for that. One just could not designate it a skid. After a few feet on the walk, I sailed off onto the grass. It didn't appear to be as smooth; so I caught my breath for the fall and tried to guess whether I would fall flat on my face, or on my back. Brian was helpless—partly with laughter—and could hardly keep up with me. I crossed a good stretch of grass. I cannot say that I navigated it. Still erect I felt a difference in my path.

I had arrived at a driveway. It funneled me right onto the street. I could no longer see Brian, not even from the corner of my eye. Then I reached the path left clear by the morning vehicular traffic; it too must have been spotty, for I still didn't fall, but coasted to a stop. Brian caught up with me, unable to speak immediately. He had been delighted with entire production, true; but, to give him credit, I must admit that he was also delighted that I escaped totally uninjured. We went about our day's work.

That's how I feel today, as if I were sailing, upright, and rapidly, and out of control into the wild blue yonder.

Mind you, I expect to stay on my feet again this time. ❧